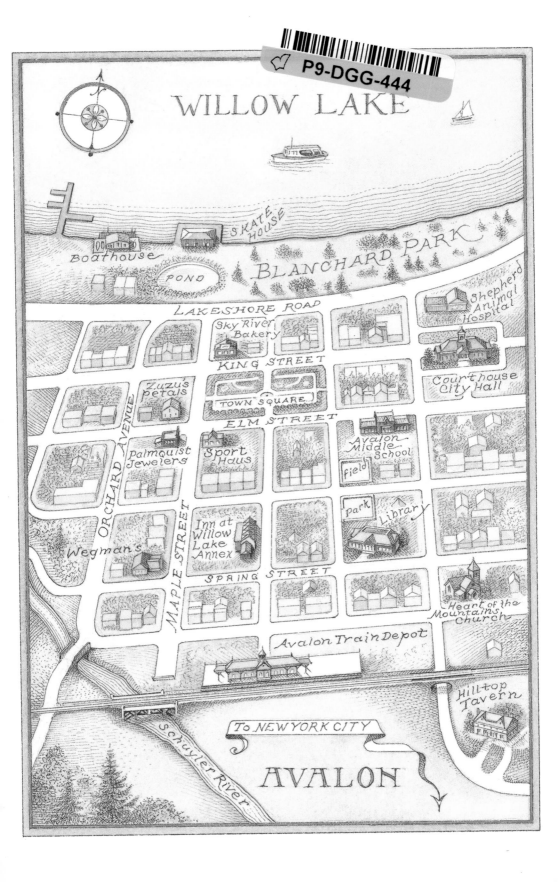

Return to Willow Lake

SUSAN WIGGS

THE
Lakeshore Chronicles

Return to Willow Lake

HARLEQUIN®
entertain, enrich, inspire™

ISBN-13: 978-0-7783-1384-7

RETURN TO WILLOW LAKE

First printing: September 2012
10 9 8 7 6 5 4 3 2 1

To imakepesto from beachwriter

PART
1

SONNET ROMANO'S
MUST-DO-BEFORE-AGE-THIRTY LIST

✔ college degree

✔ overseas internship

✔ bond with estranged father

✔ find a better apartment

＿ fall in love

A Scout is never taken by surprise;
he knows exactly what to do when anything unexpected happens.
—ROBERT BADEN-POWELL (SCOUTING FOR BOYS, 1908)

CHAPTER
1

Moments before the wedding was to begin, Sonnet Romano shuddered with a wave of nervousness. "Mom," she said, hurrying over to the window, which framed a view of Willow Lake, "what if I screw up?"

Her mother turned from the window. The late afternoon light shrouded Nina Bellamy's slender form, and for a moment she appeared ethereal and as young as Sonnet herself. Nina looked fantastic in her autumn-gold silk sheath, her dark hair swept back into a low chignon. Only someone who knew her the way Sonnet did might notice the subtle lines of fatigue around her eyes and mouth, the vague puffiness of her skin. Just prior to the wedding, she'd attended the funeral, up in Albany, of her favorite aunt, who had died the week before of cancer, and the grief of goodbye lingered in her face.

"You're not going to screw up," Nina said. "You're going to be fabulous. You look amazing in that dress, you've memorized everything you're going to do and say, and it's going to be a wonderful evening."

"Yes, but—"

"Remember what I used to say when you were little—your smile is my sunshine."

"I remember." And the memory did its magic, bringing a smile to her face. Her mom had raised Sonnet alone, but only now that she was grown did she appreciate how hard that had been for Nina. "You gave me lots of memories, Mom."

"Come here, you." Nina opened her arms and Sonnet gratefully slipped into her mother's embrace.

"This feels nice. I wish I had a chance to come back here more often." Sonnet turned her face to the warm breeze blowing in through the window. The sheer beauty of the lake, nestled between the gentle swells of the Catskills, made her heart ache. Though she'd grown up in Avalon, the place felt foreign to Sonnet now, a world she used to inhabit and couldn't wait to leave.

Despite her vivid memories of her childhood here, playing in the woods with her friends or sledding down the hills in winter, she'd never truly appreciated the scenery until she'd left it behind, eager to find her life far away. Now that she lived in Manhattan, crammed into a closet-sized walk-up studio on a noisy East Side street, she finally understood the appeal of her old hometown.

"I wish you could, too," Nina said. "It's time-consuming, isn't it, saving the world?"

Sonnet chuckled. "Is that what I'm doing? Saving the world?"

"As a matter of fact, it is. Sweetie, I'm so proud to tell people you work with UNESCO, that your department saves children's lives all over the world."

"Ah, thanks, Mom. You make me think I do more than write emails and fill out forms." Sonnet often found herself wishing she could actually work with a child every once in a while. Buried in administrative chores, it was easy to forget.

On the smoothly-mown lawn below, guests were beginning to take their seats for the ceremony. Many of the groom's friends were in military dress uniform, adding a note of gravitas to the atmosphere.

"Wow," said Sonnet, "it's really happening, Mom. Finally."

"Yes," Nina agreed. "Finally."

A chorus of squeals came from the adjacent room, where the rest of the bridal party was getting ready.

"Daisy's going to be the prettiest bride ever," Sonnet said, feeling a thrum of emotion in her chest. The bride was Sonnet's best friend as well as her stepsister, and she was about to marry the love of her life. To Sonnet it felt like a dream come true… but also, deep in a hidden corner of her heart, a loss of sorts. Now someone else would be the keeper of Daisy's most private secrets, her soft place to fall, the person on the other end of the phone in the middle of the night.

"Until it's your turn," Nina said. "Then *you'll* be the prettiest bride ever."

Sonnet gave her mom's hand a squeeze. "Don't hold your breath. I'm busy saving the world, remember?"

"Just don't get so busy you forget to fall in love," Nina said.

Sonnet laughed. "I think you need to embroider that on a pillow. How about— *Hello.*" Her mind drained of everything but the sight of the tallest groomsman in the wedding party, escorting the grandmother of the bride to her seat in the front row.

In a dove-gray swallowtail tux, he moved with long-limbed grace, although his height was not the most striking thing about him. It was his hair, as long and pale as a banner of surrender, giving him the otherworldly look of a mythical creature. She couldn't take her eyes off him.

"Holy cow," she said. "Is that…?"

"Yep," said her mother. "Zach Alger."

"Whoa."

"He's finally grown into his looks, hasn't he?" Nina commented. "I'd forgotten how long it's been since you last saw him. The two of you used to be so close."

Zach Alger. Surely not, thought Sonnet, practically leaning out the open window. This couldn't be the Zach Alger she'd grown up with, the whiter-shade-of-pale boy who lived down the street, with his big goofy ears and braces on his teeth. Her best friend in high school, the freakishly skinny kid who worked at the Sky River Bakery. This couldn't be the college geek working his way through school, obsessed with cameras and all things video.

Zach Alger, she thought. Well, well. Since high school, he and Sonnet had gone in different directions, and she hadn't seen him in ages. Now she couldn't take her eyes off him.

After helping Daisy's grandmother to her seat, he pulled a flask from his tux pocket and took a swig. All right, thought Sonnet. *That* was the Zach she knew—a guy with more talent than ambition, a guy with a troubled background he couldn't seem to shake, a guy who was part of her past, but had no possible place in her future.

Movement in the next room reminded her she had an important job to do today. She peered through the doorway at Daisy, who was surrounded by the hairstylist, makeup artist, wedding planner, her mom Sophie, the photographer and several people Sonnet didn't recognize. "What do you say?" she asked her mother. "Shall we go help Daisy get married?'

Nina grinned. "She wouldn't dare make a move without you."

"Or you. Honestly, when you married Daisy's dad, she hit the stepmom jackpot."

Nina's grin turned to a soft smile, and her dark eyes took on an expression that pulled Sonnet into days gone by, when it had just been the two of them, making their way in the world. Nina had turned a teenage pregnancy into a small but lovely life for herself and Sonnet. Yes, she was married now—unexpectedly, in the middle of her life—but their two-against-the-world time together belonged solely to Nina and Sonnet.

"You're going all mushy on me, aren't you?" Sonnet said.

"Yeah, baby. I am. Just wait until you're the bride. I'll need CPR." The shadows in the room were just starting to deepen; evening was coming on.

"No, you won't, Mom," Sonnet assured her. "You'll rise to the occasion. You always do."

Nina took her hand again, and together they stepped through the door.

CHAPTER
2

The wedding wound down like a noisy parade fading into the distance. In its wake was the curious mellow quiet of a just-passed storm. Sonnet stood on the broad lawn by the pavilion at Camp Kioga, surveying the petal-strewn aftermath and holding onto a well-earned sense of accomplishment.

As maid of honor, she'd been intimately involved with every aspect of the event, from coordinating Daisy's bachelorette party to picking the colors of the table linens. But today hadn't been about table decorations or small appliances. It had been about friends and family and a celebration so joyous she could still feel its echo deep inside her.

Rather than feeling exhausted after the long, emotional day, she was chased by a feeling of restlessness. It was strange, coming back to the place she'd once called home, seeing people who looked her over and remarked, "I remember when you were *this tall*" or "Why hasn't some guy snatched you up by now?" as if being twenty-eight and unmarried was taboo in a town like this.

She smiled a little, pretending she didn't feel the tiniest dig of impatience with her personal life. No. She wasn't impatient. It was hard, caught up in the wedding whirlwind, to ignore the fact that nearly everyone in sight was coupled up.

Taking a deep breath, she went back to savoring the success of the day. The bride and groom had just departed. Her maid of honor duties were done. In the glow of twinkling fairy lights, the band was breaking down its set. The catering crew got going on the cleanup. The last of the wedding guests were slowly melting into the darkness of the perfect fall evening, the air redolent of crisp leaves and ripe apples. There had been a bonfire at the lakeshore, but it had burned to glowing embers by now. Some of the visitors headed for the parking lot, while the out-of-towners wended their way to the storybook pretty lakefront bungalows of the Camp Kioga, which through the years had been transformed from a family camp to a kids' camp to its present iteration, a gathering place for celebrating life's events. A good number of the guests were, like Sonnet, pleasantly tipsy.

A bright moon peeked over the dark hills surrounding Willow Lake, throwing silvery shadows across the still water and trampled grass. Childish laughter streamed from somewhere close by, and three little kids chased each other between the banquet tables. In the low light, Sonnet couldn't tell whose kids they were, but their joyous abandon lifted her heart. She adored children; she always had. In a place deep down in the center of her, she felt a soft tug of yearning, but it was a yearning that would likely go unfulfilled for a very long time. Maybe forever. She had big plans for her future, but at the moment, those plans did not include settling down and having kids of her own.

In the first place, there was no one to settle down with. Unlike Daisy, who had found the love of her life and was going forward with clear-eyed certainty, Sonnet had no vision of who might be that person for her, that one adored man who would become her whole world. In all honesty, she wasn't a hundred percent sure such a person existed. There was nothing missing from her life, nothing at all. It wasn't as if she needed to add someone like the final piece of a puzzle.

Greg Bellamy, Sonnet's stepfather, came walking across the now-trampled lawn, heading for the gazebo to shell out extra tips for the band. As father of the bride, he was all smiles. Sonnet went over to him, teasingly holding out her hand, palm up. "Hey, where's the tip for the maid of honor?"

Greg chuckled, looking handsome but tired and slightly disheveled in his tux, the black silk bow tie undone and hanging on either side of his unbuttoned collar. "Here's a tip for you. Take a couple of aspirin before you go to bed tonight. It'll counteract those Jell-O shots you did at the reception."

"You saw that?" She grinned. "Whoops."

"It's okay. You've earned it, kiddo. Great job today. You looked like a million, and that toast you made at the reception—hilarious. Everybody loved it. You're a born public speaker."

"Yeah? Aw, thanks. You're not so bad yourself, for an evil stepfather." Sonnet loved her mom's husband. Through the years, he'd been a great mentor and friend to her. But he wasn't her dad. Sonnet's father, General Laurence Jeffries, played that role, although he had been virtually absent from her childhood, making a career for himself far from the bucolic charm of Avalon. When Sonnet went off to college at American University and then graduate school at Georgetown, however, she and Laurence had reconnected; she had dived into his world of public service and strategy and diplomacy, eagerly soaking up his knowledge and expertise.

She was the first to admit that hero worship made for a much more complicated relationship with Laurence than she had with Greg.

Nina came over to join them, her heeled pumps dangling from one hand. "What's this I hear about Jell-O shots? You were doing them without me?"

"Trust me," said Greg, "the champagne cocktails were a lot more fun."

"I trust you. And you were an amazing father of the bride," she said to Greg, smiling up at him.

"I cried like a baby girl." He offered a sheepish grin.

"We all did," Sonnet assured him. "Weddings seem to have that effect on people. Daisy's even more so, because of all the trouble she's had."

"Speaking of trouble, I need to go make sure we've settled up with everybody else," Greg said.

"I'll come with," Nina said. "You might need propping up when you see some of the final bills."

Greg slipped his arm around Nina. "In that case, how about we have one last glass of champagne together? For courage."

"Good plan." Nina helped herself to a couple of flutes from one of the tables. "Join us down by the lake?"

Sonnet found a half-empty bottle and poured herself a glass. "I think I'll stick around here and…" She paused. After all was said and done, the maid of honor had no further duties. "…drink alone."

"Ah, baby." Her mom offered a soft smile. "Your time will come, just like I was saying before the wedding. No one can say where or when, but it'll happen."

"Gah, Mom." Sonnet grimaced. "I'm not mooning about my love life. That's the last thing on my mind."

"If you say so." Nina lifted her glass in salute.

"I say so. Go away." Sonnet made a shooing motion with her free hand. "Go drink with your husband. I'll see you in the morning, okay? I'm planning to be on the noon train to the city." She watched her mom and stepdad wander down the gentle slope toward the lake, their silhouettes dark against the moonlight.

They paused at the water's edge and stood facing the moonlit surface, Greg holding Nina protectively from behind, his hands folded over her midsection. Sonnet sighed, feeling a wave of gladness for her mom. Yet at the same time, the sight of them embracing made her heart ache. Sonnet tried to imagine herself in that role—the bride. Would her own father walk her down the aisle, the tears flowing freely down his face? Doubtful. General Laurence Jeffries, now a candidate for the United States Senate, was more figurehead than father.

And when she pictured herself walking down the aisle, she couldn't form a mental image of the guy waiting at the end of it. She wasn't going to hold her breath waiting for him.

"I hate weddings." Zach Alger sidled over and slammed back a bottle of Utica Club. "I especially hate weddings that require me to behave myself."

Sonnet had spent most of the day sneaking glances at Zach, trying to accustom herself to this new version of her oldest friend. They hadn't had a chance to talk at the wedding; the evening had sped by with her still doing her duty as maid of honor. Now, mellow from drinking and dancing, she regarded him through squinted eyes. It was hard to get her head around the idea that he had been a part of her life since preschool. That, perhaps, was the only reason she didn't swoon sideways when he walked past, the way most women did. Still, it was hard to get used to his unique, striking looks—so blond he was sometimes mistaken for an albino, and now built like a Greek athlete, yet oddly oblivious to his effect on the opposite sex.

She gave him a superior sniff, falling into her old role as sidekick. "You mean there's a kind of wedding that *doesn't* require you to behave yourself?" She plucked an untouched flute of champagne from one of the tables that hadn't yet been cleared.

"I'm a wedding videographer. I've filmed more weddings than I've been to baseball games. I haven't seen a Saturday night in five years. And what do I do when one finally rolls around? I go to a freaking wedding."

"*Daisy's* wedding."

"Any wedding. I hate them all."

She scowled at him. "How can you be hating on Daisy Bellamy's wedding?"

Just hearing herself say the words aloud filled her with a sense of wonder—not because Daisy had married the man of her dreams. That in itself was wonderful. But the real miracle was that Daisy had gotten married at all. Her parents' divorce had been so hard on her. Back when Daisy's dad and Sonnet's mom were first getting together, both girls had agreed that marriage was too perilous and restrictive, and they'd made a pact to avoid it at all costs.

Now Daisy was soaring off to wedded bliss, and Sonnet was stuck keeping her end of the pact. She cringed at the picture of her own romantic future. Thanks to her impossibly busy career as a director at UNESCO, she had almost no time to date, let alone get swept away and fall in love. She dreamed of it, though. Who didn't? Who didn't want the kind of love Daisy had found? Or her mother and Greg Bellamy? Or the head couple of the Bellamy clan, Jane and Charles, who had been married for more than fifty years.

Of course Sonnet wanted that—the love, the security, the lifelong project of building a family with her soul mate. It sounded so magical. And so unreachable. When it came to a serious relationship, she had never quite figured out how to get from Point A to Point B.

Lately, though, there was a glimmer on the horizon from a most unexpected source. Her father—yes, her superaccomplished, goal-oriented father—had introduced her to a guy. His name was Orlando Rivera, and he was heading up the general's run for office. Like the general, he'd attended West Point. He was in his thirties, ridiculously handsome, from the eldest son of a monied Cuban-American family. He had the dark appeal of a Latin lover and was fluent in English and Spanish. And, maybe most importantly of all, he was in the tight inner circle of satellites that revolved around her father.

"I'm allowed to hate anything I want," Zach said, grabbing the champagne from her hand and guzzling it down.

Defiantly, she picked up a half-empty bottle that was bobbing in an ice bucket and took back the glass. "It was Daisy's big day, and if you were any kind of gentleman, you'd be happy for her. And for me," she groused at him. "I got to stand up at the altar for my best friend—"

"Hey," he groused back. "I thought *I* was your best friend."

"You never come to see me." She feigned a dramatic sigh. "You don't call, you don't text… Besides, I can have more than one."

"Best is a superlative term. There can only be one."

She refilled the glass and took a gulp, enjoying the lovely head rush of the bubbly. "You and your rules. Both you and Daisy are my besties and there's nothing you can do about it, so there."

"Oh yeah? I can think of something." He grabbed her hand and pulled her down toward the dark, flat expanse of Willow Lake.

"What the heck are you doing?" she said, twisting her hand out of his.

"The party's over, but I'm not tired. Are you tired?"

"No, but—"

"Hey, check it out." He led the way down the slope to the water's edge.

"Check what out? I'm going to ruin my shoes."

He stopped and turned. "Then take them off."

"But I—"

"Lean on me," he said, going down on one knee in front of her. He slipped off one sandal and then the other. She felt an unexpected frisson of sensation when he touched her. "That's better, anyway."

She sniffed again, unwilling to admit that the coarse sand on the lakeshore felt delicious under her bare feet. "Fine, what are we checking out?"

"I saw something...." He gestured at the water lapping gently up the sandy slope.

She saw it, too, a glimmer in the moonlight. Then she frowned and lifted the hem of her dress to wade out and grab it. "A champagne bottle," she said. "Somebody littered." Holding it up to the light, she squinted. "There's a message inside, Zach."

"Yeah? Open it up and check it out," he said.

"No way," she said. "It might be someone's private business."

"What? How can you find a message in a bottle and not look at it?"

"It's bad karma to pry into it. I won't be party to snooping around someone else's emotional baggage." Defiantly, she flung the bottle as far as she could. It landed unseen, with a decisive *plop*. "What kind of idiot leaves a message in a bottle in a land-locked lake, anyway?" she asked.

"You should have looked," he said churlishly. "It might have been important. Maybe it was a cry for help and you just ignored it."

"Maybe it was some teenager's angsty poetry and I did her a favor by getting rid of it."

"Right." He grabbed her hand and pulled her toward the dock jutting out into the lake.

She pulled back. "Wait a minute. *Now* what are we doing?"

"I told Wendela I'd take the boat over to the boathouse."

Wendela was the wedding planner, and Zach did most of the videography work for her. In addition, she often enlisted him to do other odd jobs at events. In a small town, it was a way for him to cobble together a living, Sonnet supposed. He was talented at what he did; during the reception, Wendela had told her he'd won some prestigious awards for his work. But like all artists, he struggled. Awards didn't translate into a viable income.

"You're here as a wedding guest," she protested. "Wendela wouldn't expect you to work tonight."

"What, driving a boat is suddenly work? Since when?"

"You have a point. What is it with guys and boats?"

"There are some things that cannot be resisted." He slipped off his bow tie and opened the collar of his tuxedo shirt, his Adam's apple rippling as he sighed with relief.

Good Lord, had he been working out? She didn't ask, because everyone knew that was just code for "I think you're hot."

And she didn't. How could she? He was Zach—as familiar as a lifelong friend, yet suddenly…exotic.

"I shouldn't have done those Jell-O shots," she murmured. Pulling her attention elsewhere, she stood on the dock and looked out at the moon-silvered water. The sight of the lake never failed to ignite a rush of memories. She had been here before, many times through the years.

During her junior high and high school years, when Camp Kioga had been closed down, she and Zach used to sneak onto the premises with their friends on hot summer days, swimming and reliving the glory days of the resort, which dated back to the 1920s. And every once in a while, the two of them would slip into the boathouse and pretend to be smugglers or pirates or stuntmen in the circus. Sometimes, even as youngsters, they would fall so deep into the fantasy that they'd lose track of time. She remembered talking with him for hours, seemingly about nothing, but managing to encompass everything important. When she was with Zach, it never felt strange that she didn't have a dad, or that she was biracial, or that her mom had to work all the time to make ends meet. When she was with Zach, she just felt…like herself. Maybe that was why their friendship felt so sturdy, even when they almost never saw each other.

An owl hooted from a secret place in the darkness, startling Sonnet from her thoughts. "It's getting late," she said softly. "I'm leaving."

He gently closed his hand around her wrist. "Come with me."

A shiver coursed through her, and she didn't resist when he drew her close, slipping his arm around her waist and edging her

toward the boat moored at the end of the dock. It was a vintage
Chris-Craft runabout, its wooden hull and brass fittings polished to a sheen so bright it seemed to glow in the moonlight.
The old boat had been used in the wedding, mostly for a photo
shoot but also, and most romantically, to transport the bride
and groom to the floatplane dock, where they'd been whisked
away to their honeymoon at Mohonk Mountain House. A Just
Married sign was tied to the stern.

"Hang on to me," Zach whispered. "I don't want you falling in."

"I won't fall—whoa." She clung to him as the boat listed be-
neath her weight. The open cabin smelled of the lake, and the
flowers that had been used to decorate it, and the fresh scent
made her dizzy. The second wave of champagne was kicking in.

"Take my jacket," he said, wrapping it around her shoulders.
"Chilly tonight."

She took a seat in the cockpit, feeling the peculiar intimacy of
his body heat lingering in the folds of the jacket. She reveled in
the slickness of the satin lining, which smelled faintly of men's
cologne and sweat. Oh boy, she thought.

There was an open bottle of champagne in the cubby by her
knees, so she grabbed it and took a long, thirsty swig. Why not?
she thought. Her official duties for the wedding were done, and
it was time to relax.

Zach untied the boat and shoved off. He turned on the running lights and motor, handling the Chris-Craft with expert
smoothness. He'd always been good with his hands, whether
handling a vintage motorboat or a complicated video camera. As
they motored across the placid water toward the rustic wooden
boathouse, Sonnet admitted to herself that although she loved
living in New York City, there were things she missed about
the remote Catskills area where she'd grown up—the moon on
the water, the fresh feeling of the wind in her face, the quiet and

the darkness of the wilderness, the familiarity of a friend who knew her so well they didn't really have to talk.

She had another drink of champagne, feeling a keen exuberance as she watched loose flower petals fluttering through the night air, into the wake of the boat.

She offered the bottle to Zach.

"No thanks," he said. "Not until I moor the boat."

She sat back and enjoyed the short crossing to the boathouse, which was bathed in the soft golden glow of lights along the dock.

Over the buzz of the engine, he pointed out the constellations. "See that group up there? It's called Coma Berenices—Berenice's hair. It was named for an Egyptian queen who cut off all her hair in exchange for some goddess to keep her husband safe in battle. The goddess liked the hair so much, she took it to the heavens and turned it into a cluster of stars."

"Talk about a good hair day." She was beyond pleasantly tipsy now. "I'd never cut off my hair. Took me years to get it this long."

"Not even to keep your husband safe in battle?"

"I don't have a husband. So I'll be keeping my fabled locks, thank you very much. Berenice's hair. I swear, your mind is a lint trap for stuff like this. Where do you learn it?"

"The internet. Yeah, I like geeking out over trivia on the internet, so sue me."

"I'm not going to sue you. Whatever floats your boat, ha ha."

"You can find out anything online. Ever watch that video of the Naga fireballs?"

"I haven't had the pleasure."

"Too busy overachieving?"

"Since when is that a crime?"

"Never said it was." Zach guided the boat inside, cutting the engine to let it nudge its way into the moorage, gently bumping against the rubber fenders.

"There," he said, taking the champagne from her, "I've done my good deed for the day. Here's looking at you, kid."

"Too dark in here to see," she pointed out. "Oh, right. That's a movie reference. I forgot, you're a walking movie encyclopedia."

"And you're movie illiterate."

"No wonder we bicker all the time. We have nothing in common."

He handed back the bottle and rummaged around the console of the cockpit. Then a match flared and he lit a couple of votive candles left over from the photo shoot. Taking the bottle again, he said, "*Now* here's looking at you."

She looked right back at him, unsettled by feelings she didn't understand, feelings that had nothing to do with the amount of champagne she'd consumed. Like Willow Lake, and the town of Avalon itself, he was both deeply familiar and, at the moment, unaccountably strange. There had been a time, many times, when they had truly been best friends, but after high school, their lives had diverged. These days, they saw each other infrequently and when they did, their visits were rushed, or they were busy, or one of them had a train to catch, or work, or…

Not tonight, though. Tonight, neither of them had anywhere they had to be, except right here in the moment.

She fiddled with a dial on the boat's dashboard. "Is there a radio?"

"It's a stereo." Leaning forward, he hit a switch. Sonnet recognized an old tune from the days of her grandparents—"What a Wonderful World."

"What's this?" She pointed out a small screen.

"A fish finder. Want to turn it on and see where the fishies are?"

"That's okay. And this?" She indicated a small cube-shaped object mounted in the center.

"A GoPro. It's a camcorder, mostly used for sports." He turned up the music. "You didn't dance with me at the reception," Zach said.

"You didn't ask me." She feigned a wounded look.

"Dance with me now."

"That's not asking."

He heaved an exaggerated sigh and offered her his hand, palm up. "Okay. Will you dance with me? Please?"

"I thought you'd never ask." She stood up and the boat rocked a little.

"Careful there. Maybe ease up on the champagne."

He drew her up to the dock next to him. She was a full head shorter than he was. It hadn't always been that way. She remembered the year of his growth spurt—junior year of high school. They'd gone from seeing each other eye to eye to her getting a crick in her neck from looking up at him. He'd been skinny as a barge pole, and she'd taken to calling him Beanstalk.

He wasn't a beanstalk anymore. As her mother had pointed out, he'd finally grown into his looks. In the candlelight, he looked magical to her, Prince Charming with a boyish smile. She kept the surprising thought to herself, knowing instinctively she didn't want to go there.

He held her lightly at the waist and they swayed to the music, their movements simple and in sync. At the wedding reception, she had danced with a few guys but dancing had never felt like this before.

"You've been wanting to do this ever since our glory days in seventh grade," he said softly.

"Oh, please. You were short and obnoxious, and I had a mouthful of metal."

"I know. But I remember wanting to stick my tongue in there several times."

She shoved him away. "I'm glad you never told me that. It would have meant the end of a beautiful friendship. You're still obnoxious. And I wouldn't have let you, anyway. I'm sure you would have been a terrible kisser."

"You don't know what you missed out on, metal mouth. I was good. I *am* good. Let's hope you've honed your skills."

"Oh, I have mad skills," she assured him, then realized that she was flirting, and whom she was flirting with. Extricating herself from his embrace, she said, "I want to get back to the pavilion. I missed out on wedding cake."

"You're in luck." He reached down into the boat's hull and took a large domed platter from under the dash. The music changed to "Muskrat Love," a tuneless horror from the seventies.

"Zachary Lee Alger. You didn't."

"Hey, it was going to go to waste. A cake from the Sky River Bakery. That would be a federal crime." He picked up a hunk with his fingers and crammed it in his mouth. "Oh, man. I just died a little."

He held out another piece and she couldn't resist. The chocolate slid like silk across her tongue. She closed her eyes, savoring it along with the bits of hazelnut that had been kneaded into the buttercream icing. "Oh, my. Are you sure this is legal?"

"Would you care if it wasn't?"

"Nope." She helped herself to another bite. "And how cool is it that the Sky River Bakery did the cake?"

The old-fashioned family bakery had been a town institution for generations. It was also the place where Zach had worked all through high school, dragging himself to town before dawn to mix the dough and operate the proofing machines and ovens.

"You used to bring me a pastry in the morning," she reminisced.

"I spoiled you rotten."

She washed down a bite of cake with a slug of champagne. "It's surprising I didn't get as big as a house."

"Not surprising to me. You could never sit still for more than ten seconds. Are you still that restless?"

She considered this for a moment. "I guess I was really eager to get going on something."

"Always the overachiever. Always striving."

"You say that like it's a bad thing."

"It is when it takes you away from what's important."

She frowned. "Such as...?"

"Well, let's see. Such as this." With a gentle tug of his hand, he pulled her against him, planting a long, hard kiss on her surprised lips. She wasn't sure what shocked her more—the kiss itself or the fact that it was coming from Zach Alger. Equally shocking was the fact that he hadn't been lying about his expertise. Holding her with gentle insistence, he softened the kiss and touched his tongue to a secret, sensitive place that took her breath away. It struck her that this might be the best kiss she'd had in ages. Maybe ever.

The biggest surprise of all was that she was kissing Zach Alger—the same Zach Alger whose apple she had stolen from his lunchbox in kindergarten. The one who had tormented her when she was in the fourth grade. The boy who had pushed her off the dock into Willow Lake innumerable times, with whom she'd shared homework answers and after-school snacks, repeat viewings of *Toy Story* and *Family Guy,* and on whose shoulders she'd cry each time her heart was broken—and the first one she called with good news, whenever good news came around: "I got into college. My mom's getting married. The internship program in Germany accepted me. My birth father finally wants a relationship with me. They're making me a director at UNESCO...."

Their points of contact over time were innumerable. They'd shared big moments and small, joy and grief, silliness and seriousness. He was the friend who had been there through all the moments of her life, yet the present moment felt entirely different, as if she were meeting him for the first time. Now she was with him in a way that felt completely new, and the world seemed to shift on its axis.

Through the years she had known him every way it was possible to know a guy and yet…and yet… Now there was this. It was some crazy emotion more intense than she could fathom, brought on by the champagne but by something else, too—a need, a craving she had no power to resist.

She fought herself free of the intensity and pulled back, though both of her fists stayed curled into the fabric of his dress shirt. "I had no idea you had that kind of kiss in you," she whispered in a shaky voice.

"I've got more than that in me," he replied, and bent down to kiss her again, lips searching and tasting, his arms holding her as if she were something precious.

Lost in sensation, she simply surrendered. She was melting and it was confusing because this was Zach—she had to keep reminding herself it was *Zach,* the very essence of the boy next door, as familiar as an old favorite song coming on the radio. But suddenly she was seeing him in a way she hadn't noticed before. Particularly when he started doing what he was doing now—holding her arms above her head and whispering, "You taste delicious. Kissing you is like eating a fresh peach pie," which made her laugh, and then they would start again. Tucked away in the back of her mind was the knowledge that this was a supremely bad idea that could turn out very badly for her. But all the standard objections stayed tucked away, hovering at the far edges of consciousness.

"We're making a huge mistake," she said, "but I'm too…I don't know how to stop it," she said.

"Then quit trying," he said simply.

"Zach, I don't think—"

"Exactly. Don't think."

He made it easy to drift away from rational thought. There was something about the soft night and the lush leather bench seat of the vintage boat, and him, and the two of them together again after such a long time. His kisses tasted of champagne and chocolate cake and memories so old she couldn't tell if they were memories or dreams.

He pulled back and parted the coat he'd wrapped around her, sliding it away. His hands glided over the form-fitting dress as he whispered, "I want to take this off." Without waiting for her to respond, he reached for the side zipper of the silk dress.

Somewhere, floating amid the mind-fogging kisses and the champagne and Jell-O shots, a tiny *no* formed, waving its arms like a drowning victim. Then the *no* floated away and disappeared, and what was left was something she had never before said to Zach Alger in this situation, even though she'd known him all her life.

"*Yes.*"

PART
2

Must-Do List (revised)

✔ graduate degree

✔ win a fellowship

✔ find excuse to avoid

   10-year high school reunion

_ really fall in love

Achievement brings its own anticlimax.
—Maya Angelou
(born Marguerite Ann Johnson, April 4, 1928)

CHAPTER
3

If there was such a thing as a better day than this, Sonnet Romano couldn't imagine what that might look like. Brighter sunshine? Clearer air? Theme music playing as she crossed Central Park en route to 77th Street subway station? Street performers scattering flower petals as she passed by?

She didn't need any of that, not today. Her own news was good enough. The beautiful spring weather was the icing on the cake. New York City was at its best, crisp and clear and lovely as a fairy tale. Great things hovered over her head like air traffic over LaGuardia.

She took out her mobile phone, because the only thing missing at the moment was someone to share her good news with.

Great Thing #1: Her father was taking her and Orlando to dinner at Le Cirque. Time with her father—whose senatorial campaign was now in full swing—was precious, and she was eager to catch up with him and share her news.

Great Thing #2: Orlando. The ideal boyfriend, the kind of

guy who seemed too good to be true. Everyone said she and Orlando were great together, and they were only going to get better. Just this morning, he had given her the key to his apartment. Correction: the key to his stunning East Side pre-war co-op, which had closets bigger than Sonnet's entire studio. Orlando was not the kind of guy who gave out keys lightly. He'd told Sonnet she was the first, and that had to mean something. Also, he was proof that she'd moved on from the Zach incident, that singularly bad decision she'd made at Daisy's wedding last fall.

So why then, she wondered, did her finger hover over his name on the screen of her phone, like the planchette of a Ouija board? Why, even now, did she think of him first when she had big news?

The big news was Great Thing #3: Perhaps the greatest—the fellowship. Out of a field of thousands of candidates, she—Sonnet Romano—had been chosen for a Hartstone Fellowship. It was probably the biggest personal news she'd ever had, and she was dying to share it with someone. She quickly scrolled past Zach's name—and why, pray tell, asked a little voice inside her, have you not deleted him from your contact list?—and went to her mother's name—Nina Bellamy. As usual, her mom's voice mail picked up. During the workday, Nina was too busy running the Inn at Willow Lake to take a call. Sonnet didn't bother leaving a message; her mom tended to forget to check. They'd catch up later.

She called Daisy next, and Daisy, bless her, picked up on the first ring. "Hey, you," she said. "How's my wicked stepsister?"

"Good. *So* good. In fact, Mrs. Air Force Babe of Oklahoma, you need to stop me from making a fool of myself. I'm in the middle of Central Park and I'm tempted to burst into song about what a Great Day this is. I'm about to become a one-woman flash mob. Stop me because I'm supposed to be cooler than that."

"You're a New Yorker. You *know* you're cooler than that. But it does sound like you're having a good day."

"I'd say so. The *best*."

"That's good. So, you've got news? What's going on?"

"God, just…everything. I got the fellowship, Daze. I got it. Out of everyone they could have picked, they picked me."

"That's great. So what does it mean? Besides more laurel wreaths being laid at your feet? You know you're making the rest of the family look bad, right?"

"Hardly." She knew Daisy had to be kidding. A talented photographer, she'd been given a citation as an emerging artist, and her work had been in a special show at the Museum of Modern Art. She'd set the bar high. Sonnet was just glad the two of them worked in completely different fields. "What the fellowship does is put me in charge of a program to give indigent children a chance in life. It's incredible to think I could really make an impact. I don't know yet whether I'll be assigned to a domestic program or overseas, although it doesn't matter. There's need everywhere."

"Wow, that's really something, Sonnet," Daisy said. "There was never any doubt, not in my mind, anyway. You're amazing. So, uh, will you be traveling somewhere far away?"

Despite the enthusiastic words, Sonnet heard something in Daisy's tone. "You sound funny," said Sonnet. "What's up? Is Charlie doing any better in school?" Daisy had the most adorable son, but the kid was having a hard time with school this year.

"It's a process," Daisy said. "So hard to see him struggle, but we're working on it. It's just… Hey, have you talked to your mom today?"

"I tried calling her but she didn't pick up. She never picks up. Why do you ask?"

"Oh. You should call her. She…"

"God, is Max in trouble again?" Daisy's younger brother, now in college, had always been something of a challenge.

"It's just…call, okay?"

"Don't be going all cryptic on me. I—"

"Hey, you're breaking up."

"Oh, you big faker—"

"Sorry. Can't hear. And I need to check on Charlie—"

The line went dead. Sonnet instantly tried her mother again, and then the Inn at Willow Lake, but was told Nina was out. Frustrated, she glared down at her phone. There was Zach Alger's name, at the top of the contact list. Prior to the night of Daisy's wedding, he would have been one of the first people she would call with her news, good or bad. That had all changed, though. She'd never call him again, not after that glorious, sweet, impossible mistake she'd made in the boathouse six months before.

Stop. It was a known fact that ruminating on regrettable past events was an unhealthy habit. Better by far to accept what had happened, set it aside and move on. Ruminating kept the incident alive in one's head, meaning the hurt, anger, humiliation and regrets felt like fresh wounds, even after time had passed.

Sonnet knew these things. She'd read the self-help books. She'd sat through college courses in human psychology. She knew the drill. Knew how to protect her own heart. Therefore, it was disconcerting to realize she hadn't been able to push past what she'd come to refer to in her head as the Zach incident.

Having sex with him had been a moment of madness. The sex had been outstanding, but she couldn't let herself dwell on that. In his arms, she'd felt protected and adored and special... and she couldn't think about that, either. Because no matter what sort of crazy connection they'd found that night, there was no chance for a romantic relationship for the two of them, and they both knew it. The fellowship and her career were just too important to her; she couldn't compromise everything she'd worked for just because skinny little Zach Alger had morphed into a sex god.

Particularly in light of what had happened after. The humiliation still made her cringe. After their mad lovemaking, they'd been lounging on the bench seat of the boat, speechless with the lush saturation of sexual fulfillment. Finally, Zach had tried to say something. "That was…that…God, Sonnet."

She hadn't done much better. "I think we'd better… I'm… Is there any more champagne?"

He reached for the bottle. He paused, and she saw him frown in the dim light. "Shit, it was on."

She was still limp with pleasure. "What was on? You mean that camera thing? No way. Oh, my God. Can you fix it?"

He laughed. "Relax, I'm a professional." He'd popped out the camera's SD card. "Your secret's safe with me."

"You totally have to erase that, Zach. I don't care if it recorded anything or not. You have to promise."

"Of course I'm going to erase it," he said. "What do you take me for? Hey, I can do better than that." He flicked the tiny card into the lake. Then he had turned to her, this sexy stranger who had once been her best friend. "Now, where were we?"

And the mind-blowing sex had continued. Dawn had crept in, and they'd sneaked away from the boathouse, only to encounter Shane Gilmore, president of the local bank and the town gossip, out for his morning jog by the lake. Her mom's ex, of all people. And there had been no mistaking the expression on his face.

Sonnet cringed all over again as she reached the edge of Central Park, heading for the subway to catch the train to the restaurant. She emerged from the lush gardens of the park onto Fifth Avenue, where the sidewalk was crammed with hurrying pedestrians who all seemed to be in a pointless race with one another.

To refocus her thoughts, she slipped her hand into her pocket and closed it around the key. No one else in the surging stream of humanity had any clue what the key meant to her or even why. Despite the warmth of the day, she felt a chill.

It was a chill of excitement. Of anticipation. The key had been given to her by Orlando, aka the ideal boyfriend. He was one of those guys who really was as good as he looked on paper—

background, education, career path, manners, looks. And because her father had introduced them, Orlando had arrived in her life preapproved. And he said he was in love with her.

He was the first man to say so. Hearing the declaration hadn't been the exhilarating free fall of emotion she'd imagined as a girl. It was better than that. He was mature, he knew what he wanted, and he wanted to share his life with her.

As the crowd on the sidewalk halted for a traffic light, she gave a couple of bills to a guy strumming "While My Guitar Gently Weeps" on a ukulele. A block farther, she played a secret game of peekaboo with a toddler being jiggled on his mother's shoulder. Oblivious, the mother gabbed away on her phone about a fight she was having with her boyfriend. The baby had cheeks like ripe apples and eyes that looked perpetually startled, and a wisp of blond hair rising from his forehead like the flame of a candle.

He looked like half the dolls Sonnet used to play with when she was a little girl. The other dolls looked more like the little African-American girl in the umbrella stroller a few feet away. When Sonnet got older, her mom had explained that baby dolls who looked like Sonnet were hard to come by. Santa's elves, apparently, had not caught up with the times. Mixed race babies were common enough; dolls that resembled them, not so much.

The light changed and she walked on, her fingers clenched around the key until its teeth bit into the palm of her hand. She wasn't so sure herself. The way her career was going at UNESCO, there was scarcely time to squeeze in a trip upstate to see her own mom, let alone raise a kid.

On the other hand, her twenty-eight-year-old body was awash in hormones raining from an invisible emptiness inside her, just begging to procreate.

She wondered what Orlando would say if she brought it up. He'd probably bolt for the nearest exit. They were still too new, key or no key. He had told her long ago that he wanted to postpone having kids. There would be plenty of time for that un-specified "someday."

As far as she was concerned, nothing could dampen her spir-its today. She had the ultimate good news to share, and she was about to share it with the two people who would totally get how cool it was.

She'd been racing around madly all day, trying to get ready for this new chapter in her life. A Hartstone Fellowship. She, Sonnet Romano, from the tiny town of Avalon on Willow Lake, had been chosen for the honor. People who won the Hartstone Fellowship tended to change the world. She'd always been eager to measure up to her father's expectations. Personal accom-plishments were so important to her father. She could under-stand that. They validated you, told the world you did things that mattered.

As usual, she was in a hurry. It was her normal mode. She had hurried through school, graduating with a 4.0 GPA and zoom-ing ahead to her dream school, American University. From there she'd pursued a double major in French and international stud-ies, then raced ahead to grad school. Sometimes she asked her-self what the hurry was, but mostly, she didn't slow down long enough to wonder.

And it was working well for her. The letter in her satchel was proof of that, for sure.

As she hurried down the stairs to catch the train—she was on the verge of being late, an unforgivable offense in her father's book—her phone chimed, signaling an incoming text message, sneaking in just before she lost the signal underground. At the same time, she heard the train rattling into the station. She rushed to slip her pass through the turnstile and proceed into the fecund heat of the underground station.

The train's moon-yellow headlights were filmed with the ever-present dirt of the subway, and its brakes gave a tired-sounding squeal. The doors clanked apart, disgorging streams of passengers. Just as quickly, people on the platform boarded. She paused and bent down to help a woman with a stroller over the gap between the platform and the train car.

At the same time, she thought about the text message that had come in. She didn't know what made her grab for her phone just in that moment; she got text messages all the time. Habit, probably. Or it could be Daisy's cryptic comment about checking in with her mom.

As Sonnet stepped across the gap and took out her phone, someone jostled her from behind. Both the phone and the key dropped from her hand. She saw a coppery flash as the key disappeared onto the tracks, and her heart sank along with it. The phone screen stayed lit momentarily. Before it slipped from her hand, she saw the name of the sender of the incoming message: Zach Alger.

A crush of passengers pressed in from behind. The doors clanked shut, and the train lurched away.

Sonnet grabbed a safety pole and clenched her jaw. Her stomach turned to a ball of ice. *You made me drop the key,* she silently seethed. *Prepare to die.*

His name on the screen reminded her that she should have taken him off her contact list months ago. Unfortunately, that didn't mean she could erase him from her mind. She used to look forward with pleasure to his text messages, but now the thought of him made her shudder.

Given where she was now, her relationship with Orlando moving ahead, Zach could ruin everything. Having sex with him the night of Daisy's wedding had been the ultimate bone-headed move on both their parts, and she bloody well knew it. As soon as she'd floated back down to earth, as soon as the pink cloud of champagne and wedding bliss wore off, she had felt a terrible twist of foreboding in the pit of her stomach. In one foolish act, they had changed their friendship irrevocably, and not for the better. Her father had just introduced her to

Mr. Wonderful; she needed to focus on Orlando, not get drunk with Zach Alger.

She hadn't spoken to him since. He'd called a bunch at first, sent text messages, and she finally texted him back and said, Don't call me. Don't text me. Can we just leave it at that?

His calls had stopped, and she told herself she was relieved. There was nothing to say. What were they going to say? Sorry I screwed up a beautiful friendship? Have a nice life?

Willfully she pulled her mind away from the lost phone and focused on the more immediate problem. The missing key. Now, there was a boneheaded move for you. When your boyfriend finally gives you a key to his amazing midtown east apartment, losing it immediately is a bad move. Sure, it was an accident, but the symbolism was hard to ignore.

On top of that, she was going to be late. Both her father and Orlando were sticklers for promptness, yet somehow she'd fallen behind. And now she didn't even have a way to send Orlando a text.

Her stomach clenching, she found a vacant seat and sat down. Across from her sat a teenage girl and her mother. Sonnet studied their reflection in the window glass of the subway car. The two of them looked alike, except for the way the mother's Nordic coloring and blond hair contrasted sharply with the girl's nappy hair and café-au-lait skin. She wore her mixed heritage like an ill-fitting garment. Sonnet related to that kind of discomfort because once, not so long ago, she'd been that girl— biracial and wondering just where she belonged.

The girl had her iPhone turned up too loud, and through the earbuds, Sonnet recognized the thud and angry tones of Jezebel, the latest hip-hop sensation. The chart-topping song was called "Don't Make a Ho into a Housewife" or some such nonsense. Though she was no fan of the genre, Sonnet was aware of Jezebel from the scandal blogs and magazines. She was the latest of many to be doing time for something or other.

The girl listening to the music looked angry, too. Maybe she was having a bad day. Maybe she was ticked off at her mom. Maybe she was wondering why her dad only got in touch with her on Christmas and on her birthday, and half the time he forgot the birthday. Maybe she was trying to figure out what she was supposed to do in order to get his attention.

In the window glass, her gaze met the girl's. Both glanced quickly away, perhaps recognizing in each other a kindred spirit.

You'll be fine, Sonnet wanted to reassure the girl. Just like I'm fine. *Fine.*

As she approached her stop on the subway, Sonnet tried to come up with something plausible to tell Orlando about the key. Saying she'd dropped it on the subway sounded so…so careless. And she did care. Having access to his apartment, his private space, was a huge step for them as a couple. It meant something, something big.

The very thought of it made her heart skip a beat. To Sonnet, this was not a pleasant sensation.

Zach Alger stared down at the screen of his iPhone. He shouldn't have sent that text to Sonnet. He really, *really* shouldn't have sent it. What was he thinking? He wasn't thinking.

Maybe being in church affected his judgment. Although he wasn't *in* church, attending services. He was doing wedding prep work at Heart of the Mountains Church, getting ready for a big video job here. So at the moment, it didn't count.

He wrote down a couple of measurements—they were cramming too many people into the sanctuary, but he'd deal—and then paused to check his phone. Good, no reply. He scrolled to email, and his queue was full of work stuff. Endless work stuff, sandwiched between a few notes from women. Yeah, he was "dating." In a town like this, with a population that couldn't fill a high school stadium, that simply meant he was keeping his options open. On the menu today—he could go to the climbing gym with Lannie, and there were worse things than staring at her cute butt while holding the belaying rope. Or, he could go to Viv's for dinner. She was a sous-chef at the Apple Tree Inn, and she had trained at the Cordon Bleu. Third option—an open invitation from Shakti, who practiced a form of yoga she liked to call Yoga Sutra.

His buddies on his mountain biking team envied him the attention from women. And hell yeah, he loved women. He loved their soft hair and their curvy bodies, the flowery scent of them and the lilt of their laughter. He loved them all, yet to his dismay, he wanted only one. And the one he wanted was Lady Insanity herself, Sonnet Romano.

No. Correction. She was not the one he wanted. She was the one he wanted to avoid.

Contacting her had been a bad lapse, and it was convenient to foist the blame on something other than himself. He hadn't spoken to her since that night. Yeah, *that* night. But he'd felt compelled to contact her today because something weird was going on. After the epic night of sex, he'd been pretty sure it was their secret.

Yet now he was not so sure.

His friend Daphne, aka the ace internet mole, had alerted him this morning that something was up. A web-based rumor mill had published a nasty little bit hinting that the daughter of a certain candidate for the U.S. Senate was into, ahem, post-wedding hookups.

Politics was a dirty business. In the race for public office, nothing was off-limits, not even the candidate's family. In making a run for national office, Laurence Jeffries was putting everyone in his orbit in the spotlight. Zach wondered if the guy had thought about that when he'd decided to go for it.

Zach's own father—still serving time for defrauding the city of Avalon—certainly hadn't taken Zach into consideration. Sometimes, Zach thought that was what tied him to this little town, long after he should have left. He had something to prove; he wanted to show people that he wasn't anything like his father.

Upon seeing the link to the hookup story, Zach had impulsively sent Sonnet a text message. A heads-up; it was the least he could do. He didn't actually worry too much on his own behalf. Thanks to his father, Zach was beyond the point of embarrassment. But Sonnet had always been super sensitive about her reputation.

Yet the moment he'd hit Send, he started wondering if the rumor mill had simply made a lucky guess, or if they really knew something. Or if there had been a different wedding... and a different guy.

He batted at a fly buzzing around his head and got back to work.

She probably wouldn't respond. Ever since the wedding— the post-wedding-champagne-fueled sex they'd enjoyed—Sonnet had been in hiding. To be honest, Zach was okay with what had happened—hell, he'd liked it, but Sonnet insisted they weren't a match. No way they were a match, despite the mind-blowing boathouse encounter, and she claimed they were both old enough to realize it. She wanted them to go back to being friends, the way they'd been since kindergarten.

He wanted more. She wouldn't let him convince her, though. She made it clear that being with him would put a crimp in her future plans. Fine, then, he thought. He had plans, too.

But he missed her. Shit, he really did. He missed the friendship, the easy feeling of being with someone he felt completely comfortable with. Most guys had a family to lean on, but not Zach. He was the son of a bad man who was behind bars. His mom had left when he was a kid, remarried and then died of cancer. So he was not exactly a member of the all-American family. Through the years, Sonnet had become his default go-to person, the one he could call or text at all hours, the one who knew his history and didn't judge him for it, the one who loved hearing his good news. Correction—she used to love it. Now she didn't even pick up the phone.

Inside the church, he ran into the pastor, a paunchy, sober man who took great pleasure in marrying starry-eyed couples in his storybook-cute church.

"Hey, Reverend Munson," he said. "I'll be out of your way shortly. Just needed to make a plan for Saturday's ceremony."

"Take all the time you need, Zachary. I know how important the video is to the bride."

"Yep," he said. "You're right about that."

"Jenna's back from her mission trip to Korea," said Reverend Munson, referring to his youngest daughter. "I imagine she's going to want to tell you all about it. She always did like you, and she took a lot of video footage over there. I'm sure she'll be in touch."

She'd already been in touch, Zach reflected. It was awkward as hell making small talk with the reverend, who was clearly unaware that not so long ago, Zach had spent a few pleasant hours sipping Zima from his daughter's navel. And doing some other things as well.

"I think I've got everything I need," Zach said with hearty decisiveness. "See you on Saturday, sir."

"I'll be camera ready." Reverend Munson playfully framed his face with his hands. His clean pale hands, the ring finger encircled with a band of gold. For some reason, Zach started feeling guilty.

What the hell, he thought as he left the sanctuary. He'd been working as a videographer and editor for Wendela's Wedding Wonders since college. Nothing wrong with the gig except that he was forced to work crazy hours, endure bridezillas and their maniac moms, and he hadn't seen a Saturday night since he'd become old enough to drink.

And what Zach wanted, what he longed to do, was tell stories. Not his own. God, no. Other people's stories. He'd been doing it ever since he was old enough to hold a camera. He had a knack for capturing a subject's emotions on film, finding their hidden vulnerabilities, peeling away the layers to reveal truths that were often raw, but beautiful. He wanted to go out into the world and find those stories. He ought to get out of Avalon before he got stuck here forever.

But that took dough, lots of it. For a long time, it had seemed like an impossible dream as he dug himself out of student loans, made regular payments to the town of Avalon in an attempt to make up for what his father had stolen and gambled away, and simply went about the business of living. There was no law requiring him to make restitution for the damage his father had done, but the night with Sonnet had reminded him that this was not a dress rehearsal.

In order to move ahead in the field, he needed to go where the work was. L.A. or New York. He'd been sending out his portfolio for the past couple of years. So far he'd won loads of admiration and a prestigious award or two, but no offers of paying work.

Pissed at his thoughts for circling around to Sonnet again, he scrolled through his contacts, the digital equivalent of a little black book, and without much thought, hit on one. Shakti. She always picked up.

"Hey, what are you doing?" he asked.

"Waiting for you to call." She gave a soft, ego-stroking purr.

"I'll be right over."

Later that night, Zach went to the Hilltop Tavern, an Avalon watering hole favored by locals. Two of his buddies were there—Eddie Haven, a talented singer and songwriter who had settled in town to hide from his past as a troubled child star, and Bo Crutcher, a pitcher for the Yankees who used to play bass in Eddie's band, and kept a vacation cabin on the lake. Zach had filmed both guys' wedding videos, and they'd become friends along the way.

"I got girl trouble," he said, sliding into the booth with them.

"My favorite kind," Bo said, filling Zach's glass from a frosty pitcher of beer.

Eddie raised his glass of root beer. "What's up, my brother? Shit, don't tell me somebody's pregnant."

"No," Zach said instantly, shuddering with a chill at the very thought. "It's complicated. See, I kind of...you know, I've always been one to play the field."

"Boy slut," said Eddie. "We've all been there."

"That's why I'm telling you this," Zach said. "So now—and I never thought I'd be saying this—it's getting old." He thought about Shakti, who had rolled out the welcome mat earlier in the evening. He hadn't taken advantage of the welcome. Instead, he'd bought her dinner, dropped her off at her house, and called this meeting with his friends to confess that he was losing his mind.

"Dude," said Bo. "Welcome to adulthood. We all take a while to get there, but we get there. I know I did."

"You did it by marrying a woman who looks like a supermodel," Zach said. "That must have been so hard for you."

Bo laughed. "I reckon it was harder for Kim. So what's on your mind?"

"Who, not what. Sonnet Romano. Yeah, *that* Sonnet Romano. The one I've known since she was Willow Lake's hopscotch champion. We had...we did..."

"Nina's girl? You finally nailed her? Awesome," said Eddie, high-fiving him. "Doesn't sound like so much trouble to me."

"Then you don't know Sonnet. She could make a copper penny complicated."

"Let me guess," said Bo. "You nailed her, and now she wants a...what's that word? Oh, yeah. *Relationship*. It never fails. Give 'em a few X's and O's, and next thing you know, they're picking out the china pattern."

"Jesus, you're a tool," said Zach. "How come a tool like you gets to marry a supermodel?"

Bo glanced from him to Eddie. "What?"

"Here's the complication," Zach said, "and believe me, it pains me to admit this. *I* want the relationship."

To his relief, Bo and Eddie did not look too aghast, merely interested.

"Okay," Zach went on, "maybe not the china pattern, but yeah, all the stuff most guys want to run away from. I can't stop thinking about her, even when I'm trying to move on to another girl."

"In my very educated opinion," Eddie said, "other girls tend to be distractions from what you really want."

"Yeah," said Bo. "What is it you really want?"

Zach took a large gulp of beer and let out a lengthy belch. "The whole thing—love and family, stability, even kids one day. Yeah, kids. I want kids, how crazy is that?"

"It's not crazy at all," said Eddie. "Maureen and I are having loads of fun working on that. Kids are awesome. It's the parents who screw them up. All you got to do is promise you won't be that kind of parent."

"That's getting ahead of things. We're not even back on speaking terms these days."

"Why the hell not?"

"After we... After I—"

"Nailed her," Bo supplied.

"Yeah, it was in the boathouse up at Camp Kioga. Shane Gilmore figured it out, I think."

"Now, there's a tool for you. Can't stand that guy," Eddie said. "What the hell do you care?"

"I don't, but Sonnet's father is running for Senate, and

Gilmore's driving around with a Delvecchio bumper sticker on his car, so he's supporting the opponent."

"Whoa, I didn't know she was Jeffries's daughter," Bo said.

"Like I told you, she's complicated. Anyway, I saw a stupid rumor about the candidate's daughter hooking up at a wedding—did I mention we hooked up at Daisy Bellamy's wedding?"

Bo refilled Zach's beer glass yet again. "Drink up. It's gonna be a long night."

Sonnet rushed into the restaurant approximately ten minutes late to find Orlando in the foyer, jabbing his finger at the keypad of his phone.

"Sorry," she said, slightly breathless. "I got caught in the rush-hour craziness."

He put away his phone and bent to brush her cheek with a kiss. He was impressive, a tangible presence, exuding the class and polish of his Ivy League graduate degree, his looks an attractive balance between his Cuban mother and African-American father. After fulfilling his service requirement for West Point, Orlando had gotten an advanced degree in political science from Columbia and had become an expert at managing electoral campaigns. He was known as one of the best in the business, stopping at nothing to advance his candidate's cause.

"Just curious," he said in his half-teasing way, "does rush hour come unexpectedly every weekday?" He softened the critique with his trademark smile.

Sonnet furrowed a hand through her hair—it was now a fuzzy mess, thanks to the rushing and the rain. Yes, she had emerged from the subway to find the sunshine had turned to rain—and of course she had no umbrella.

"I got caught in the rain," she confessed.

"You should carry an umbrella."

She hated seeming scattered and disheveled around Orlando,

who was always the soul of organization. And here she was, committing the trifecta of blunders. She had lost the key to his apartment. She had lost her mobile phone. And to top it all off, she was late.

"I don't blame you for being mad," she said.

"Hey," he said, "it's okay. Nothing to get mad about. I'm on-time enough for both of us."

She summoned a smile and took his hand. Orlando Rivera was brilliant, professional and knew the importance of being prompt. No wonder he was in charge of getting her father elected to Congress.

It was surreal to Sonnet, the idea of her father becoming a U.S. senator. But it was not surprising; Laurence Jeffries had always been a larger-than-life figure. Although he was her birth father, he'd taken on the proportions of myth. Yes, she admitted that. But it never kept her from hoping they would build something sturdier on that foundation.

As a kid, she'd fantasized about having him in her life more than a couple of times a year. Then she'd been accepted to a major college, and everything had changed. Suddenly she had done something remarkable, winning a scholarship for a world-class education, and her father not only took note, he'd reached out to her. She still remembered the expression on her mom's face when Nina had handed her the phone. "Laurence wants to speak to you."

Her father almost never called. There was usually a stilted conversation on Christmas, late in the day after all the presents and feasting, and sometimes on her birthday, when he remembered. So for him to call out of the blue had been extraordinary.

"You've made me proud" were his first words to her that day.

Her heart had taken wing. Sure, she knew she'd be justified in asking him why he'd never been more than a modest monthly check to her up to this point, or asking him why he couldn't have been there for her during her not-so-proud moments, like when she'd been caught skipping gym class, or when she'd stolen a sex manual from the library, or was left on the curb after her first date, because she'd refused to put out.

But instead of hurling recriminations, she'd opened her heart to her father. They'd talked at length about her future and her goals. She'd once thought she wanted to teach or somehow work with children, but her dad had convinced her that she would have more of an impact on the world with an international career. He was passionate about global affairs and about the possibility of bringing about positive change in the world, and that passion was infectious. Broadening her focus, Sonnet had pursued international studies with single-minded determination, intent on proving herself every bit as worthy as the two trophy daughters her father had with the woman he'd married.

She pulled her mind away from her dad's "other" family— his legitimate family. Angela, his lovely and accomplished wife, and his daughters, Layla and Kara. Sonnet herself had a glorious family on her mother's side—the big Romano clan of Avalon—and for that, she would always be grateful, just as she was grateful for her vibrant career and this new, huge opportunity offered by the fellowship.

Maybe in the excitement over her news, Orlando would dismiss the fact that she'd lost his key.

"I can't believe you lost my key," Orlando said after she'd sheepishly explained what happened. He shrugged out of his cashmere overcoat and handed it to the coat check girl.

"I'm really sorry." Sonnet handed over her coat as well. "I don't know what else to say. I'll have another one made."

"You can't. It's a co-op. The building supervisor has to get a duplicate. I'll take care of it."

"Sorry," she said again, probably for the dozenth time. He was being nice about it, but she almost wished he'd tell her it was a huge pain in the ass and get the scolding over with.

"I know. I'll deal with it. But listen, since we're taking this step, there's something we need to talk about." He paused, took her hand and lifted it to his lips.

She smiled, taken in by the warmth in his eyes. "Kissing my hand in public, Orlando? I'm a fan."

He smiled back. "And I'm a fan of you. I just wanted to talk about the whole key thing—the whole sleeping-over thing."

She bit her lip. Maybe the fellowship was not going to be such welcome news to him after all. "I love the sleeping-over thing. I love that you gave me a key."

"I love it, too, don't get me wrong. That's why I need to ask you…"

…*to marry me.* Sonnet heard the words in her head, and even though they hadn't been spoken aloud, she got chills. She pictured herself saying yes, flinging her arms around him, being hoisted off the floor and spun around as they shared a joyous kiss.

"…because of all the attention he'll be getting as we get closer to election season."

"I'm sorry, what?" She flushed, embarrassed by her own flight of fantasy.

"I was just saying, let's try to be discreet about you staying at my place."

"Right. This is the twenty-first century, after all."

"You and I know that. But there are still plenty of voters who could take issue with the idea that the candidate's daughter—"

"—who happens to be a grown-up with a life of her own—"

"Sorry, I don't make the rules. Honey, all I'm saying is let's try to keep our private life just that—*private.*"

"Are you afraid I'm going to, what, post our status on Facebook?"

"Of course not. I'm afraid some dumb-ass from the opposition is going to try to make an issue of it."

"Then why did you bother giving me a key—oh. I get it now. You gave me a key so I didn't have to be buzzed up every time, which is totally indiscreet, right?"

"Honey. I gave you a key because I want you in my life. I might want you there permanently, if you know what I'm saying."

"God, Orlando, how did you get so romantic? 'I might want you there permanently?' Seriously?"

"It's true, I might. But I'm not going to break down and propose right here and now in the middle of a crowded restaurant."

"Well, that's a relief."

"But I am going to propose. And it is going to be romantic and you're going to say yes."

Goose bumps suddenly covered her arms. But then, questions and second-guessing kicked in. Was he going to propose because he loved her and couldn't live without her, or because it would make his candidate's daughter look less like a slut to the electorate?

She brushed aside the cynical thought. When had she turned into such a skeptic? Or had she always been this way?

A large, imposing silhouette filled the doorway.

"Hey, my father just got here," she said. "Can we talk about the key later?"

Orlando was already striding across the foyer, his hand outstretched. "Laurence, how are you?" No comment about General Jeffries being tardy.

Sonnet felt a swell of pride and excitement as the two men shook hands. Her father was every inch the military man, looking as polished as the brass buttons on his swirling greatcoat.

Standing between the two of them, she felt like a princess, flanked by visiting royalty. The host led them to their table, where he held the thronelike upholstered chair for her.

"So there's news," Sonnet said once they were all seated. "Good news."

"I'm always up for good news." Her father regarded her warmly.

She paused, savoring the moment. "I got the Hartstone Fellowship," she said. "The call came today, and I have an official letter."

Orlando gave a low whistle. "That's fantastic."

"Sonnet, I'm so proud of you." Her father ordered a bottle of champagne. "I can't say I'm surprised, but proud as hell."

"Thanks. I'm still pinching myself." She beamed at them both as the sommelier brought a bottle of Cristal and poured three flutes. "It's so great that we're together, celebrating. I was going to send you an email but I wanted to tell you in person." She'd been brimming over with the news all day.

"You deserve it," said Orlando. "I know how hard you worked for this."

"He's right," her father agreed. "We're going to miss you when you're overseas."

Sonnet blinked. "How do you know it's an overseas assignment?"

He glanced up at the chandelier. "That's usually the case. Am I wrong?"

"Never," she said, but he failed to catch the note of irony in her voice.

"With your background and language skills, you'd excel in a foreign location." He waved a hand to summon the waiter. "I think we're ready to order."

"I have the final numbers on the fundraiser." Orlando handed Laurence a printout. "I thought you'd like to see."

"We exceeded our goal for this stage of the campaign," said Laurence.

"That's great, Dad. It's good news all around," Sonnet said. She really wanted to talk more about the fellowship, but didn't want to monopolize the conversation. "Maybe we should buy lottery tickets."

"I've never been one to leave things to chance," her father said. "Better to make your own luck."

"Agreed," said Sonnet. Her father was something of a control freak. He had been ever since she'd gotten to know him during her college years.

Orlando and her father talked shop—polls, demographic studies, campaign strategies, and she listened attentively. When their meal came, there was a pause to appreciate the perfectly prepared food, served with deftness by a waitstaff that worked like a well-oiled machine. She flashed on a memory of her childhood—Sunday dinners at her Romano grandparents' home, with all the aunts, uncles and cousins diving into delicious but simple food, served family style. The food was simple but plentiful, the family noisy but bighearted.

"Wow, it's crazy to think that by next year, I'll be the daughter of a U.S. senator." Sonnet took a bite of the wild mushroom risotto, savoring the sherry and cream flavorings.

Laurence tried the wine and accepted it with a curt nod. "I assume you mean crazy in a good way."

She smiled as the waiter filled her glass. "Of course. It makes me really proud."

"I wish I could say the election is going to be a slam dunk." He sliced into his steak.

"We don't hear you saying that," Sonnet said.

"I have to be honest with you," said Laurence. "Delvecchio is getting desperate, and he's known to fight dirty when he's slipping in the polls."

"Are you saying he's slipping in the polls?"

"He most definitely is."

"So we can expect him to fight dirty," said Orlando.

"We can." Laurence swirled a bite of rare meat in the Bearnaise sauce. "And Sonnet, I have to tell you, he's bound to send someone snooping into every corner of my life."

"Including me, you mean." A knot of tension formed in the pit of her stomach.

"I wish I could deny it. Delvecchio is a master at negative spin. He could find a way to make Santa Claus look bad."

"How bad?" Sonnet pushed her plate away and regarded them both.

Orlando handed her a printout from a political blog. She scanned the article, horror rising along with the bile in her throat. She stared at her father. "They're bringing up your illicit affair as a West Point cadet with an underage local girl. Of a different race. Which, by the way, is not exactly fiction."

The article further characterized her father as a ruthlessly ambitious career operative who ignored his own child and moved ahead with his own agenda. At the bottom of the article was a link—Jeffries's love child...post-wedding hookups?—that made her nearly gag. How had that leaked?

"All fiction, of course," Orlando said confidently.

She shuddered with distaste, pushing aside the page. "They left out the bit about you having horns and a tail."

"I'm sorry," her father said. "I hate that you had to be sucked into this."

"How will you respond?"

"It's taken care of. I issued a statement with the truth, explaining that I wasn't aware that I'd fathered a child. Once I learned I had a daughter, I was elated by the gift I'd been given, and I supported you and your mother to the best of my ability. I'm proud to say you've grown into an accomplished young woman with a passion for service and a bright future ahead of her." The hookups notwithstanding, she thought with a shudder.

"Depending on their politics, readers will decide which version to believe," said Orlando.

"And if someone contacts me?" Sonnet suppressed a chill of terror.

"Tell them the truth," her father said easily. "*Your* truth."

"Sure," she said, envious of his sangfroid. "Right." In her heart, she knew she would gloss over certain key facts—such as the fact that she used to cry herself to sleep at night, wishing she had a daddy like other kids, even a part-time daddy. Or the

terrific, secret envy she felt toward his other daughters, Layla and Kara, the dual heiresses to his dynastic marriage. Yes, he'd married the perfect woman to enhance his career. Sonnet wanted to believe it was a love match, but sometimes she wondered if his marriage to the daughter of a famous civil rights leader had been by design or happenstance. Sonnet wouldn't say a word about these matters because she could scarcely admit them to herself. Love had never seemed like her father's top priority. He shied away from it, perhaps because it was the kind of thing that couldn't be controlled, like a battalion of soldiers or a department in the military.

"I'm a big girl," she assured them. "I can take care of myself."

"There was never a doubt," said her father. "But again, I'm sorry."

An uncomfortable thought struck her. "Did they harass my mother?"

"I would hope not, but unfortunately, we're dealing with Johnny Delvecchio."

"If he contacts her, she won't have anything bad to say." Sonnet spoke with complete assurance. Nina had always owned her part in the situation, too, and she'd never expressed any bitterness or resentment against Laurence. Not to Sonnet, anyway.

The conversation drifted to other campaign matters, the topic sneaking further away from Sonnet's big news. She tried not to feel cheated. This was supposed to be a celebration of her getting the fellowship. Of course, in the company of her father, she was used to being eclipsed. He had a big career and a big life, and running for Congress only made it bigger.

Like everyone else in his circle, she admired and respected him for his drive to succeed. Judging by the things he had achieved in his career, the propensity was working well for him. He lived a considered and well-crafted life.

The only misstep he'd ever made was Sonnet herself. She was the result of a youthful indiscretion, one for which the world had forgiven him. Some people were lucky that way. They got away with things.

Other than that, his resume was stellar. Through sheer determination, he'd risen from humble roots as the son of a single mother who got by on public assistance. In school, he excelled at both academics and sports, winning a coveted appointment to West Point. From there he'd climbed the ladder of leadership through the ranks of the military. He married well, in terms of his career, and as far as anyone knew, it was a loving partnership. His two lovely daughters wore the polish of private schools and an international lifestyle. Sonnet was the only blot on an otherwise spotless record.

She hated being the blot.

"How is this going to work?" Sonnet asked Orlando later that night as they got ready for bed. He'd calmed down about the key, and she felt excited to be at his place, carefully placing her belongings in a small corner of his walk-in closet. "With you being here and me going overseas?"

"Guess we'll rack up some air miles."

"I don't mean booking flights. I mean, how will it work?"

"You mean how will we stay in this relationship."

He'd called it a relationship. He'd teased her about a proposal—or was it more than teasing? They were making progress, she felt sure of it. Progress toward a goal—that was a good thing, right?

He was the most cautious guy she'd ever known, choosing his words as if they were going to be chiseled in stone. Saying something like "relationship" was serious business to a man like Orlando. She tended to be more impulsive, and he balanced her.

"Thank you," she said. "That is precisely what I mean."

"Besides visiting, there's email and Skype," he pointed out.

"And that's enough for you?"

"It will have to be. Unless you're willing to give up the fellowship."

"Or you're willing to give up the campaign," she said.

"Don't be silly. It's not an either/or situation."

She tried to figure out what she was feeling. Neither of them seemed too upset by the prospect of a lengthy separation. Yet they were in a relationship. He'd given her a key to his place, and even though she'd promptly lost it, they were still a couple. Weren't they?

"As a matter of fact, it's probably a good thing we don't give Delvecchio one more thing to latch on to."

"Orlando—"

His phone rang, and he grabbed it. She gritted her teeth. Couldn't he for once let it go to voice mail?

He answered, listened briefly, then handed her the phone. "It's your mother. She's been trying to reach you."

Sonnet grabbed it. "Mom, hey. I, uh, lost my phone today—"

"Oh, no wonder I couldn't get you. Sorry to call so late."

"Is everything okay?"

A beat of hesitation passed. "Why do you ask?"

"Daisy said you had news. Geez, Mom."

"She's right, honey. I've got a little news. Are you... Um, is this a good time to talk?"

"It's fine. Just tell me, Mom. You're freaking me out."

"Have a seat, Sonnet."

Sonnet carefully set the phone receiver back in its cradle. She felt strangely disoriented as she approached Orlando. He was now busy checking his email on his iPad. "Um...there's been a change of plans."

He barely looked up from his screen. "Yeah?"

"Are you listening?"

"Yeah. Sure, babe."

She hesitated, so filled with the news from home she couldn't

think straight. She wished she felt closer to Orlando in this moment. She longed for their relationship to be further along, so
that she could tell him anything and everything. But when she
tried to come up with the words to explain, she felt frustrated
before she even began.

Meanwhile, he'd gone back to reading on his iPad, the bluish
glow of the screen outlining the angles of his chiseled features.

"Orlando."

"Uh-huh?"

She abandoned the idea of explaining everything to him. So
she simply told him, "I have to go back to Avalon."

CHAPTER
4

"How about a cream-filled delight?" The waitress named Glynnis leaned toward Zach Alger and moistened her lips, just in case he missed the suggestion.

He didn't miss it. Kind of hard to miss a rack like Glynnis had. She was one of several women he'd dated, but she wanted something from him he had no capacity to give. Not to her, anyway. There wasn't a thing wrong with her…except that she was wrong for him.

"I'm good, thanks," he said, swirling the coffee in his mug.

"God, Zach, don't you know I'm hitting on you? You used to be fun. What's the matter with you?"

Great, he thought. She's going to make me say it. "Hey," he said, "that's really cool and you know I like you, but—"

"Whoa." She held up her hand, palm out. "I'd just as soon you didn't finish that thought. I can already see where you're going with it."

He tried not to show his relief. "I'm sorry. It's not you."

"Clearly not. God, I need to get the hell out of this burg. Don't you ever get the feeling you're fading away?"

Honestly, he didn't. Right here, in the middle of this small town, was where he felt most alive. Which probably meant there was something the matter with him.

"Me? Fading?" he said, trying to lighten the moment. "No way."

"Have the cream-filled delight anyway." She shoved a thick white china plate onto his table. "And don't forget to tip your server," she added as she went back to the counter.

Not only would it be rude to refuse the treat at this time, it would be foolhardy. No one in his right mind refused a pastry from the Sky River Bakery.

His love affair with the Sky River Bakery had begun way back when he was a tiny kid. Now it was still his favorite place to sit with a big mug of coffee and a cruller, getting into work mode for the day. The place looked virtually the same as it had all those years ago, although it had been stylishly updated by Jenny McKnight, the owner. There were café tables made from rounds of maple wood, a changing display of work by local artists, and a black-and-white checked floor. It still had an old-fashioned feel to it, and the warm, fragrant atmosphere created an air of nostalgia. Zach sometimes used it as the setting for wedding videos or personal narratives. The morning crowd was present—locals grabbing a bite, retired folks chatting over the day's *New York Times,* a couple of tourists perusing an area map.

In fact, the family-run shop was the site of his earliest memory. His mom was taking him to the first day of kindergarten and he was practically catatonic with terror. She'd grabbed his hand and ducked into the bakery, which was just a block from the primary school. He could still remember the sugary, buttery smell of the place, the smell of comfort.

His mom had bought him an apple kolache and a cup of hot chocolate, and she'd told him that going to school was a big adventure for a little boy, and that he was going to love it. And she'd filmed the whole thing. That was his mom's thing—documenting her life. She'd been compulsive about it, capturing moments on her video camera. His mom had filmed everything—his first day of school, his first lost tooth, his exploits on the soccer field, his disastrous attempts to emulate Jimmy Page. She didn't put herself in the picture much but her voice often came from behind the camera, always encouraging and sweet-toned. It was as if she'd known she wouldn't be around that long, and wanted to capture the two of them together for posterity. And sure enough, one day the filming had stopped, and she had moved away. Far away.

He hadn't seen it coming that day, and he hadn't been fooled for a minute by her pep talk about kindergarten. His head was full of nightmare visions of snarling teachers, an endless maze of hallways, rooms full of strangers. But then, as he was chewing on a bit of kolache, Sonnet Romano had breezed into the bakery, completely by herself. She wore a pink backpack with pockets and zippers, and pencils all lined up like bullet cartridges in an ammo belt. She wore her curly black hair in twin braids, and a pair of horn-rimmed glasses perched on her nose.

All by herself, she marched up to the counter. Her pointy little chin barely reached the edge. "One iced maple bar, please. And can you put it in a nice box? It's for my teacher. Today is my first day in kindergarten and I'm bringing her a treat." She carefully placed her money on the counter. "My mom said this is the right amount. She had to work today."

Zach stared at her in amazement. His mother nodded with approval. "It's that nice Sonnet Romano from play group. Why don't you go say hi?"

Zach recoiled in horror. He nearly gagged on his pastry.

While Sonnet waited for her parcel, she turned, zeroing in on him like a laser. "You're Zach," she said. "You're in Miss Nelson's class, same as me."

He couldn't think of anything to say, so he blurted out the first thing that popped into his mind. "Why are you wearing those glasses?"

"They make me look smarter," she said, tilting up her chin with pride. She turned abruptly, pigtails flying out like helicopter rotors. Then she picked up a pink cardboard box sealed with string, and went to the door.

She paused and turned to Zach. "Well? Are you coming?"

His mom had given him a hug. "Go ahead, sweetheart. It's going to be a wonderful day."

Zach shook his head at the memory. *Even then*. At the age of five, Sonnet knew exactly where she was going, and he was expected to follow along.

He sipped his coffee and frowned at the screen of his iPhone. He was supposed to be getting organized for the day, and instead he'd let his mind wander to a time back in ancient history. With a will, he made himself focus on the present.

The present wasn't a bad place to be. Here and now, with the future glimmering ahead like a sunrise on the horizon. He needed to move in that direction, not dwell in the past.

Through the shop window, he watched the town getting ready for the day. Shopkeepers rolled out their awnings and displayed their wares on the walkways. Delivery trucks disgorged supplies to restaurants, and people walked briskly toward the train station. Like any small town, an atmosphere of familiarity colored the scene. Zach had always liked that about Avalon. Being part of a small community filled in somewhat for his crappy family situation.

He had been on his own ever since high school, when his father was led away in handcuffs, the town disgrace. Zach was left with a house in foreclosure, a mountain of unpaid bills and a reputation in tatters. Matthew Alger had defrauded the town of Avalon. He'd picked the pockets of people who could scarcely buy groceries, let alone pay their local taxes.

Zach had made a vow that day. He would make restitution to the people his father had defrauded. It would surely take years, but he would do what he could. It wouldn't happen on his salary from Wendela's, though. Through the years, he had been depositing whatever he could into the city treasury, trying to chip away at his father's debt, bit by bit.

He was going to miss this place. But he had to go, and soon. How else was he going to find his life? Filming weddings and bar mitzvahs and retirement parties was a way to make ends meet. But being a filmmaker...that was his life. And he couldn't very well do that in Avalon. Sure, the town looked as pretty as a picture on a postcard, so pretty it made your heart ache. But pretty didn't pay the bills. To do that, he needed to go where the work was. But he was stuck in a conundrum. Due to lack of funds, he had not gone after what he wanted.

Zach's phone rang, and he did a double take. The name that came up was the one he least expected—the longest of longshots: Mickey Flick.

"Who's Mickey Flick?" demanded Glynnis, peering at the screen of his phone. She not only had a rack; she was the nosiest waitress on the planet.

He ignored her, and skimmed his thumb across the screen in order to take the call. "This is Zach Alger."

"Mickey Flick here." A crisp, easy familiarity mellowed the voice. The guy sounded as if he and Zach talked every week.

Zach held his breath. Mickey Flick headed up an outfit in Century City noted for its wildly successful celebrity reality shows. Zach was no fan of the genre, having little interest in watching has-been actors in some ludicrous setup. He was, however, a fan of the success of the shows. He'd been in contact with Mickey Flick Productions, knowing it was a crazy roll of the dice. There had been several emails back and forth with various assistants, but still, he hadn't expected anything to come of it. Now here was the guy, calling him out of the blue.

"Hey," he said, trying not to fumble. "Thanks for calling me back."

"Not a problem. We were glad to hear from you. We've been going over the samples you sent in."

Zach felt himself teetering on the brink. He knew, he just knew his life was about to change. "Wow. Well," he said, "I'm flattered you had a look. I hope you liked what you saw."

"Hell, yeah, we liked them. You've definitely got the technical expertise and the eye we're looking for, so I wanted to see if you're available for a new production that's about to start filming."

Available? Available? Was he available for Mickey-freaking-Flick?

"Could be," he said, hoping to sound measured. Interested, but not too eager. "Tell me more."

"For the time being, I can't say much. You'll get more details from Clyde Bombier, my production exec. It'll be a reality show, all under wraps until we're ready to go wide with it. What I can tell you is that it's a sixteen-week gig, it involves a major talent and a name director. You'd work directly with him."

"Okay," Zach said. "You have my attention."

He tried not to hyperventilate as he listened to the terms being offered. The money alone made his head spin, but the real excitement kicked in when Flick said he was sending a formal letter of offer and a contract via email.

Zach thanked him and hung up, looking around the bakery at the coffee drinkers, the tourists and locals, the little kids smearing their hands on the glass cases, the old guys with their crossword puzzles. These people had no idea that the world had just shifted for him. Finally the dream was coming into reach. He'd been trying to get a break forever, sending out his portfolio of digital clips, emailing them into what seemed like a black hole of digital ether. He'd been networking through people in the business who were at least six degrees away from West Coast and New York producers. Each award he won, each scrap of recognition, hoisted him another rung up the ladder, but until now, nothing had materialized.

The opportunity was still so new, he had only the sketchiest idea of what was in store for him next. He knew for certain Mickey Flick had a reputation for doing things in a big way. The guy had mentioned that this opportunity was a major production. *Major.* It was the biggest thing that had ever happened to Zach, for sure.

The current project was so top secret he would only learn the details when everything was in place. All he knew was he'd been offered a fortune to work on the production. He wondered why they'd picked him, given all the talent in the business. He wouldn't quibble. The money was nice, it was more than he'd dreamed of making, but that wasn't the part that excited him. What really excited him was the crazy array of possibilities that now lay before him.

Speculating on what the secret plan for the show might be, he dreamed of Malibu, maybe filming a surf competition. Or perhaps there would be a crew of castaways on Fiji, mountaineers in Colorado. Or a rock group in Amsterdam. Yeah, that'd be awesome. Mickey Flick was known to work closely with some of the biggest names in the music business. His last hit had involved a world-class heavy metal star's collaboration with a classical pianist, culminating in a triumphant performance in Carnegie Hall.

Zach couldn't wait to see what was in store for him. And at the end of it all, he'd finally have the seed money to start living his dream.

The people in the café carried on, oblivious. Just for a second, Zach felt a twinge of frustration. He wanted to call somebody, tell somebody, share this amazing news. And the person he most wanted to share it with was the last one who wanted to hear.

PART
3

Must-Do List (revised, again)

- ✔ sublet apartment

- ✔ return library books

- ✔ repay student loans

- ✔ realign priorities

- __ really fall in love (no, seriously)

---

*What we remember from childhood
we remember forever—permanent ghosts, stamped,
inked, imprinted, eternally seen.*
—Cynthia Ozick, American writer, b. 1928

CHAPTER 5

Sonnet awakened as the train from the city lurched into the station at Avalon. Just for a moment, she felt fuzzy and disoriented, her sleepy mind flipping through all her many homecomings. As a new, homesick college student, she'd arrived with a sense of relief, eager to be enfolded in the comfort of her mother's arms. During her various internships overseas, she'd visited less often, but always with appreciation. Yet as time went on, the town where she'd been born and raised seemed smaller and smaller to her, with less and less to tie her to the pretty lakeside hamlet. While her world was expanding, Avalon remained the same.

She felt strange about this homecoming, for a lot of reasons. It made her seem like she was going backward into a world where she no longer fit or belonged.

Grabbing her bags from the luggage rack, she stepped down to the platform and looked around. Same little burg, with its picturesque square, the old brick buildings huddled shoulder-to-shoulder, their striped and scalloped awnings shadowing the shops and businesses she'd walked past every day as she was growing up.

She noticed a bit of commotion on another car as a group of people got off, lugging hard cases of equipment and rolls of cable on hand trucks. There were a couple of guys and women, dressed mostly in black, looking around as if they'd stepped off a spacecraft onto an alien planet. One of the guys wore a black baseball cap with the logo MFP, and the equipment boxes were marked Mickey Flick Productions.

Sonnet thought they might be a camera crew. Back when her mother served as the town mayor, she'd set up a volunteer film commission to attract business. A place like Avalon didn't see much action, but every once in a while a crew came through to create footage of the quaint town, or of fall foliage or sometimes aerial views of the area. It was a place that seemed frozen in time, achingly pretty, useful for establishing a historic or generic small town setting. A few years back, there had been a public television documentary on the annual Christmas pageant that had created quite a stir.

The PBS camera crew hadn't looked like this bunch, however. These people had that edgy East or West Coast look. They consulted smartphones and lit up cigarettes before moving en masse to a large panel van parked in the commuter lot.

Seeing a camera crew reminded her of Zach Alger. He was the last person she wanted to think about, but she couldn't help herself. God, those kisses. Those hands. The things he'd whispered in her ear. Even now, she felt an unbidden spasm of desire at the mere thought of him. It was ridiculous, feeling turned on by a man she had no business thinking about.

Squaring her shoulders, she took out her new phone and sent a text to Max Bellamy, her stepbrother, who had offered to pick her up. In the parking lot, he texted back. Need help with bags? She indicated that she did not, and rolled her luggage toward Max's slightly beat-up Subaru.

Max stood in his shirtsleeves, one hand in his jeans pocket, his hip cocked at a jaunty angle. He attended college in Hamilton, where he liked to say he majored in beer and girls. With his surfer-blond good looks, he took after his dad, Greg Bellamy, though his air of easy charm was something that belonged to Max alone. Sonnet liked him well enough, but she would never understand him. He came from a great family—he was a *Bellamy,* for heaven's sake—yet he seemed to be in no hurry to find his life.

"Hey, you," she said, giving him a hug. He'd topped six feet a few years ago, and he moved with easy grace as he loaded her bags in the back. "Thanks for picking me up."

"Sure. Your mom's going to go nuts when she sees you."

"She's already nuts. Seriously, Max. *Pregnant?*" It felt weird just saying it aloud. Her mother—her over-forty mother—was pregnant. When Nina had first told her, Sonnet had been speechless with disbelief. Then she'd accused Nina of telling a bad joke. "I'm still in shock. How about you?"

Max rolled out of the parking lot and headed toward the Inn at Willow Lake, which Nina and Greg owned and operated. "It's cool with me. I mean, yeah, it's weird because we're so much older than little Junior or Juniorette is going to be, but..." He shrugged. "Red Bull?" He offered her a sip of his drink.

"Uh, no, thanks." She tried not to ingest things that had ingredients she couldn't pronounce. She looked out at the scenery—the covered bridge over the Schulyer River, the hills draped in sunlit green. As they neared the inn, she glimpsed the lake in the distance, shining like a jewel. "Hey, I saw a camera crew get off the train. Know anything about that?"

"Some kind of top-secret production is going to be starting. That's the word, anyway," Max said, flashing his thousand-watt grin. "Maybe they'll make me a star."

"You wish."

He turned into the gravel-paved lane leading to the Inn at Willow Lake. As always, it was lush and gorgeous, perfectly planted and maintained, a testament to Greg Bellamy's skill as a landscape architect. "There's some producer named C. Bomb staying at the inn," Max said. "He's like the head of the outfit or something."

"C. Bomb?"

"That's what he calls himself. Clyde Bombardier or something like that. Spends all day glued to his laptop, gabbing on his Bluetooth."

"So, not your typical guest." The inn was known as a place for romantic getaways. "And he's not telling people what he's up to?"

Max shrugged. "His business. I guess we'll find out soon enough."

"And my mom? My pregnant mom?" Sonnet was still trying to get her mind around the concept. When she'd told Orlando, he'd merely wondered why Sonnet had to go haring off to Avalon simply because her mom was expecting. Orlando didn't get it. It wasn't every day a grown woman discovered her mother was going to have a baby.

"*Her* business," Max said reasonably enough. "I'm sure the two of you will be up half the night discussing it."

Nina was sound asleep. Sonnet tiptoed into the house, which had once been a caretaker's cottage on the estate that had become the Inn at Willow Lake. She found her mother on a daybed in the living room, covered in an afghan, softly snoring. Quietly setting down her things, she paused to study Nina. Did she look different, or was that just Sonnet's imagination? She just looked like…Mom, with her pretty Italian features and thick black hair, which she'd grown long enough for a ponytail, her dark eyelashes shadowing cheeks that looked slightly gaunt. You're pregnant, Sonnet thought. You're supposed to be glowing.

"Mom," she said softly.

Nina's eyes fluttered open. Her mouth unfurled into a smile. "Hi, baby." Her favorite pet name for Sonnet now took on new meaning. "Thanks for coming."

Sonnet hurried over to the daybed and they hugged. Her mother smelled like Pond's lotion, a warm scent that took Sonnet back to her girlhood. She shut her eyes, and in a swift sequence she remembered all the hugs they'd shared through the years. During her childhood, the two of them had been inseparable, making their way through life together. There were tough years, there were times Sonnet yearned for a father or for something that looked like a two-parent family, but ultimately, the two-alone dynamic brought them closer. They were more than just mother and daughter; they were best friends.

"It's the middle of the day and you're sleeping," Sonnet said.

"The prerogative of pregnant ladies."

It felt completely surreal to Sonnet. "So you weren't kidding about being pregnant."

Nina scooted up to a sitting position. "Not kidding. Not the sort of thing any woman kids about."

There was a bottle of prenatal vitamins and a prescription bottle for something Sonnet didn't recognize next to a glass of water on the end table. Reality started sinking in. Sonnet's mother was pregnant. "Are you showing yet?"

Nina smoothed a hand down her midsection. "Not too much."

Sonnet couldn't help staring. "Not there, anyway. But wow, Mom. You've had a visit from the boob fairy. Your girls are looking good."

Nina waved her hand and glanced away. "I'm not really focused on that."

"Well then…congratulations. It's really exciting, Mom. Just unexpected. You caught me off guard. The last thing I thought I'd hear from you is that you're having a baby."

Nina smiled. "You'll get used to the idea. Greg and I are so happy."

"That's great." Sonnet was surprised to feel the tiniest twinge of jealousy, followed by a cold wave of shame. Her mother and Greg were totally in love, they were having a baby together, and she *was* happy about it. Yet there was a small, selfish part of her that wished she'd had the childhood this baby was going to have—two doting parents, a storybook-pretty life in this cottage near the lake. It was a stark contrast to the drafty rentals she and Nina had lived in, with Nina working all the time, trying to make ends meet.

"How are you feeling?" Sonnet asked, shifting gears into good-daughter mode. "Besides tired, I mean."

"I feel…I'll be fine," Nina said firmly. "Perfectly fine."

"So is it a boy or girl?"

"We considered leaving that unanswered, but I just had to know. I've already had the amnio, and what we know so far is that the baby is healthy and growing on schedule. And it's a boy."

"A boy." Sonnet felt a genuine smile unfurling on her lips. "I'm going to have a baby brother. That just seems so incredible."

"Okay, I'm getting a little insulted by how incredible you think it is. For a teen mom, I didn't do half bad, right? As an older mom, I'll manage," Nina said. "So, welcome home, my prodigal child," she added. "How long can you stay?"

"Today, plus the weekend. I wish it could be longer, but there's work."

"And the fellowship. Oh my gosh, baby, I'm so thrilled that you got the fellowship. You're amazing, do you know that?"

Sonnet hugged her mother again. "I'm feeling like a pretty big deal these days."

"You should feel like a big deal every day. I'm ridiculously proud of you. This is a huge opportunity, isn't it?"

"The biggest. I have a meeting next week to find out my assignment. Two years overseas…somewhere. I can't wait to find out."

A shadow flashed across Nina's face. Maybe Sonnet imagined it. Then she guessed her mother's thoughts. "Oh, God. I won't be here when the baby comes. Mom—"

"Stop right there. You don't need to be here for the birth. The baby won't know the difference."

"But you will. Mom, I could ask—"

"No," Nina interrupted again. "This is the opportunity of a lifetime. You've been working toward this since the day you left home. No way are you going to pass it up."

Sonnet felt her eyes misting up. "You're the best, you know that?"

"I've always told you so." Nina stood up and folded the afghan.

Sonnet studied her mother. "I thought pregnancy was supposed to make you fat. You look tiny, Mom. Are you eating okay?"

Nina fussed with the blanket, arranging it on the back of the chaise. "I've been having morning sickness. Come on. Let's go find Greg. He promised to make his famous barbecued chicken tonight. You want to see if Zach can come over?"

Sonnet bit her lip. It was completely normal to invite Zach to dinner. Absolutely, completely normal. Through the years, he'd been like a family member. "Maybe another time," she said.

"Am I hearing you right? You haven't been home since Daisy's wedding, and you're not seeing Zach?"

"Uh, not tonight, okay?"

"Sure, suit yourself." Nina winced a little as she started toward the door.

"Are you sure you're all right?" Sonnet asked.

"I'm fine." Nina squeezed her hand.

Yet as Sonnet followed her out of the room, she was struck by the strangest notion that something was afoot. She'd been away far too long.

CHAPTER
6

Zach paced the sidewalk in front of the bakery, trying to stay cool as he waited for his upcoming meeting with a producer who called himself C. Bomb. It was mystifying to Zach that the producer had come all the way to Avalon to meet with him, and to explain what the top-secret subject of the upcoming show was going to be.

Meanwhile, he had another client who'd asked to see him. He didn't usually get nervous about meeting potential clients. Usually they were the nervous ones, jittery brides wanting him to turn their special day into a piece of beautiful cinema worthy of an Academy Award. And the funny thing was, sometimes he did. Sometimes he captured a moment, elevated it to a lasting moment. Other times, he was lucky to record a few decent sequences before the event unraveled thanks to drunken groomsmen, warring relatives, or tearful brides having a hissy fit.

Today's client wasn't a bride. She was a married woman. Who just happened to be the mother of Sonnet Romano. What

Nina Romano Bellamy wanted with Zach was not likely to be a gauzy wedding video.

She showed up at the appointed time, a bit rushed and breathless. Sonnet's mother was attractive in a no-nonsense way, with olive-toned skin, balanced features and brown eyes, dark hair. The similarities between her and Sonnet were subtle but Zach could see the resemblance in the way they carried themselves and a certain energy that emanated from within. Nina looked a little frayed around the edges this morning, but she was the kind of pretty that shone through regardless. Sonnet took after her in that way; Zach couldn't help making the observation.

He couldn't remember a time when he hadn't known Nina. After his mom had left, he'd always been welcomed by her and the whole Romano clan, for that matter. There had always been room for one more place at the table, or in front of the TV for Friday night movie-and-popcorn. Later, when Zach's dad had been convicted, Nina had all but adopted him. Maybe that was why everything was so weird with Sonnet. After Nina had been so nice to him, he should have known better than to go banging her daughter in a boathouse.

"Thanks for meeting me, Zach." Nina smiled, her kind expression only deepening his guilt.

"Anytime. Is everything okay?"

She headed for the bakery. "I'm going to grab something to drink, and then we can walk. It's too nice a day to stay inside."

"Sounds good." He followed her inside and they got in line to order.

While they waited, at least five people said hello to her. Nina had served two terms as mayor of Avalon. She'd taken it on the chin when Zach's father had defrauded the town, because for a while, it appeared the lost revenues were caused by the mayor's mismanagement. Zach always appreciated that she didn't hold him responsible for his father's misdeeds.

"Sonnet's here for the weekend," said Nina. "Have you seen her yet?"

He kept a poker face. He had no idea what Sonnet had said to her mother about the wedding incident. He and Sonnet were… what? They were nothing anymore. They'd gone from friends to nothing in one night.

Damn it. He missed her.

He wondered what she'd said to her mother. That they'd had a falling-out? That they'd had a one-night stand, which made it impossible to go back to being friends, or…anything?

Before that night, he might have asked Nina how Sonnet was doing. Then again, he wouldn't have to, because he'd know. Because they would have called or sent text messages or emailed the way they'd always done.

"Uh, no," he said. Brilliant, dude. Just brilliant.

"Well, she'll probably call you."

"Probably," he said noncommittally. Obviously Sonnet hadn't clued her mother in. That was good, then, he told himself. The internet rumor hadn't shown up on her radar, which meant it was probably nothing to worry about. "What's up?"

"I have a little business proposition for you," she said. "I need to make a video."

"You came to the right place." He tried to sound enthusiastic. She probably needed a promo video for the Inn at Willow Lake, one of those "escape and find yourself" pieces with soothing music and water sounds. Not exactly Zach's favorite genre, though he'd done plenty of it, and he was good at it. With the Mickey Flick gig on the horizon, it was hard to focus on anything else.

"Herbal tea, please," said Nina to the girl behind the counter. "I'm avoiding caffeine," she told Zach. "About the video—this might seem a little self-indulgent…."

"Try me." He waited while she drizzled honey into a cup of

tea that smelled more like flowers than tea. When she finished, he said, "So what can I do for you?"

She snapped a lid onto the paper cup. "Let's walk." They headed up the street toward Blanchard Park, a swath of green space bordering the lake. Between the trees, the sunlight shimmered along the path, a byway for joggers or people with strollers, the occasional slouching teenager or skateboarder. At midmorning, it was uncrowded, the air filled with birdsong and the distant whistle of the commuter train.

"Okay, on to business," Nina said. "I want you to document my pregnancy."

Zach nearly tripped over his own feet. "Sorry…what?"

She lifted her chin and kept walking. "I'm pregnant. And don't act so shocked. Women my age commonly have kids."

"I didn't mean—"

"Don't worry. I'm just teasing. Everyone's going to be surprised when they hear. That's why Sonnet came up from the city this weekend."

"Okay, so, uh, congratulations," Zach said, feeling totally uncomfortable. Document a pregnancy? Nina's pregnancy? All right, he'd entered the Twilight Zone. No matter how fascinating gestation might be to those directly involved, to anyone else, it was likely to be as boring as watching paint dry.

"I'd do it myself," she said, "but I want this to be really good. Professional quality. I'd like to make a video diary."

"Nina, I wish I could help you out, but—"

"Zach, it's something I need to do. See, the pregnancy is… well, there's a complication. Not just due to me being an older mom, but something else came up, and I really need to document this process, and do it well. You're the best, Zach. I've seen your work and you're exactly the one I need."

He grinned. "You're making it hard to say no."

"Then my plan is working. Zach, before you make up your

mind one way or the other, I need to let you know about the complication."

Any pregnancy seemed complicated to Zach. "I'm listening."

"The prospect of having a baby is a wonderful thing. It's fabulous news. But there's some not-so-good news as well. It's kind of hard for me to say this, but…" Her voice wavered, then trailed off.

He glanced over at her, and saw that she was blinking fast, the skin taut across her cheekbones. After having filmed hundreds of weddings, he knew that face. It was the face of a woman fighting tears. Great.

"Hey, are you all right?" he asked. Lame. People on the verge of tears were not all right.

"I'm…I will be. Zach, I just… Oh, I have to come out and say it. I have cancer."

Oh, geez. Zach knew he winced visibly. Cancer. *I have cancer.* Probably the three worst words in the English language. The three words no one ever wanted to say…or hear.

"Nina, I'm sorry."

"It happens. You of all people know that, because of your mom. I hesitated about coming to you because of that."

"It was a long time ago," he said. "I'm glad you came to me. If you're going to do something like this, I'm the one you want."

She offered a faint smile. "Agreed."

"I'm sorry," he repeated. "I don't know what else to say."

And he didn't, just like he hadn't known what to say when his mom came to see him from Seattle, where she'd gone after leaving him and his dad. He had been a confused kid at the time, desperate to see his mom. The prospect of a visit from her had filled him with joy. Then when she'd told him, "I have cancer," his world had come crashing down. She'd still looked like his mom, still sounded like his mom. But cancer was the worst disease he'd ever heard of. He'd dared to ask: "Are you going to get better?"

"That's the plan," his mother had told him. "I have to take a lot of medicine and work really hard at it."

Three months later, she was dead.

"It's breast cancer," Nina continued.

Zach's throat ached. He felt himself being sucked into the distant past. His own mom had sunk down on her knees in front of him. He could remember how her eyelashes were spiky, and her breath smelled of Doublemint gum. She'd been wearing her winter gloves, and she'd taken off one of them. *I have cancer.* His mom had had breast cancer.

"It's treatable during the pregnancy," Nina added. "There's every expectation of a good outcome."

"So this video diary…" He suspected he knew what she had in mind, but something in him needed to hear her say it.

"Is for my children," she said, unfazed. "Look, nobody gets a cancer diagnosis without going there—to the worst-case scenario. There's a chance—a small one, I'm told, but a chance—that I won't survive. If that's the case, I would like to leave something behind for my kids, especially for the little one. I want to record my thoughts, and some things about my life. Ever since the diagnosis, I've been lying awake at night thinking…I want to create something to prove I was here and that I mattered. It's not about my vanity, Zach, or my ego, I swear it's not."

"I would never think that." Her words struck at him. How could she think she needed to prove something like that? He thought again about that little boy, living with his too-quiet dad and filled with fear and sorrow. How he'd wished for someone, anyone, to comfort him. "How did Sonnet take the news?"

Nina looked away. The wind whipped her hair across her face. "She's adjusting to the idea that she's going to have a little brother."

"I don't mean the baby," he said.

"I, uh, I haven't told her about the diagnosis."

"Wait a minute. She doesn't know?" Zach felt a chunk of ice forming in the pit of his stomach. "Nina—"

"I can explain."

"No, you can't. This isn't the sort of thing you keep from your own daughter. And she's more than a daughter to you. Both of you have always said that. You're each other's closest friend. What do you think, that she's not going to find out?"

"If you'd just calm down and listen, I *can* explain. She's got one shot at this fellowship, and I don't want to be the cause of her missing this amazing opportunity."

"Hang on—fellowship? What fellowship are you talking about?" It was a fair question. Sonnet, with her stellar academic record, was constantly pursuing—and receiving—various scholarships and fellowships.

"She didn't tell you about the Hartstone Fellowship?" Nina stopped walking in the middle of the path."

"Nope."

She gave a little laugh. "It's the biggest thing that's happened to her. I can't believe she hasn't told you yet."

"I don't get what this has to do with you not telling her about the…about your diagnosis."

"I'm just worried she'll make a hasty decision and decline the fellowship just to be with me."

Now it was his turn to laugh. "You think?"

"I'm serious, Zach. There's no crisis, nothing for her to do here but worry, and that's the last thing I want for her."

"Then tell her what's going on and let her decide."

"I already know what she'll decide. That's why I'm not telling her."

CHAPTER
7

Sonnet dreaded running into Zach again now that she'd returned to Avalon, but she didn't expect the encounter to happen so soon. First thing in the morning, before she'd put in her contact lenses, or brushed her teeth, or brought some sort of order to her hair. And before—dear God—she had washed off the green mint facial she'd found in the guest bathroom. Hearing someone down in the kitchen, she'd assumed it was Greg or Max.

"Hey," she said, adjusting the clip that was keeping her hair out of the facial mask. "I was wondering if you could show me how to use the coffeemaker. I tried earlier, but I couldn't get it to work. Those little pod thingies are— Oh, God." She stood with her feet frozen to the floor of her mother's old-fashioned country kitchen, staring at Zach Alger in all his tall, shimmering blond glory.

"Sorry, can't help you with the coffeemaker," he said easily, as if they'd just seen each other last week. As if they hadn't fool-

ishly hooked up at Daisy's wedding. He stared at her for a moment. Two moments. Then he lost it, bursting out in guffaws.
"Sorry, but you look scary."

Sonnet tried to muster some dignity as she adjusted the la-
pels of her oversized bathrobe. "Okay, how about knocking,"
she suggested. "It's a good idea to knock before barging into
someone's house."

"I've always had barging privileges here." His laughter sub-
sided to chuckles.

She wanted to smack him. Did he never act his age? "I know,
but that was…" *Before*. "You should respect people's privacy,"
she said.

"Oh, so now you're *people*. Got it."

She sighed. "Have a seat, Zach. Let me… I need to go and
change, and I'll be right back."

"Don't take all day."

"I'll take as long as I please."

"Still your same charming self," he commented, managing
to make her feel both ridiculous and small.

She marched from the kitchen. As soon as she was out of
sight, she sped upstairs to her room. Zach had come to see her.
Zach, whom she was supposed to be done with. At the end of
their crazy night together, she'd told him they'd made a huge
mistake. In the long silence afterward, she had concluded that
their friendship had run its course, they weren't kids anymore,
and both were going to move ahead with their lives in different directions.

As she stood at the sink and scrubbed furiously at her face, she
had multiple flashbacks going all the way back to early childhood. There had never been a time when Zach was required to
knock at the door. He'd been family—her mom used to say so
often. As a child, Sonnet hadn't realized how difficult Zach's
home life had been. She barely remembered his mother, though
she remembered when Zach realized Mrs. Alger had left and

wasn't coming back. He had built a fort in the woods at the edge of Blanchard Park, and he'd hid out there for a day and a half before anyone noticed he was missing.

After that, Sonnet's mother had swooped in—that was her specialty, swooping in—and brought him into the fold. He was allowed to come over anytime—at mealtime, bedtime, before school, after school. He and Sonnet became constant companions, as close as brother and sister.

The trouble was, they'd grown up and grown apart, and he didn't *feel* like a brother to her. The night of Daisy's wedding, she could only see him as a grown man who was intriguing and far too…sexy.

"I don't think he's sexy," she said to the mirror, where the image was slowly turning into something not quite so scary. She caught her hair back in a messy ponytail and threw on a pair of jeans and a T-shirt with the slogan Jeffries for Senate, a pair of flip-flops and headed downstairs.

It occurred to her that she would never dress like this around Orlando. He was big on appearances, even around the house. Jeans were okay if paired with a silk top and heeled sandals. Sonnet respected that about him, that he understood appearances mattered.

Not around Zach Alger, though. If he had a problem with her dressing like a slob, so be it.

The thing was, she knew he didn't care how she dressed, the same way she didn't care how he dressed. Okay, so the grooms-man's tux had turned her head, had turned her, truth be told, into a temporary maniac. But in general, she didn't focus on what he was wearing. He was just…Zach. He'd always been just Zach. She wished she could put the sexual encounter behind her and reclaim their friendship, but she had no idea how to do that.

In the kitchen, he'd helped himself to a soda and was standing by the door. "Let's take one of the boats out," he said.

Last time they got in a boat together… She pictured the two of them having a leisurely Saturday morning paddle with the sunlight glittering on Willow Lake. It was one of those days when the water was so still it made their voices echo, as if they were the only people in the world. "I have a better idea. Let's not."

"That's not a better idea. Come on." Without waiting for an answer, he headed out the door and across the lawn. A few guests of the Inn at Willow Lake were strolling the grounds or seated in Adirondack chairs, reading, just enjoying the sunshine or watching their kids play in the shallows. People came from all over to be here; for some it was the kind of vacation they dreamed of all their lives. Growing up here, Sonnet could remember only dreaming of leaving.

Yet she felt proud of what her mother and Greg had created here, an oasis of tranquil beauty and luxury, the sort of place people visited and returned to, year after year. The inn itself was a nineteenth-century mansion with a belvedere surrounded by lush, rolling grounds expertly designed by Greg, who was a landscape architect. At the edge of the property was a vintage boathouse with a dock. The upper part of the structure housed private guest quarters—the bridal suite when the inn was the venue for a wedding, which it was most weekends in the summer. Rowboats, canoes and kayaks for the guests' use were moored at the dock, and inside the boathouse itself was a restored wooden runabout, not unlike the one she and Zach had made such illicit use of after Daisy's wedding.

Pulling her mind back from thoughts of that night, she tried to keep up with Zach's long, lanky strides.

"I can't stop thinking about that night," he said suddenly, as if he had crawled inside her head with a clipboard, making notes.

"I never think about it," she said.

"Liar. I bet you think about it as much as I do."

"Listen, if this is what you came here to talk to me about, you're wasting your time. And mine. Is that why you sent me that text message?"

"The one you didn't reply to?" he asked bluntly. "No. That was…a wrong number."

"I'll just bet it was." In spite of herself, Sonnet felt good around Zach. She didn't have to act a certain way, or dress a certain way. She just had to *be*. And that, she realized, was what they had destroyed with their foolishness on the night of the wedding. "We both agreed we shouldn't have…"

"Shouldn't have what? Made each other come? Again and again?"

"That's it," she said, pivoting on her heel. "I'm leaving."

He grabbed her arm. Just that touch, that uninvited pressure, felt far too good, and she pulled away. "Zach—"

"Wait a second. I'm sorry, Sonnet. I didn't come here to re-hash all that. We can talk about that another time."

"No, we can't. I'm done talking about it."

"Get in the boat." He tossed her a life jacket and held her hand to steady her.

Something in his tone, or maybe in his intent expression, convinced her. In so many ways, she knew him well, knew that intensity he communicated with his pale blue eyes and the tautness in his jaw. Without another word, she took a seat in the small wooden rowboat. As kids growing up in Avalon, they used to go boating nearly every day in the summer, paying seventy-five cents to rent a paddleboat by the hour. They were pirates, explorers, merchant marines back in those days, their fantasy worlds more real than reality itself. Back then, it was easy to escape the fact that Sonnet had a single mom who had to work all day, and Zach's dad was as emotionally absent as if he was on another planet. It was easy to be together, too, communicating without words, a subtle look or hand gesture enough to be understood. She hadn't realized then what a gift it was, that level of intimacy with another person, but looking back, she did now.

That was another time, though, and they were different people. Now, she had no idea what his purpose was. She still had Daisy, of course, but Daisy's life as an air force wife was taking her farther and farther away. Their friendship was strong, but it had changed.

Sonnet's friendship with Zach had done more than change. It had…imploded. Or maybe morphed into something else. They sat in the boat facing each other. He picked up the oars and started rowing. Her gaze was drawn to the long, ropy muscles of his arms, and the flowing motion of his shoulders as he propelled the boat away from the dock.

"Where are you going?" she asked.

"Away. It's easier for me to talk when my hands have something to do."

"Talk. You want to talk." She felt a nudge of resentment. He'd been silent for months after that night, and *now* he wanted to talk.

"It's not what you think. I came to talk about your mom."

This was the last thing she had expected to hear from him. "What about my mom?"

"She's the reason you came back."

"Of course she is. In fact, I was planning on meeting her for lunch after her doctor's appointment, so I hope this won't take long."

"You're planning on staying through the weekend."

"Not that it's any of your business, but yes."

"Your mom told me you were selected for some big fellowship, and you're moving overseas."

"That's none of your business, either, but you're correct." Thanks, Mom, she thought. "What are you getting at, Zach?"

"There's something your mom's not telling you. Something I think you need to know."

"And you're going to be the one to tell me."

"I sure as hell don't want to be, but if the situation were reversed, I would want you to level with me. The truth is the truth. She's sick, Sonnet."

"She's pregnant, Zach. Last time I checked, that didn't qualify as an illness."

"No, I mean it." He stopped rowing and let the oars go slack. His gaze didn't waver as he said, "Nina's got cancer. She told me this morning."

As Sonnet studied his expression, she felt a chill slither through her, tightening around her stomach. Despite the fact that she no longer had a friendship with Zach, she had never known him to lie to her, or to make such a tasteless joke.

"Oh, my God," she said.

The water lapped quietly and rhythmically against the hull of the boat.

"Zach?"

"Shit. I'd give anything to not be having this conversation. I told Nina she should tell you but she refused to listen."

"Cancer? Oh, my God, Zach. My mom has *cancer?*" It was right up there with her worst nightmares.

"It sucks to have to break a confidence, but I know some things. I know because of my own mom. They kept her illness from me when I was little, and it was wrong. I know she thought she was protecting me, but all it did was make it a lousy shock when I finally found out. You're her daughter. Despite what she's thinking, you need to know. And you need to know now, not after you've moved away."

"What is she thinking?" Sonnet asked desperately. "What in the world is she thinking?"

"She didn't want to tell you because she doesn't want you changing your plans for her sake."

A trembling began inside Sonnet. Everything felt heightened, more intense. She could hear the water trickling past the hull, the sharp call of killdeer in the trees along the shore, the sunlight dancing along her bare arms. "My mom has cancer," she whispered.

"I'm sorry," Zach said quietly, still watching her. "I'm sorry as hell. She said she didn't want to worry you—"

"My mom's pregnant, and she has cancer, and I'm not supposed to worry?" Sonnet nearly reared up out of the boat. "And how does anybody know she's going to be all right?"

He didn't answer. She saw his gaze shift and darken, as though a shadow passed over him. Then a memory struck her, an echo of a time long past, a time she'd nearly forgotten. Zach, still just a boy, standing alone in the brick-paved driveway of his father's house, bouncing a pink rubber ball against the garage door, again and again in a rhythm as regular as a heartbeat.

Sonnet had gone to visit him on her bike. It was an afternoon in early fall, the leaves of the maple trees in town edged with the colors of fire. They made a peculiar dry sound as the wind rustled through them, punctuated by the rhythm of Zach's thrown ball.

"Want to go climb up to Meerskill Falls?" she had asked him. It was one of their favorite things to do, riding their bikes to the trail at the edge of town and then hiking up the steep gorge to the top of the falls, spanned by a hanging bridge where, according to local legend, two lovers had once jumped to their death nearly a century before.

"Nah," he said. Sunlight glinted off his hair.

"Come on. It's not a school night. We don't have any homework." She knew this because they were in the same class, Mr. Borden's sixth grade.

"Can't," he'd said.

"What do you mean, you can't?"

"I have to go to Seattle."

"Seattle? That's where your mom lives, right?"

"That's where my mom died." The rhythm of the ball never faltered.

Sonnet dropped her bike with a crash, letting her library books spill across the driveway bricks, ignored. "Oh my gosh, Zach. That's so sad. That's the saddest thing in the world." Mothers weren't supposed to die. Grandparents, sometimes. And great-grandparents definitely, like Nonna Romano, who had been so old there was actually a celebration with people dressed in costumes from the various eras of her life. Sonnet and her mom had worn flapper dresses.

That was what a mom did—she went to parties with you, or dressed you to go on your own. Every once in a while, a mom got a divorce and moved away, like Zach's had. But she wasn't supposed to die.

Zach still hadn't said anything. He kept bouncing the ball.

"It's just wrong." She barely remembered Zach's mother. Pale blonde like Zach, quiet, hard to know. Zach had adored her, and he'd been shattered when she moved away. And now...

"What can I do, Zach?" she asked in desperation.

He hadn't answered. The shattering showed in his eyes, like a million pieces of ice breaking on a blue blue pond.

"I wish I was magic," she said. "I wish I could make this not be happening."

But no one had been able to stop it. That was the thing about a disease once it took hold. Sometimes there was no stopping it.

Memories of that day haunted Sonnet now, morphing into a new nightmare, one in which her mother was the victim. "Zach, what am I going to do?"

"Nothing but the docs and meds can make it go away, or make it stop hurting, or make you stop waking up at night scared out of your mind," he said, his words as blunt and harsh as a sudden hailstorm. "You can't *do* anything. You can just be there for her."

"I'm not sure I know how to do that. How will I just...be?"

"You'll figure it out," he said. "You always do."

"I've never had to figure out what to do when my pregnant mom has cancer," she said. Her own words killed her. "God," she whispered. "Oh, my God. If I lose her…Zach, I just don't know if I can handle being that sad. I don't know if I can survive it." She caught her breath, then burst into tears.

"Hey." Zach set aside the oars and stepped over the bench seat. His long arms enveloped her, and she melted, swept up in a wave of hurt and fear. "Hey, I'm sorry. I'm sorry as hell." He murmured other things but she didn't hear him. She just knew that for this moment, his chest felt like a wall of strength, and he smelled amazing, like the lake-freshened air, and his voice, speaking words that held no comfort, sounded as sad as a tragic song on the radio.

"Zach told you?" Nina dropped the wooden spoon she'd been using to stir the red gravy. It wasn't actually gravy, but a delicious, rich tomato sauce that had been made by the Romanos since the beginning of time. The deep aroma of slow-simmered tomatoes and herbs took Sonnet back to the days of her childhood, when they went to Nonna's for Sunday dinner, to a house filled with aunts and uncles and cousins, noisy and chaotic with laughter and chatter. She hadn't thought of those days in years. She'd been so eager to leave Avalon, to find her life in the world beyond this little town.

Now she stood in the kitchen with her mother, and wished she had cherished those times more. She wished she'd listened to her grandfather's stories more attentively, or watched more closely when Nonna and Zia Antonia made the red gravy. She wished she'd tucked the memories away in a special part of her heart, rather than letting them flow past, unheeded.

"Yes," she said, her throat tightening with fear and grief. "He told me you have cancer."

Nina gripped the edge of the counter. "He shouldn't have said anything. It's not his story to tell."

Sonnet had been dreading a chance meeting with Zach, but her feelings about their oh-so-sweet mistake at Daisy's wedding melted away in the face of the horrible news. She was grateful to him now. "I'm sure he would agree with you," she said to Nina. "Why would you burden him with this?"

"I didn't think it was a burden—"

"It should be *my* burden," Sonnet said. "He didn't want to be the one to tell me, but he knew it was the right thing to do. My God, Mom. How could you keep something like this from me?"

"I didn't want you to worry about me."

"Worry about you? *Worry about you?* You're making me crazy. Did you think you were going to hide a cancer diagnosis?"

"It's not a question of hiding anything. I'm just…controlling the flow of information."

"What gives you the right to do that?" Sonnet felt like a teenager again, yelling at her mom. "You're my mother, and when something like this is going on, I get to be informed."

"All right, fine. You want the gory details? I'm a walking encyclopedia now. I found a lump. So when I went to my twelve-week prenatal visit, I had the doctor check it out." Nina paused. "Ah, her face, Sonnet. I think I knew the second she palpated it. I had an ultrasound and my lump had a name—a three-centimeter lobulated mass. So I had to have a core biopsy, which I would *not* wish on my worst enemy. You're clamped into a mammogram machine, lying down in an awkward position on a bench. You get a local anesthetic with a hideous needle. That was the worst part of it. After the numbing, they stick you with an even more hideous biopsy needle. I'll never forget the sound it made—a loud click."

Sonnet cringed. "Mom, that's awful. Why the hell didn't you call me?"

"It all happened really fast. Greg was my rock. He still is."

"I know, but I'm your *daughter*. Okay, so the biopsy…"

"Then there was a sentinel node biopsy, CT scans, MRI. Consider yourself informed. And stop worrying. I'm going to get through this."

"Not without me, you aren't."

Nina bent and picked up the dropped spoon, rinsing it at the sink. "Sonnet, you have amazing things happening in your life. I don't want you to miss a moment of it."

"How about this?" Anger surged through her, cutting cleanly through her terror. "How about you let me be your daughter and tell me what's going on with you?"

"Because I know you. I know you're going to freak out—"

"You think?" She felt the acid burn of tears in her eyes. "You really think I'd freak out about my mom having cancer? Gosh, whatever gave you that idea?"

"I don't want you to put your life on hold and try to good-daughter me to death."

"In case you're wondering, the decision is already made." Sonnet felt a horrible tearing sensation in her gut, knowing her plans for the future were about to crumble. The fellowship was a once-in-a-lifetime opportunity. No one was given a second chance. It simply didn't work that way. "There's not going to be any fellowship, no moving overseas. I'm staying with you until you get through this. I'm not leaving your side, Mom."

"And I love you for that, but it's not what I need from you. I need you to go for your dreams, not stand around wringing your hands with worry about me."

"Do you think for one second my dreams matter more than your life, Mom?"

"Ah, baby." Nina wiped her hands on a tea towel. "No, I don't think that. But I also don't think it's going to help either of us for you to change your plans because of this."

"It's my life. My decision."

"You gave everything you have to getting this fellowship," Nina pointed out. "I'm not letting you give it up for me."

"Fine. Then I'll give it up for *me*. I'm not going to do the world one bit of good if I'm sitting in some foreign country worried sick about my mom."

"You won't be worried. I have a fantastic team of doctors, and there's a treatment plan...."

Sonnet swallowed. Treatment plan. "Will the chemo..." Sonnet couldn't figure out how to say it. "Will it affect the baby?" *Are you going to lose the baby?*

"No." Nina's reaction was swift and vehement. "That's the first question I asked. This baby is mine and Greg's. It's your sibling. I can't think of anything but protecting and loving him. The cancer can be treated without harming the baby. There's a type of chemo that will be filtered by the placental wall. I just can't have radiation until after he is born."

"But would radiation be more effective against the cancer?"

"It's not an option," Nina said firmly.

For a split second, Sonnet resented the baby, the little stranger that was keeping her mother from getting the most aggressive treatment available. Easy, she told herself. Calm down. Parents risked their lives for their kids all the time; it was part of being a parent. "So what's the plan?"

Nina's gaze shifted to the floor, then out the window over the sink, which framed a sparkling view of Willow Lake. "I'm starting chemo before the surgery."

"The surgery." Sonnet swallowed hard. "You mean..."

"A mastectomy, yes. I couldn't say it out loud at first, either, but I'm getting used to it. Then...we'll see."

Nina picked up a tea towel and scrubbed at an invisible spot on the counter. "Well, I could have a lumpectomy—to start. But the doctors say a mastectomy is probably the best option."

"Oh, Mom." A mastectomy. To fundamentally change her body—forever. The very idea shook Sonnet to her core, leaving her nauseous with disbelief. She took the towel from Nina's hand and hugged her. "I'm so sorry. Tell me what I can do."

"You can carry on with your life and let me and Greg and the docs handle this so I can get better."

"I already told you, my life is on hold until you get through this."

"What's your father going to say?" Nina demanded. "He knows what it took to get you where you are. What will he think when you throw it away?"

"He'll understand."

"Will he?" Nina drilled her with a stare. "Will he?"

Sonnet's stomach twisted into knots. No, she thought. No. Her dad believed in duty over personal concerns, all the time. He'd built his life around serving his country and the world at large, and sometimes the family had to take a backseat to that. She cringed inwardly, imagining his reaction when she told him she was going to forfeit her fellowship because her mom was sick.

"I can't worry about what Dad will think or say," Sonnet stated firmly. "I'm staying with you, Mom. I'll think about everything else after you're better."

"Ah, sweetheart. You're already good-daughtering me. Do me a favor and don't make up your mind right away."

"Too late. Mom—"

"No, listen. A cancer diagnosis doesn't mean the same thing these days as it once did."

Sonnet wanted to believe it. But she kept thinking about Zia Antonia, the favorite aunt in Albany. One thought kept drumming through her head, and had been ever since Zach broke the news to her: *My mom has cancer. My mom has cancer.* She walked over to the sink where Nina was standing. "So then," she said in a soft, broken voice she scarcely recognized, "what *does* it mean?"

Nina took a deep breath. Sonnet studied her, not wanting to believe her cheekbones stood out more, or that her eyes were circled by fatigue, or that, when she turned to lower the flame under the pot on the stove, she winced a little.

"That needs to simmer for an hour or so," Nina said. "Come on out to the sunroom. I've got a little project started there."

"But Mom, we've barely begun to discuss what's going on. I have a lot of questions—"

"And you can ask them. Of course you can. But when I was diagnosed, I made a promise to myself. I don't have to be a cancer patient every minute of every day. I get to be me, and to forget about it and just be normal some of the time. Got it?"

Sonnet nodded, trying to keep it together. "Sure. Let's have a look at your project."

True to its name, the sunroom was flooded with daylight. It was one of those bonus rooms in the house that had been turned into a staging place for boxes, parcels and odds and ends of furniture that didn't have any other place to go.

"Let me guess," said Sonnet. "The nursery."

"That's what Greg and I are thinking. Between the Bellamys and the Romanos, we've got more than enough stuff for the little guy, so the trick is to sort everything out and arrange it. But there's a problem. I don't know where to start." She made a helpless gesture with her arms.

The stacks of boxes were intimidating, some labeled, most not. Mismatched items of furniture were shoved up against the walls—a chest of drawers, pieces of a crib, nightstands and lamps. The air smelled of sunshine and dust and disuse.

"A wise woman once told me to do the next indicated thing," Sonnet reminded her. "Oh, that's right. That would be my mother."

"Gosh, I was annoying, wasn't I?"

"Only because you were usually right."

"Don't be nice to me just because I have cancer."

Sonnet hated hearing those words. She hated them with a vengeance. But it only made her more determined to stay positive. "How about I'm nice to you because you're my mom and you're awesome?" She opened the first dusty box, which was marked "baby things" in her mother's handwriting. Brittle leaves of tissue paper covered the contents. She pulled the tissue aside to find a collection of folded clothes and blankets. There was a tiny smocked shirt with whales swimming across the chest, a pair of hand-knit booties, woven blankets and little toys and teething rings.

"Those were yours," her mother said, her eyes misting up. "Wow. I haven't seen these things in ages." She held up a yellow romper with an owl on it. "Look how tiny you were."

"And now you're doing it all over again," Sonnet said. "That's exciting, Mom. It's very cool."

"It's such a blessing, Sonnet. Such a gift, I can't even describe it. I *am* excited."

Sonnet tried to imagine what that must be like, expecting a baby and dealing with cancer at the same time. The only thing she felt was sick to her stomach. "So what do you want to do with this stuff?" she asked. "Store it away, or keep it for the new baby?"

"Well, if it's a boy, some of this won't work, but I'd love to pass on some of your favorite things. Unless you'd prefer I save them for *your* babies?"

Sonnet rolled her eyes. "I'm not even close to thinking about that."

"I'm just assuming you will be, one day."

"Maybe." Sonnet's "one day" seemed as distant as a dream. "Don't save anything for me, Mom. Use whatever you like. I think it's great that you get to do that."

"All right, then. I'll make two stacks. Then we can— Oh, Sonnet. Look." She held up a doll-sized gown, with white-on-white embroidery, the front covered in tiny pleats. Held to the light, the fabric seemed as wispy as a cloud. "It's your christening gown. You wore this at your baptism at St. Mary's. Oh, my gosh. What a day that was." Her gaze softened as she studied the delicate garment, her finger tracing a line of embroidery. Nina had been a single mother, but one with a big, supportive family who probably all gathered for the event.

"You were so young," Sonnet said quietly. "Did you even understand how your life would change?"

"Not a clue. What kid that age has a clue? I was that cautionary tale, the girl they all pointed at and whispered about, you know? 'That Romano girl' became code for 'town slut.'"

"Ah, Mom, that makes me hurt for you."

"Don't feel sorry for me. I was—and still am—blessed with an incredible family who supported and loved me no matter what. And in the end, I got to claim the ultimate reward—you."

"Yes, but I hate what you had to go through."

"I don't remember hating it. Your father was a cadet at West Point when we met at Avalon Meadows Country Club. Cadets were the ultimate forbidden fruit, because they weren't allowed to marry while they were at West Point. There was nothing to hate, just a beautiful evening, a boy who…well, without going into too much detail…"

"Thanks." Sonnet braced herself.

"I want you to know, you weren't a mistake, but a blessing. I'm sure your father sees you the same way."

"I'm not sure how he sees me," Sonnet confessed.

"He's a very responsible person. The only reason I didn't let him know I was pregnant with you was that he would have insisted on taking responsibility for you, and that would have forced him to withdraw from the U.S. Military Academy."

"Did he ever object to the fact that he never got the chance to choose for himself?"

"Yes, but ultimately, I think he was relieved that he didn't have to make a really difficult choice."

Sonnet didn't love the idea that she'd been anyone's difficult choice. She was grateful to her mother that Nina hadn't hesitated to turn a moment of hormone-driven madness into a lifetime commitment. That wasn't the right choice for every teen mom, but Sonnet was one of the lucky ones.

"So you waited to tell him until he finished West Point and got his commission," she said.

"Yes, and at that point, he sent child support like clockwork. I don't think his opponent in the campaign is going to be able to make much out of this," Nina said. Her dark eyes softened with memories. "I was still only a kid myself. Nowadays, I'd be on an MTV series."

"Thank God you weren't." Sonnet shuddered. Although grateful her mom had always been completely open about her conception and birth, she was also glad to safeguard her privacy. She prayed her dad's campaign would not breach that wall. Sonnet had been the result of a night of irresistible impulse and raging hormones, and a decision that changed the course of Nina's life. "You gave up so much for me," she added.

"I gained so much more from being your mom than I sacrificed."

"Aw, Mom. Thanks." Sonnet gave her another hug. "And thanks for never letting me feel like a mistake."

Nina tightened her arms around Sonnet. "Let's get one thing straight, missy. You were never a mistake."

CHAPTER
8

Zach regarded the people at the meeting with horror. "Are you *serious?*"

It probably wasn't the most diplomatic thing to say about a reality show concept that had been months in the making, but he couldn't keep his thoughts to himself.

C. Bomb slapped his hands on his knees and laughed. "We knew you'd love it," he said. "Don't we all love it, people?"

Around the long table in the conference room at the Inn at Willow Lake, heads nodded emphatically. It was just Zach's luck that C. Bomb's headquarters turned out to be the inn belonging to Nina and Greg Bellamy. Nina was beyond pissed at him for telling Sonnet about her cancer, though he knew he'd do it all over again given the chance. A person deserved to know something so basic and so serious about her mother. If Sonnet ever discovered that Zach knew the truth and didn't tell her, there would be hell to pay.

The producer of the reality series did not look as cool as his name. He wore pleated khakis and a golf shirt, and he constantly had a Twizzler half in and half out of his mouth, or held between his fingers like a cigar. However, he ran the meeting like a precision machine, although he didn't seem to realize Zach's comment wasn't meant as a joke. He was sincerely appalled. The title and concept of the show felt like twin nightmares to Zach.

He glanced around at the other personnel gathered at the conference table, checking to see if anyone else was as appalled as he was. Instead, everyone—from the art director to the field director to the location manager to the story specialist—leaned forward, seeming to hang on C. Bomb's every word.

"*Big Girl, Small Town*. You gotta love it, right?" C. Bomb exclaimed, beaming as if he'd just discovered a cure for male pattern baldness. "It all takes place right here, in this little piece of Americana called Avalon."

And there you had it, Zach thought glumly. He was staying right here in Avalon, like a migratory bird that had lost its way. When the production company first got in touch with him, he'd imagined a move to New York or out to L.A. to find his dream job. Instead, the job had come to him.

"And that's not all," the producer continued. "We've secured a deal to film at another location nearby—a resort called Camp Kioga." He clicked on his computer keyboard, and a slide show started on the big screen of the conference room. Appropriate gasps arose from the team.

"That's stunning," said the art director, a woman clad entirely in black, with a pierced eyebrow and several visible tattoos. Murmurs of agreement rippled around the table.

Zach didn't need to look. Not only did he know Camp Kioga like the back of his own hand; the photos in the brochure had been done by Daisy Bellamy, the owners' granddaughter. Besides that, he'd shot umpteen weddings there.

He'd nailed Sonnet Romano in a boathouse there. That, maybe, was his favorite memory of the place.

Still, that didn't mean he was going to like working on this crazy series. He'd been looking for something new and different. This was going to be like one unending wedding, presumably one with an overweight bride who was going to be shedding pounds week by week. Zach tried to picture himself trying to document her angst-ridden journey, complete with late-night meltdowns, tearful phone calls to the folks back home and over-produced hissy fits. He gritted his teeth, suppressing a shudder.

"All right, C.," said the director of photography. "Let's hear about the talent you've got lined up for the show." The DP was a guy Zach had actually heard of, Myron Wu, a big name in the world of reality shows. Zach had been stoked about meeting him. He was still stoked, but…Christ. Avalon. Willow-Freaking-Lake. How much worse could it get?

There was a knock at the door, and then it opened. Sonnet Romano stepped into the room. "Sorry I'm late," she said, brushing back an indigo coil of hair. She handed a small computer storage drive to C. Bomb. "Here are the images you requested."

Zach felt his jaw practically hitting the table. *Sonnet.* What the hell was she doing here?

"People, I'd like you to meet Sonnet Romano," C. Bomb said, beaming at her like a proud papa. "She just joined the team this morning, and thank God for that. We've been needing a casting and location coordinator, and Sonnet just happens to have grown up right here at Willow Lake."

Sonnet took them all in with a warm, professional smile—everyone except Zach. When her gaze reached him, a subtle sheen of defiance came over her eyes. He was pretty sure he was the only one who could read her look; she'd always been clever about masking her moods.

Zach's stomach twisted into a double knot. Fantastic. Fan-effing-tastic. So not only was he stuck in Avalon for as long as the show lasted—and Mickey Flick productions were known for being long-lived—he was also going to be working with Sonnet Romano, of all people. If he'd thought things were complicated before, they were suddenly even more so.

"So you were saying," the DP prompted him. "About the talent…? Who's our big girl, Clyde?"

"Ah, the talent. That's the best part." The producer selected a fresh Twizzler from a bowl on the table, then gestured at the screen. "Check it out."

He touched the keyboard, and a strong beat thudded from unseen speakers. A video in grainy Super 8 format appeared on the screen, the first image a black girl's furious face, filling the screen. Zach recognized the piece even before the words appeared on the screen: "Luv Made a Mess o' Me" by Jezebel, the latest hip-hop sensation on the national music scene.

The reason he recognized the piece—and the artist—was that she was so damn mesmerizing, you couldn't look away. From her first album, she'd been a sensation. She'd burst onto the music scene a few years back, angry and unapologetic, and unselfconsciously…large. Her lyrics were anthems of fury and injustice, thumping like a sledgehammer.

Then came the seemingly inevitable battle with fame and notoriety. Zach wasn't quite sure what had happened to Jezebel, but he knew by the end of the video, he'd find out.

"She's good, eh?" asked C. Bomb.

"The best," agreed the art director. "Whatever happened to her?"

"That's my favorite part. She was with this loser guy, a second-rate hipster named Goose, who she claimed beat the crap out of her. Defrauded her of her earnings, too." C. Bomb advanced the image on the screen to show an issue of the *New York Daily News,* its headline screaming Hip-Hop Star Arrested for Battery, Destruction of Property, Grand Theft Auto. Next came a video clip of her arrest. As fierce and defiant as a combat soldier, she glared straight into the camera with her one good eye and one swollen eye.

"So they're fighting, her and this Goose character," the producer explained. "I'm thinking she gives as good as she gets."

"Better," murmured a woman named Cinda.

"Yeah, and she seems to hit him where he lives. She messed up his two most prized possessions—his BMW Z4 and his Tibetan mastiff."

"Oh, my God, she hurt a dog?"

"Nope. We couldn't feature anyone who hurt a dog." C. Bomb showed another visual. "She spray-painted her favorite obscenity on his side, in DayGlo orange paint."

There were high fives and fist bumps around the table. "You're right," someone said. "She's awesome."

The producer took them through the rest of the sordid story. After doing time at Bedford Hills, Betty Lou Watkins—aka Jezebel—was released under house arrest, on condition that she didn't leave the state. An electronic ankle-bracelet monitor ensured her cooperation.

"Holy cow," said the DP, turning to high-five C. Bomb. "Nice going. So you're...what? Going to set her loose on the unsuspecting town of Avalon?"

Zach glanced over at Sonnet. She sat statue-still, staring at the final image on the screen, a shot of Jezebel looking as livid and defiant as ever, leaving some courthouse or other and heading toward a shiny black Hummer.

"Better than that," said the producer. "We got a lot of tricks up our sleeve."

When the meeting broke up, everyone dispersed, laden with assignments, which had been handed out with brisk efficiency by Sonnet herself. She was already indispensable to the producer; Zach could see that. It was one of her gifts, that knack she had for anticipating what needed to be done and then doing it before she was even asked. It used to drive him crazy when they were kids. In school, she'd be the one getting her homework done when the rest of the class didn't even see the assignment coming. Senior year, she'd been voted the girl most likely to succeed, though he used to tease her, calling her the girl most likely to annoy.

Overachieving had served her well—academically and career-wise, at least. As the photography unit was getting organized to head for the train station to shoot Jezebel's arrival in town, Zach cornered Sonnet.

"Seriously?" he demanded. "Are you serious?"

She clutched her clipboard against her chest. It seemed she'd been carrying a clipboard since the second grade. "I needed a job," she stated defensively.

"Aren't you a little overqualified for this?" He thought about her years at college and grad school, the internship overseas, the work at the UN.

"It's a way to be near my mom. That's all that matters." A shadow flickered over her face.

And just like that, his annoyance vanished. She'd always had that power over him, the power to move him, somehow reaching his heart and touching it in a spot only she seemed to have access to.

"Let's go," someone on the team called. "Who knows the way to the station?"

"I'll show you." Sonnet held Zach's gaze for another moment, then dashed away to the lead van. Zach followed in his work van with Perla Galleti, his newly hired assistant. They'd only just met a couple of days ago when she'd arrived from the city. Though she dressed like a Catholic schoolgirl, she had the mouth of a dock worker and a degree from NYU's Tisch Film School. Now that he realized the show was going to be about a disgraced hip-hop star, he understood why Perla had been assigned to him. Her resume contained a list of music videos a mile long.

Not only that, she was a digital geek. He'd always considered himself pretty good at multitasking, but she truly had a gift. At any given moment, she could juggle up to three devices. She might be tweeting on her iPhone while taking a call, at the same time scheduling something on her iPad and uploading a video to the internet. He was in awe of her for that.

"What's the scoop on Jezebel?" he asked, putting the van in gear. "Ever worked with her before?"

"Yep, I assisted on a shoot for 'Hell Hath No Fury' a couple of years back. It was an MTV video of the year."

"What's she like?"

"Oh, just you wait. You're gonna love her."

"Get the hell outta my way," bellowed Betty Lou Watkins. These days, the hip-hop icon went by one name only, a stage name summing up her image. With the presence of visiting royalty, she brushed aside a guy in a black sweatshirt who seemed to be with her security detail. Then she descended from the train to the platform, planted her hands on her hips and scanned the area with narrowed eyes. Thrusting on a pair of thick-framed sunglasses and tossing back her mane of shining braids, she struck a powerful stance, projecting a do-not-mess-with-me message. Despite the mismatched stack of amulets encircling her arms, and the house-arrest bracelet unabashedly displayed on her ankle, she had the look of a queen surveying her domain.

Sonnet had always admired black girls who were comfortable being black. She wished it had been that simple for her, wished she could simply look in the mirror and feel comfortable in her own skin. She remembered being ten years old and wondering if she could use a magic marker to change the color of her eyes from deep brown to blue. As a teenager, she'd spent the better part of her allowance on smoothing and straightening products for her hair. And of course, the only thing she looked like was a mixed race girl trying to look like a white girl.

Now she tried to maintain a professional demeanor as she watched the scene unfold. The camera crew—with Zach at the helm, stepping into his role with a mastery she'd never seen from him before—surrounded Jezebel, who seemed completely at ease with three high-tech lenses and several mikes aimed at her. She'd been on a special called *Hip-Hop Horrors,* Sonnet recalled. All she could remember about the show was a lot of bleeped-out dialogue and smashing of scenery.

"Where's my ride?" Jezebel asked, heading for the stairway.

Zach moved smoothly along with her. Sonnet had always liked watching him work before. She'd always known videography was more than simply pointing a camera at someone and pressing the record button. Zach seemed to have an innate understanding of the grace and subtlety it took to capture a sequence.

Jezebel's luggage was a collection of couture bags and what appeared to be army surplus duffel bags and rucksacks. Sonnet watched with fascination as the entourage moved en masse toward the parking area. Jezebel stopped at the curb and looked around. "My ride?" she repeated with an imperious tone.

A couple of the production workers traded glances, then shrugged.

"Did anyone order a car?" asked one of the producers.

No one responded.

Jezebel gathered herself to her full, impressive height. "What the f—"

"I've got this," Sonnet said. "We can go in my van." She was driving one of the Inn at Willow Lake courtesy vehicles used for shuttling guests around town. "Over here." She gestured at Jezebel.

The star glared at Sonnet as if tempted to eat her alive. Sonnet waited, determined not to be intimidated. Just because Jezebel was a giant—physically, and in the music world—and just because she'd done time in prison and had a reputation for violence, Sonnet intended to hold her ground, even though she wanted to run and hide. Something told her that if she did that, Jezebel would run roughshod over her throughout this whole process.

"Are you coming?" she asked, then turned and walked to the van.

To her relief, Jezebel followed and climbed in the passenger side, while luggage was loaded into the back. Zach and an assistant joined them, camera rolling. Sonnet hadn't been expecting that. Actually, she had no idea what to expect, but now that she thought about it, the whole point of this production was to document Jezebel's every move, so it made sense.

Jezebel pulled a seat belt around her considerable girth. "You in trouble, girl," she said, cracking open a bottle of BluMania, a new energy drink on the market.

"Me?" Sonnet started the engine. "Why?"

"I was about to have a shit fit about the ride."

"Look, it wasn't anyone's fault they forgot to figure out your ride in advance. Everyone just got here, and we're still getting organized."

Jezebel snorted. "No, I was *supposed* to have a shit fit. Hell, I was just getting warmed up."

"Why were you— Oh. I get it. They like tantrums."

"Uh-huh."

Sonnet kept her eyes on the road, though she couldn't resist glancing at Zach in the rearview mirror. "I've always thought so. Sorry. But I'm sure you'll find lots of stuff to make a fuss about."

"Make a fuss about?" She snorted again. "Who are you, anyway, Creampuff? Who talks like that?"

"I'm Sonnet Romano." She didn't much care for the nickname Creampuff. "Born and raised here."

"Sonnet. What the hell kinda name is Sonnet?"

"My mom was into Shakespeare when she had me—a May birthday. I'm named after Sonnet number 18. Do you know it?"

"'Shall I compare thee to a summer's day,'" Jezebel quoted, her voice taking on the cadence and tone of the syncopated sound that had made her famous. "'Thou are more lovely and more temperate: Rough winds do shake the darling buds of May, And summer's lease hath too short a date. Sometimes too hot the eye of heaven shines...' You mean that one?"

Sonnet was surprised and charmed by the recitation, which took on unexpected life with Jezebel's delivery. "Exactly."

Jezebel offered a regal sniff. "Don't be acting so shocked."

"I'm not shocked. But impressed, for sure. I studied Shakespeare in school but I can hardly remember any of it."

"Yeah, well, I didn't learn it in school."

"On your own, then?"

Jezebel's laugh sounded like a crack of thunder. "Right. The Bedford Hills School For Young Ladies, that's where."

"Oh. Uh. Well, it's very impressive and I hope I get to hear more." Bedford Hills was a maximum-security prison for women in Westchester County. It was amazing to Sonnet that Jezebel had memorized Shakespeare's sonnets while behind bars. Maybe that was where she had also learned to hold up her attitude like a riot shield, and where her anger had hardened into a shell of toughness.

"Born and raised here?" Jezebel repeated, staring out the window as they passed through the tiny downtown area of Avalon. Old brickfront buildings, window boxes spilling flowers, colorful awnings shading the shops and restaurants. On a sunny day like today, the town was sweetly pretty, with an air of days gone by. Jezebel's lip formed a curl of contempt.

"That's right," Sonnet replied. "There's not a lot of excitement here, but that's what some people like about it." Personally, she loved visiting new places. It was a wonderful feeling, stepping out of a taxi or train and finding a whole new, unexplored world. The thought triggered a pang of regret. If she'd accepted the fellowship, she'd be arriving in a foreign country this week.

She quickly suppressed the pang. She was here for her mother, and for the time being, nothing was more important than that.

"You live here now?" Jezebel asked.

"I've been living in New York, and just moved back."

"Did you work in the business in New York?" asked Jezebel.

"Not even close," Sonnet admitted. "I worked for UNESCO, an agency of the UN."

"And you gave that up to be a damn PA?"

"For the time being, yes."

"Why?"

Sonnet steered toward the lakeshore road. "Personal reasons," she said.

"Huh. Just tell me it's none of my damn business." Jezebel gave another sniff.

"It's not, but..." Sonnet paused, uncomfortably aware that they were being taped. "I'm back because my mom is pregnant. She's, um, older than most expecting moms, so it's a high-risk pregnancy."

"I got a half sister who's half my age," Jezebel said. "It's fun, but it's not like having a sister."

Sonnet kept her eyes on the road as she wondered how much more to say. There always seemed to be an element of shame when it came to cancer. People lowered their voices and whispered the truth: Her mom has *cancer*. Like it was something to be hidden away. And it wasn't, she told herself. "And there's another complication," she told Jezebel. "My mom just found out she has cancer. So I want to be nearby for her sake."

"Hoooo." Jezebel made a musical sound. "That's some bad shit, there."

"Right," Sonnet agreed. "It's some bad shit."

"She gonna be okay," Jezebel said. It wasn't a question.

Sonnet glanced over. The surly expression was gone from Jezebel's face. "That's the idea. I'm here to do what I can."

"You can do a lot," Jezebel said. "Believe me, I know."

"Know what?"

"Family's important. It would have saved me."

She spoke softly, sounding so unlike the angry hip-hop star that Sonnet glanced over at her. "Saved you from what?"

"From a lot of the shit I did. A lot of the shit I let people do to me. Maybe I wouldn't have done the stuff I did to get me this." She indicated the ankle bracelet. Then she indicated the scenery out the window, clearly ready to drop the subject. "That Willow Lake?" she asked, studying the view of the water, sparkling in the midday sun. The graceful trees that gave the lake its name dipped their fronds at the shoreline around the town dock.

"Yes. We're headed for the north end, to Camp Kioga." According to the production notes, Jezebel was to stay in one of the cabins and a good portion of the show would be shot there. The producers had made a deal with Olivia Bellamy Davis, who ran the resort. In exchange for filming at the location, Mickey Flick Productions would fund the entire summer at camp for twenty-four inner-city kids.

"Camp Kioga." Jezebel snorted. "I never been to a summer camp."

"It's really beautiful up there," she said. "You'll see."

"So you went there, Creampuff?"

"No. It was closed when I was a kid. The Bellamy family reopened it a few years back and turned it into a destination resort." Growing up, Sonnet had taken the mythic beauty of the locale for granted. When you passed paradise on your way to school every day, it didn't seem so special. Yet for a kid who had never known anything but the bustle of city life, and maybe for Jezebel, it was going to seem like a magical world.

"I'm gonna be so damn bored my head'll explode," Jezebel warned.

Maybe not so magical, Sonnet thought. She glanced in the rearview mirror to see what Zach thought of this, and was startled to see he was still filming. Scowling, she turned her eyes back to the road. It was his job, she reminded herself. And it was hers to support the process. Still, it was unsettling to realize how easy it was to forget she was being recorded.

Jezebel took another sip of the energy drink and grimaced. "Ooh, that's nasty."

"There's bottled water in the back," Sonnet said.

"I gotta drink this stuff," Jezebel explained. "For the cameras, at least, on account of them being a sponsor."

"Oh, right." Sonnet was way out of her element, and she knew it. This could not be more different from a typical day at the UNESCO Liaison Office at the UN. However, at the end of the day, she was going home to her mom, and that was everything.

Just the thought of her mom made her palms sweat. She was still adjusting to the idea that her mother was facing a life-threatening situation. The news had made Sonnet feel panicky and vulnerable, like a little girl again in many ways. She realized that no matter how old she got or how far she traveled, she would never stop needing her mom. Now, staring her in the face, was the possibility of a loss so devastating Sonnet didn't see how she could survive it.

So far, Nina was being a stoic, but Sonnet knew her mom, maybe even better than Greg did. Nina had a habit of compressing her worries into a little parcel and shoving it deep down inside her. Sonnet knew this because she caught herself doing it as well. While that seemed admirable, it was probably not healthy. And if ever Nina needed to be healthy, now was the time.

She turned down the narrow private lane that led through the deep woods to Camp Kioga. Ancient elms and sugar maples flanked the drive, and the forest floor was bright green with ferns and blueberry plants. There was an archway at the end of the drive with Camp Kioga spelled out in Adirondack twig lettering. A flagpole circle brought them around to the main pavilion. Ordinarily, guests would stop here and check in, but this wasn't ordinary, Sonnet reminded herself. This was reality TV.

An auxiliary crew of three awaited them, no doubt to capture Jezebel's reaction as she looked around Camp Kioga for the first time. Sonnet was seeing it for the zillionth time, but now the breath caught in her throat. She found herself staring at the broad lawn where it reached to the lakeshore, and she thought, that's where he took my hand. And the boathouse: that's where he kissed me, and where we made love. The thoughts streamed through her head, out of control, impossible to rein in. It had happened only once, she reminded herself. It had been a mistake. A big, sweet, delicious mistake. She should have moved past it months ago, letting it fade into the realm of things better forgotten.

They all got out of the van, and she jerked herself back into the present. Jezebel scanned the area, with its beautiful wooded trails, the rustic cabins and outbuildings and docks, set against the sparkling backdrop of Willow Lake. Glancing sideways at Jezebel, Sonnet tried to read her mood. She was complicated, that was obvious. Sonnet had never met anyone like her—crude, smart, angry, soulful, surprising.

"What the hell is this place?" Jezebel asked of no one in particular.

For some reason, Sonnet felt the need to explain. "It's been around since the 1920s. Started out as a summer retreat for people from the city. A local family runs it as a resort now. I know it's pretty remote, but there's plenty to do, once you get used to the solitude."

"It's the bomb," Jezebel said, momentarily slipping out of her angry mode. "So this is where I'm staying."

"That's right." Sonnet checked her notes on the clipboard. "You're going to be in Saratoga Cabin with the kids. You'll have the counselor's room in the back. That'll give you a bit more privacy." She noticed Zach's camera capturing her explanation. "Do you mind? I'm just getting organized here."

"Keep going," he said, not missing a beat. "You're doing great."

"Listen, I'm not supposed to be on camera, so I'd appreciate it if—"

"Check your contract, babe. I bet you signed a release." He was still filming.

"Did you just call me 'babe'? I hope I misheard you."

"Nope. You heard me right."

"Zach—"

"Listen to you two," Jezebel said with a chuckle. "I guess you've worked together before?"

"No," they said in unison.

"So you just, what, like to bicker?" She didn't wait for a reply, but tossed her braids and walked toward the cabin. "It's a form of foreplay, you know."

Sonnet glowered at Zach, who acted as if he didn't see her. She was already questioning her decision to work for the production while she was in town. Yet there was a terrible, traitorous part of her that forced her to admit there was something crazy and fun about this.

Her phone vibrated. She checked the message. To her surprise, Orlando was on his way. To Willow Lake.

"Bad news?" asked Zach, peering over her shoulder.

"Why do you say that?"

"You look like you just ate something sour."

"I do not. And aren't you supposed to be following your subject around?"

"We're wrapping for the day."

"Fine, then. I'll see you here tomorrow. That's when the campers arrive." She tried to figure out what Orlando intended, coming here in person. In her wildest dreams, he was making a sweeping romantic gesture, racing to see her because he missed her terribly.

But she and Orlando were not romantic. They were...compatible. That was more important in the long run, anyway.

Yet sometimes the truth niggled its way into her consciousness. She did want to fall in love with Orlando, but every once in a while, usually when she was lying awake at night, staring into the darkness, she forced herself to ponder some very hard questions. Did she even know what love felt like? Did he? Or was he just the means of keeping her father's attention, something she'd always craved? Was he her safe place to hide?

It was a terrible thing for her to think about herself—that her father included her in his inner circle because of her relationship with Orlando. And that this was what made Orlando irresistible to her.

"Don't be ridiculous," she muttered when Zach was out of earshot. "He's your damn boyfriend, not the holy grail."

Sonnet hadn't told her father or Orlando about her temporary job working on the production. They were mortified enough that she'd turned down the fellowship. When they heard she'd gone from a directorship at UNESCO to working on a reality TV show about a notorious hip-hop star, they'd think she'd lost her marbles.

But that's what you did for family, she reminded herself. That's what you did for your mom. You turned your back on everything else, and you stuck close, and you stayed there for as long as you were needed. The rest of life would still be waiting when the storm was past.

This became her mantra as she rode the train back to the city to sublet her apartment to a former colleague, and put her things in storage. Orlando was in Washington D.C. for the weekend, but her father had agreed to meet her at their usual spot, a coffee shop near his home on the Upper West Side. He'd explained that his daughter Layla was coming home from college today, so his time was limited.

As she let herself into the building, she thought she might feel a twinge of nostalgia, but instead, felt curiously detached. She had lived in the cramped walk-up for more than five years, yet rather than feeling like a home, it was like the other places she'd been since leaving Avalon—a way station along her journey, not meant to be permanent. The bank of mailboxes was utilitarian; she cleared out her junk mail and removed the tab reading S. Romano and it was as if she'd never been there.

Upstairs, the postage stamp-sized studio didn't take long to organize. Because the place was so small, she kept it tidy. There were only a few personal items around. She picked up a photo collage of her and her mom through the years. The oldest photo was a shot of her and Nina, who looked even younger than most teenaged mothers. Sonnet had seen the shot a million times, but now she studied it with new eyes. Nina wore an expression of desperate pride, reminiscent of a kid bringing home a straight-A report card, only instead of a card, she was holding a swaddled newborn. The shot was somehow both heartbreaking and joyous. Young as she was, Nina surely understood that she was not going to end up with the life she'd probably always dreamed of having.

Then again, did anyone end up with the life they'd dreamed of when they were fifteen? Only a select few, and Sonnet was not one of them. In her case, this was fortunate. If she'd become the person she'd dreamed of being at fifteen, she would be a prima ballerina with six kids and a horse farm.

When Sonnet got older, she came to understand the sacrifices her mother had made. Nina had worked two jobs in order to pay for her education, and Sonnet spent more time with her grandmother than she did with her mom. She had few memories of Nina giving in to despair, but one was extremely vivid. It was a school night, and Sonnet had finished her homework and had her snack and was waiting for her mother to pick her up. Nina had a couple of housekeeping jobs that made her extra late some nights. Sonnet could hear her talking to Nonna in the kitchen, and her voice was thick the way it got when she cried.

"Mama, I can't do this anymore," she'd said. "I'm so tired at night I can't even fall asleep. What am I going to do?"

"Give something up," Nonna advised. "There is no law that says you must do everything at once."

"If I don't finish my degree program now, I'll be stuck with lousy jobs forever," Nina had said. "That's no kind of life to give my daughter. The only thing worse than going on like this is *not* going on like this."

"Well, then," Nonna had said with a smile in her voice, "you just answered your own question."

Sonnet had felt very solemn and grown up as she'd walked into the kitchen. "I want to help you," she'd announced. "I know how to clean."

At that, Nina had swooped her into her arms. "Yes, you do. But you have a different job, baby. Your job is to be the kid, and to have fun and learn things and make me smile every day. Can you do that?"

"I'll try really hard," Sonnet had said. Even as a child, she'd embraced responsibility, applying herself to school and sports and music lessons with single-minded dedication.

All of the photos in the collage had been shot in and around Willow Lake. She and her mother could never afford a vacation, but with a little creativity, they'd taken imaginary trips together. There was a picture of the two of them wearing head scarves and aprons like Nonna and the ladies from the old country. They had decorated the house like an Italian village and fixed Italian food and listened to Italian music every night for a week.

Sonnet smiled at the memories as she packed away the photos in a box of personal items. There were only a few more pictures around—a portrait of her and her mom at Nina's wedding; Nina had been radiant that day, and Sonnet was ecstatic for her and Greg. There was a picture of Sonnet and her father embracing when she got her master's degree from Georgetown. Her father's chiseled profile was turned away from the camera but Sonnet wore a look shining with pride as she held him. She had a shot of Orlando striding away from the UN with briefcase in hand, the other hand lifted to hail a taxi. Sonnet had always liked the picture, not just because he looked incredibly handsome in it, but because the smile on his face was for her.

One keepsake that was in a drawer rather than displayed on a bookshelf was a picture taken by Sonnet's stepsister, Daisy. It was a classic awkward senior prom picture of Sonnet and her date—Zach Alger. They had both been dateless for prom, so they'd agreed to go together. She remembered feeling ridiculously grateful to him for that. She loved dressing up, and the thought of skipping prom had been too depressing to contemplate.

Zach looked so skinny in the photo, and so pale, like an albino scarecrow. But he had been the perfect gentleman; he'd shown up with a corsage and a boutonniere in the lapel of his rented tux. Only later did she find out how hard it had been for him that night to scrape together the money for prom.

She had thanked him with a hug, inhaling the scent of his cologne, and she'd told him everything was going to be all right. And it was. Years later, it still was. The two of them simply needed to find the equilibrium in their friendship once again. There was no reason they couldn't put the wedding mistake behind them and move ahead.

Feeling resolute about her decision, she packed up her personal belongings to take down to the storage locker and finished tidying up the already-tidy studio. By the time she was finished, it looked as neat and generic as a midpriced hotel room.

Then she set out to meet her father. She went to the fashionable old-world neighborhood where he lived, brownstones with gorgeous front gardens on a street that ended at the river. She was early for their meeting, so she grabbed a table outside where she could enjoy the afternoon sun, and ordered a chai latte.

Halfway down the block she could see his house, as staid and handsome as Laurence Jeffries himself. The garden was meticulously tended and the front steps pristine, as were the tasteful sheer curtains that hung in the bay window in front. The place didn't shout "money" but it whispered the message quite clearly. Her father's wife, Angela, came from money. Her own father had been a famous civil rights leader who later made a fortune as a broadcaster for a major network. The Jeffries girls, Layla and Kara, had always enjoyed private schools, lavish vacations and designer clothes.

When she was younger, Sonnet used to burn with envy, seeing all the opportunities offered to the younger girls. Thanks to their father's career, they traveled the world. Thanks to their mother's money, they did so in style. But during college, when Sonnet had studied abroad in Germany, she had come to realize that she was making her own opportunities, all by herself. Most of the time, that mature, philosophical attitude was enough to silence the ugly little demon inside that felt cheated.

As she sat sipping her chai, a black town car glided up to the front of the Jeffries house. Layla, the younger of the two girls got out, and the driver unloaded a couple of pieces of luggage, including a duffel bag marked with the bright red-and-white logo of Cornell. A moment later, Laurence came out. Layla sped up the stairs and threw her arms around him, and he lifted her off the ground.

Despite her mature, philosophical attitude, Sonnet felt a painful twist in her gut. It wasn't the advantages she envied, it was the access. It was having a father you could throw yourself at, one who would swing you around and be full of joy, just holding you in his arms.

Focus, she told herself. Focus on what you *can* have with

him. She could have his respect, his pride, his ear when she had something to say. But oh, how she dreaded disappointing him.

When he arrived at the coffee shop twenty minutes later, she was on her second chai. She stood and they gave each other a brief, decorous hug, like colleagues who hadn't seen each other in a while.

"How are you?" she asked him. "How is the campaign going?"

"I'm told it's going well. But even if it was going poorly, I'd be told it's going well. The only one who really tells it like it is Orlando."

"And he says it's going well."

"So far, yes." Her father smiled at her, the pride in his eyes shining like warm rays of sunshine. "You picked a good one. Orlando's one of a kind."

"I think *you* picked him," she said with a laugh.

"I'm just glad you two hit it off. You're good together."

"We are, aren't we?" She picked up her cup, set it down without tasting it. "So there's news. I wanted to fill you in."

"No way," her father said. "He popped the question?"

She burst out laughing. "I can't believe that's the first thing you thought." Just for a moment, she let herself bask in the happiness she saw on her dad's face. Orlando was a long way from popping any question other than, "Will you try not to lose *this* key?" And she was even further away from knowing how on earth she'd answer.

"Any guy in his position would be going in that direction with you, Sonnet. You're an amazing young woman."

"Thanks." She savored the warmth of his compliment, hoping he wouldn't change his opinion when she explained her plan. "I wanted to let you know I'm subletting my apartment."

"You're giving it up?" His brow furrowed, and he stirred his coffee.

"Subletting it," she repeated. "To a friend at UNESCO who's been dying to move closer to work."

"Sonnet, I know it's none of my business, but moving in with Orlando right at this time could get the wrong kind of attention from Delvecchio's campaign. I wouldn't want them starting rumors about my unmarried daughter—"

"That's not the plan," she said quickly. At the same time, she felt a twinge of annoyance. Her father always thought first of his campaign—how would something affect him, his chances at winning a seat in the Senate? "I'm not talking about moving in with Orlando. I'm resigning my directorship and staying in Avalon."

He was clenching his back teeth. She could tell by the way the side of his jaw bulged out. "And I admire you for sacrificing the Hartstone Fellowship because of your mother, but your position at UNESCO is something you should never give up."

"I don't really have a choice," she said. "I'm going to be with my mother throughout her treatment, and that doesn't mean a three-hour train commute."

"So you're taking a sabbatical," he said, steepling his fingers together.

"I'm not worried about what it's called. But there's something else I wanted to let you know. I'm going to be working while I'm in Avalon. I've got loads of student loans to pay off, and I can't afford to be out of work." She flashed on an image of his other daughter, who would undoubtedly graduate debt-free from Cornell, and the little demon of envy reared its ugly head. "Work is important to me," she hastened to add. "It always has been."

"What sort of work are you doing in Avalon?"

Here's where it got tricky. She considered telling him she was working with children, which was technically true, but it was probably best to get the explanation over with quickly, like ripping off a bandage. "I'm working in location and production on a reality show called *Big Girl, Small Town*."

The expression on his face would have been comical if she'd

been joking. "Dad," she said. "I didn't say I'd taken a job as a pole dancer. It's going to be a family show." *After certain words were bleeped out.*

"I'm not familiar with that type of show," he said, staring down into his coffee cup as if he saw something distasteful in the bottom.

"It's about a hip-hop singer called Jezebel. Heard of her?"

Even though he was a black man, her dad seemed to turn a whiter shade of pale. "No, but I suppose my daughters might have."

"You're right. Anyway, Jezebel is the star of the show. She's going to be filmed working with inner-city kids at Camp Kioga, on Willow Lake. She's outspoken and—okay, I'll be blunt. She's talented and smart, but she's also mouthy and obnoxious. I'm pretty sure the show will focus on her most outrageous moments."

"And you're working for this outfit...why?"

"There aren't a lot of jobs in a town like Avalon. The pay is incredibly good, and it's temporary."

"How temporary?"

"You mean, how soon before your opponent's camp finds out and reports that General Jeffries's daughter is working with a felon?"

"She's a *felon?*"

"Sorry, Dad. She got in trouble because of some worthless guy, but that's over. She's doing community service, working with the kids." Sonnet pictured steam coming out of his ears.

"And you considered all of these things before taking this step," he said, his voice taut with disapproval.

"Actually, no. The only things I thought about were the fact that Mom needed me and I needed a job. And if your opponent has a problem with that, they're really digging to find some way that makes *you* look bad."

He glanced at his watch. He had to go. Of course he had to

go. He had a family waiting for him. A wife and two daughters who were *not* going to embarrass him.

Sonnet decided to leave preemptively, something she never did with her father. Standing, she leaned down and placed a swift kiss on his cheek. "I have to go," she said. "I'm taking the evening train back to Avalon."

As she walked toward the nearest subway station, she hoped he would get over his anger at her. Orlando would understand. She soothed herself with the thought. He'd be a lot more understanding, and maybe he'd find a way to explain it to her father.

CHAPTER
9

"You're being completely irrational," Orlando said. So much for sweeping romantic gestures, Sonnet thought. Stepping off the train, he'd looked as handsome as a prince. For a moment she'd let herself fantasize that he had come to throw his arms around her and pledge his undying love and support. No such luck. After a quick hug, he'd scowled at her as though she was a naughty child.

"You know me better than that," she said, miffed. "I'm never irrational. And by the way, welcome to Avalon, my hometown."

He gave a cursory nod out the window. "It's cute."

"In other words, you didn't come here to see where your girlfriend grew up."

"Yes, of course, I do want to see it, but we have other things to discuss."

"Such as?"

"You're ending your career over something that is going to be resolved in a matter of months."

"First, I'm not ending my career. I'm on hiatus. And second, it's not 'something.' It's my mother. She's sick. She needs me. That trumps everything. There's really no other decision to be made. I thought you would understand."

"Darling, I do understand. You're scared. Cancer is scary stuff. But think about it. Your mom needs the best doctors in the field, the latest treatments, and I know you love her and I know you're worried, but you can't give her that."

"I can give her my support. My energy. It's hard to explain, but I really believe it matters."

She pulled up the drive. This was not the way she'd envisioned bringing her handsome boyfriend home to introduce to her mother. She'd pictured both of them a little nervous, wanting the meeting to go well, wanting her mom to see that she'd found someone she could be happy with, that her life—not just her career—was moving forward.

Instead, here was Orlando, distracted and annoyed.

"Welcome to the inn," she said, trying to keep a note of irony from her voice.

"It's gorgeous here," he said. "But you have to know what you're giving up."

She parked in front of the annex house. "And what I'm gaining. This is everything to me, Orlando. I really want you to understand that." To her surprise, she felt a sting of tears.

And to her further surprise, he reached across the seat and put his arms around her. "I do understand. I do."

She shut her eyes, silently grateful that he was finally showing some compassion. "Let's go inside. My mom's going to love you."

"Don't give me that crap." Nina's voice shot through the house with sharp edges, just as Sonnet walked in with Orlando. "I won't have it. I won't."

"Fine," Greg said, his voice taut with exasperation. "You pick what you want for your chemo playlist, then."

Sonnet glanced at Orlando, who shuffled his feet and looked as if he'd rather be in line at the DMV…or anywhere else. "Come on in," she said. "They're just getting ready for her first treatment tomorrow."

She left him waiting in the foyer and found them in the study, squaring off over a laptop and iPod. "Oh, good. You can save me from Greg's taste in music," Nina said. "He's loaded this thing with a bunch of new-agey gong tones."

"It's supposed to be soothing," Greg grumbled.

"I need Muse. I need Lady Gaga. David Bowie, the Clash, something I can stand to listen to. Something that makes me want to fight."

"Good for you. I'll take care of it tonight," Sonnet promised.

Greg looked relieved.

"Now, can we drop the subject? There's someone I want you to meet." She motioned them toward the foyer. "Orlando came to see me. He's dying to meet you." Dying. Poor choice of words. She was going to have to think before she spoke.

"Oh." Nina smoothed a hand through her hair. She looked harried, in jeans and sneakers, a shapeless top. Underneath that was the drain from her lumpectomy, though the bandages and scars were camouflaged by the blouse.

"You look fine," Sonnet said, secretly hating the idea that her mother was sick. "You're the coolest mom ever."

Greg was already with Orlando, pumping his hand and welcoming him. "And here's my amazing wife," he said, stepping aside.

"Orlando Rivera," he said, shaking her hand. "Sorry to show up on such short notice."

Sonnet held her breath. If he so much as breathed a word of their conversation about her suicidal career move, she was going to smack him.

"It's all right. Come on in and sit down. What can I get you to drink?"

"I'll take a beer, if you have it."

Greg headed for the kitchen. Orlando turned to Nina. "It's good to meet you at last. I feel as though I know you from everything Sonnet's told me about you."

Nina smiled. "I want to hear all about you, too."

The part she'd left unsaid was that Sonnet hadn't told her much about Orlando at all. She'd offered an overview of the obvious things—he was charming, successful, handsome, had an interesting job…but Nina was the kind of mom who asked hard, unanswerable questions, like does he cherish you? Does he make you laugh? Does he kiss you for no reason? When you're away from him, do you feel as if an appendage is missing?

The truth was, Sonnet didn't know these things about her and Orlando yet. They'd been together for several months, sure. He'd given her a key to his place, pardoned her when she'd lost it, and her father held him in high regard. Sonnet considered this a good start. She fully expected the other things—the cherishing, the passion, the yearning—to come with time. That was how love grew, bit by bit. It wasn't some big sudden, messy explosion like—

"I was sorry to hear about your diagnosis," Orlando said to her mom.

Sonnet cringed inwardly. Way to get to the point, Orlando, she thought. Then again, it was the elephant in the room. If not for the diagnosis, Sonnet wouldn't be here, having put her life—and yes, her boyfriend—on hold. He might as well bring up the topic and get it out of the way.

"I appreciate that," Nina said.

He handed her a manila envelope. "At the risk of being presumptuous, I wanted to give you this information on the Krokower Oncology Clinic in Manhattan. My aunt is the medical director there, and they specialize in hard-to-treat cases. If you like, I'll arrange a meeting for you."

Nina's expression brightened. "That's very thoughtful of you.

Thanks. I already have a treatment plan in place, but I'm always open to a second opinion."

"I want to do whatever I can to help," Orlando assured her.

Sonnet felt a wave of warmth for him. "You never told me about your aunt."

"Dr. Davida Rivera," he said. "She trained at Johns Hopkins, practiced at the Mayo Clinic, and was a founding physician at Krokower."

Sonnet wasn't surprised. She'd already known he came from a family of high achievers and apparently his aunt was no exception.

Greg offered Orlando a tour of the inn, including a walk around the grounds. The place had been a run-down project when Nina had taken it on, and she and Greg had fallen in love in the process of restoring it. That had been after Sonnet left for college. Her family had grown to include the Bellamys—Greg and his two kids, Max and Daisy—and she'd watched her mother's happiness expand into a kind of joy that simply hadn't existed for them before.

Sonnet had a vivid memory of Nina just before she married Greg. "Pinch me," she'd said. "Make sure I'm not dreaming this, because this feels too good to be true. I almost feel guilty, being this happy. There might be hell to pay later."

They'd laughed together, both certain the future was ripe with promise. Sonnet would go off to college, unburdened by the idea that her mom would be left alone with an empty nest. Nina would make a life with her new husband. Maybe you weren't supposed to look too far into your own future, Sonnet thought. If you did, you might talk yourself out of going toward it.

She and her mom put together a meal of tagliatelle with Nina's famous red gravy. "Well?" Sonnet asked. "What do you think?"

"He's nice. Good manners. *Very* good-looking." Nina made an exaggerated fanning motion with a tea towel. "Your father introduced you?"

Sonnet took out a block of parmigiana and the grater. No self-respecting Romano bought cheese that was already grated. "Uh-huh. He wasn't matchmaking. I don't think so, anyway. But Orlando and I hit it off, right from the start. Our first date was at a campaign fundraiser, but it was a really good date— cocktails at Smithson's, and swing dancing. He's an excellent swing dancer."

"The real question isn't what I think of him," her mother said, "but what *you* think of him."

"He's amazing," Sonnet said. "He's smart and interesting and has a cool job. Incredible apartment, too, and he comes from a good family."

"People say that all the time—he comes from a good family. What does that mean?" her mom asked, tossing a generous pinch of salt into a pot on the stove. "I wonder if people say that about you."

"If they don't, they should," Sonnet said. She thought about the one time she'd met Orlando's folks. She'd been invited to their weekend place on Long Island. They'd quizzed her about her background and education, her girlhood in Avalon, her famous father. The visit had felt more like a job interview than a social occasion.

"We're a good match," Sonnet told her mother. "It's too soon to tell if we're…God, Mom. I can't talk to you about this."

"I thought we could talk about anything."

"We can. But…Orlando and I…well, I think we're going to fall in love, but we're not there yet."

"What's stopping you?"

"Yikes, Mom."

"Seriously, if you want to be in love with him, then you should have a plan for that to happen, right? You've always been such a planner, Sonnet."

"We're both so busy with work," she said.

Nina dropped the fresh pasta into the pot. "Don't ever get too busy to fall in love," she said.

"I want to focus on you, Mom. On you getting better and giving me a baby brother. Do you know how cool it is that I'm going to be a sister?"

"It's totally cool. And good job changing the subject." She reached over and expertly turned down the flame under the pasta a split second before it boiled over.

During dinner, they talked about Orlando's work, which was a relief to Sonnet. She wasn't sure what to say about her temporary job on a reality show.

"General Jeffries is definitely the front-runner in the senatorial race," he explained. "But it's not a slam dunk."

"That surprises me," Nina said. "His opponent—Dean? See, I can't ever remember his name—"

"Johnny Delvecchio," Greg supplied.

"Isn't he in the meatpacking business?" Nina asked. "I can't imagine he's more qualified than Laurence."

"He's not," Orlando said. "Not by a long shot. But politics can be a nasty business. Lately he's been focusing on digging for dirt about the general."

"For heaven's sake, Laurence is a complete boy scout," Nina said, then stopped herself. "Oh." Comprehension dawned on her face. "You mean, *I'm* the dirt?"

"My God, no," Orlando said swiftly. "Has someone from Delvecchio's campaign approached you?"

"No," Nina said, "and if anyone did, they wouldn't hear anything negative from me. They wouldn't hear a single thing, because I'm not about to get involved."

Orlando topped off his water glass, and relief softened his eyes. "I'll drink to that. We're all going to need to drink. Because Avalon is going to be hosting the next debate."

"What?" Sonnet felt a dull thud of shock in her gut. "They're holding a campaign debate *here?*"

"Hey, back when I was mayor, I would have welcomed a senatorial debate in this town," Nina said. "The publicity would be great for the economy."

"You're not mayor now," Sonnet said. "I hate this idea. Orlando, can't you do anything about it?"

"Delvecchio's choice. He knows he's weak in Ulster County, so his people chose this town."

"Let me guess. They chose it because they're hoping to stir up trouble for my father. My God, Orlando, how could you let them?"

"It's not up to me. If we protested or fought them on it, they'd claim we've got something to hide. We need to make a preemptive move. Delvecchio's really reaching for something, and the only possible thing he can dig up is your dad's blunder when he was a dumb seventeen-year-old at West Point."

"His blunder. Excuse me, but as the result of that blunder, I'd like to term it something else."

"Good point," he said, missing her irony. "We can even put that in his talking points if the topic comes up. We'll have him call it a blessing."

"Oh, so now I've been upgraded from blunder to blessing. Thanks for that."

"We need a story line for you, too. We can't just say you gave up a directorship at UNESCO to be a script girl—"

"I beg your pardon. Script girl?"

"Whatever. Let's just call it a temporary position you took in order to help your mother through a serious illness."

"Let me get this straight. You're using my mom's cancer in order for my dad to look good to voters."

"Not at all. Your dad simply needs to tell the truth. There's nothing equivocal in this story."

"Except that it's private."

"When your father is running for national office, nothing is private. You get that, Sonnet. I know you get that."

"Just keep the controversy away from my wife and my family," Greg said. He spoke quietly, but with a conviction that made Sonnet glad all over again that he was her mom's husband.

"I'll do my best," Orlando said. "And of course General Jeffries will, too."

Sonnet studied Orlando, feeling a mixture of exasperation and confusion. He was a complicated guy, she thought. On the one hand, he'd come armed with useful information that might really help her mom. On the other hand, he was also using the opportunity to deal with a campaign matter. Nothing was ever simple with Orlando. At least she'd never be bored.

When they went to bed that night, she told him as much. Bringing a boyfriend home for the first time had never been a problem with her mom. She was always pleasant and nonjudgmental. Sonnet's dad was a different story. Perhaps that was why she never brought anyone to meet him. Except Orlando.

"What do you mean, nothing's simple with me?" he asked, carefully folding his suit jacket over the back of a chair.

She regarded him thoughtfully. "I just wonder why you came here. I would love it if you came because you missed me, and because you want to help my mom."

"I do miss you, and I do want to help your mom. Jesus, how much more simple can I be?"

"I can't help but wonder if you're also here because you're worried it's going to affect my dad's campaign if the opposition decides to focus on me and my mom."

"Look, I'm his campaign manager. It's my job to worry about everything."

It wasn't the answer she was looking for. She wasn't sure exactly what answer she was looking for.

"I doubt we'll have a problem protecting your mother's privacy. Delvecchio's not about to harass a pregnant woman with cancer."

"You sound a little too satisfied about that," she said.

"Whoa." He held up a hand. "Come on, Sonnet. What do you take me for?" He looked genuinely offended.

"Okay, sorry. I'm totally stressed out about my mom."

He fired up his laptop. "Wireless code?"

She gave it to him, then while he was absorbed in his digital world, used the opportunity to read yet another book about cancer from the collection she'd picked up at the local bookstore and library. Ever since finding out about her mother's diagnosis, Sonnet had thrown herself into a crash course on the topic of helping someone through cancer treatment, reading everything she could get her hands on. She'd spent nearly every spare moment studying up on diet and exercise, breathing techniques, side effects like nausea, mouth sores, digestive ailments, aches and pains, the ever-iconic hair loss…. Knowledge would empower her to be a better helper to her mom, she told herself, trying not to recoil as she read deeper and deeper into the topic.

She nudged Orlando. "It says here that pot will help my mom deal with nausea and increase her appetite. Do you know where to get some pot?"

"Don't be ridiculous."

"I'm not."

"She can talk to her doctors about that," he said. "Or maybe the pizza delivery kid?"

"Very funny." She went back to her reading, wondering if these books were frightening her or empowering her. She barely noticed when Orlando set aside his work and drifted off to sleep. With a laser-like focus, she read late into the night, cramming for cancer treatment the way she used to cram for exams when she was in school. She'd always been good at school. Good at work. Good at being a trophy daughter. Sometimes, though, she wasn't sure she was good at *life*.

Sonnet awoke to an empty bed, and a note atop her pillow. "Took the early train back to the city, didn't want to wake you.

Good luck with your mom today," Orlando had written in his tight, precise lettering.

She let out a sigh and turned to look out the window, pillowing her head on her arm. The sun was up, just barely, its slanting light turning the surface of the water to a field of fire. She wished Orlando had woken her, wished he'd taken her in his arms and said something comforting. But that wasn't Orlando, it just wasn't. He focused on problem solving and getting things done, and he knew as well as she did that a bunch of platitudes were not going to make her mother better. Strong medicine and good care were needed. His offer to connect her with his aunt in the city was his way of saying he cared, he wanted to help.

She sighed again and stretched, then glanced at the clock on the bedside table. It was her mom's first chemo day. The magnitude of the idea hit her, and she shuddered, pulling her arms around her midsection as she walked to the window. The wind kicked, skidding across the lake and shivering through the slender branches of the trees along the shore. Sonnet stared at the scenery out the window and at the same time pictured her mother in this setting, growing stronger and healing thanks to the sheer beauty of the world. From deep inside her, from a place she didn't access often enough and almost forgot was there, she summoned a prayer filled with every good wish and every bit of healing energy she could imagine. She pictured the prayer like a seed carried by the wind, sending it out on a breeze, certain that somehow it would find her mother.

Mom's going to be all right, she told herself. According to her reading, one in eight women will be diagnosed with breast cancer—and the other seven will know her.

She noticed two people walking down by the lake—guests of the inn? Then she frowned, leaning forward to get a better look. There was no mistaking Zach Alger's pale hair. What in the world was he doing here? And he was walking with her mom. The two of them seemed to be deep in conversation.

Sonnet hastily dressed and hurried downstairs. She spotted Zach in the parking area of the Inn. "Hey," she said, pushing a hand through her unruly hair and wishing she'd had more time to put herself together.

"Hey," he said, stowing something in the back of his work van.

"What are you doing here?"

"Stopped by to see your mom."

"To see my mom." She narrowed her eyes in suspicion. "I didn't realize the two of you were so close."

"I wanted to wish her luck today," he said, shutting the van door. "Is that a problem?"

"No," she said, nonplussed. "No, I'm just surprised."

"Yeah, that's me," he said. "Surprising. So what's your boyfriend think of Avalon?"

Ah, she thought. He'd come to check out her boyfriend. For a split second, she felt a flash of gratification. "He seemed to like it," she said. "Why? Did my mother say something?"

He leaned back against the van, propping his foot on it. "Just that your boyfriend showed up."

"And? Did she say she liked him?"

"Hell, Sonnet, why don't you ask her?"

"Because she'll tell me she likes him, but I won't know if she really does, or if she's just saying that."

He let out a brief laugh. "You two. You speak in tongues. Just say what you mean. And by the way, am I going to meet the dude?"

She gasped. "Why would I introduce you to my boyfriend?"

"Why wouldn't you?"

"Because it would be weird, Zach. For lots of reasons."

"No," he corrected her. "For one reason, and one reason only. Tell me, was he your boyfriend when we slept together?"

"Absolutely not," she said swiftly. "I can't believe you'd even ask me that. And anyway, you can't meet him, because he left already. He had to get back to the city for work."

"Quick trip," he said.

"At least he came." She took a deep breath, tasting the cool morning air. Without warning, tears sprang to her eyes. She ducked her head, hoping Zach hadn't seen.

"Hey," he said, "I didn't mean to upset you."

"You didn't."

"Then what's wrong?"

What's wrong? Two simple words. No one ever asked her that, because she was usually so vigilant, determined to prove to the world that nothing was wrong, ever. This morning, she felt scared and vulnerable and a little bit lost. And Zach—damn him—could read her like a magazine in a doctor's waiting room.

"Orlando's bugged that I'm staying here," she blurted out, needing to confess. "He's worried I won't have a career left when this is all over."

"Wait a second—Orlando? Your boyfriend's name is Orlando? Your mom didn't tell me that." Amusement tinged his voice.

"Don't start with me, Zach."

"Okay, but I get to make fun of his name later."

"Listen, you're not going to tease me out of worrying about my mom."

"Funny, what I heard was you worrying about Orlando. And your career."

"Because he might be right," she shot back. "I might not be doing what's best for my mom by being here. What if she gets sucked into all the mud-slinging of the campaign? Sometimes I feel like I'm not helping my mother at all, just getting in the way."

"Don't think for one minute you're not helping. Your being here, that's everything."

She gaped at him, because the moment the words left his mouth, she felt calmer. Where had those simple bits of wisdom come from? How had he known she needed them? Because they were friends. They'd always been friends. She'd been a fool for putting that friendship at risk, the night of the wedding. "Thanks, Zach. I know things have been weird between us lately, but really, thanks for saying that."

"No problem. And just so you know, I'm not feeling weird about us at all."

I am. She didn't say so, though, because that was her issue, clearly. "Listen, I'd better go get ready for the hospital with my mom. After she's settled, I'll be on set."

"Don't worry about the production."

"It's my job—my brand-new job—to worry about the production."

"Fine, worry about it, then. But remember the real reason you're here."

This was the Zach she missed. This was the Zach she regretted losing thanks to their night of madness. Maybe, just maybe they could go back to being just friends. She needed that now, needed it more than anything.

"I will. And, um, thanks for the reminder."

"I honestly don't need you to come," Nina said, dunking a tea bag in her mug while standing at the kitchen counter. "It's really sweet of you, but Greg and I will manage just fine."

Sonnet glanced at Greg. "Your shirt's on backward."

"Huh? Oh, yeah." He set aside his cereal bowl and ducked out of the kitchen, pulling the jersey shirt over his head.

Sonnet gave her mom an "I rest my case" look.

Nina smiled, but then the smile turned tremulous, and she pivoted away to look out the window. "I hate what's happening," she said. "I hate what it's doing to the people I love."

Sonnet took her hand and gave it a squeeze. It felt strange—and strangely right—to offer comfort to the one person who had comforted her all her life, giving her pep talks, soothing her wounds, telling her the world could be a rough place but it was no match for a determined woman. "I suppose it's okay to hate it," Sonnet said. "That'll keep us motivated to get through this, right?"

Her mom nodded. "Good thinking. How did you turn out so smart?"

She had asked that question many times over the years, and Sonnet's answer was always the same. "I take after my mother."

This morning, the reminder didn't have the usual effect. Instead, Nina tensed up and set aside the herbal tea she was supposed to be drinking. Sonnet knew she was thinking about the hereditary factor in cancer. "Knock it off, Mom, okay?" she said. "Deep breath. And drink some more of your tea. It's got chamomile and burdock. Supposed to be good for the nerves."

"I'm breathing," Nina protested. "And if I drink any more, I'll float away."

Sonnet finally asked the question that had been bothering her all morning. "I saw you with Zach earlier."

"He...um, he came by to wish me luck today."

"What else aren't you telling me, Mom?"

"Nothing." For perhaps the tenth time that morning, she checked the contents of the bag she was taking to the hospital. "I wonder if I'm bringing enough books to read."

"When have you ever read four books in one day?" Sonnet asked, dropping the subject of Zach—for now.

"I'm bringing backup books in case I don't like the others."

Sonnet detected a flash of panic in her mom's eyes. "Let's practice our breathing."

"I know how to breathe."

"Mom."

Nina heaved a sigh. "You're like a dog with a bone," she said.

"Woof, woof." She led the way to the living room, and she handed her mother a book. "Here you go."

"*The Secret Art of Dr. Seuss?* What's this for?"

"Not for reading. Just humor me. We have to lie down on the floor."

"But—"

"Humor me," she repeated, and the two of them lay side by side. "Put the book on your stomach like this." She grabbed another book from the coffee table and demonstrated. "Now, breathe in, and let your stomach lift the book as high as it'll go, for a count of five."

"That's harder than it looks."

"Therefore we practice."

Nina gave it a try, and Sonnet breathed along with her. After five seconds, they emptied their lungs for another count of five. Sonnet didn't let up until they'd repeated the exercise several times.

Greg came into the room, his shirt on properly this time. "You're on the floor with books on your bellies," he said.

Nina took one look at his face, and started to laugh. "My daughter's giving me breathing exercises," she explained, moving the book and climbing to her feet.

"She's always seemed pretty good at breathing to me," he said to Sonnet.

"Did you know," Sonnet asked, "that most people fail to breathe properly? Babies are all really good breathers. They fill their lungs all the way down to their bellies. But most of us forget how to do it right. We become upper-chest breathers and we fail to use our lungs to full capacity."

"Good to know," Greg said. "When the baby comes, we'll look for that."

When the baby comes. Sonnet was grateful to Greg for focusing on the ultimate goal, but at the moment, she couldn't think beyond the fact that her mom was about to be pumped full of toxins. She busied herself getting everything into the car—an extra pillow and blanket. A lavender sachet—the scent was supposed to be soothing. A cooler filled with drinks, snacks and gel packs for her fingers, which were likely to be damaged by the drugs. She'd put some music on an iPod—music she thought her mom would like, not the weird supposedly soothing new-age stuff that would only annoy Nina, but the kind of music she always loved listening to.

They drove separately to the hospital and met in the parking lot. Sonnet caught her mom looking wistfully at a vibrant, massively pregnant young woman heading to the obstetrics unit. Sonnet and her mom and Greg took another route—to the oncology unit.

There were blood tests, and then the drugs were prepared. The chemo room was furnished with comfy chairs for the patients, a TV and supply of magazines. Nina seemed a little nervous, her gaze flicking from Greg to Sonnet to the network of pumps and tubes and hanging bags. The nurses wore gloves because the drugs were so toxic. The docs had assured them the placental wall would filter out any toxicity, keeping the poison from reaching the baby. Still, Sonnet felt nauseous, though she was determined not to let it show.

"You look nauseous," Nina said as she took a seat in one of the big recliners.

Busted. No one knew Sonnet like her mom did. "I can only imagine how you're feeling."

"I'm staying focused on the idea that this is going to get me better."

"Good advice for all of us," Greg said.

"I'm anxious to get going with it. The nausea will come later, I'm sure."

The list of side effects was lengthy and horrible. Sonnet had pored over it, along with all the other literature she'd hastily devoured, searching for grains of hope. The worst part of chemo started after the drugs were administered. "And we'll be there for you," she said stoutly. "That's a promise."

Nina checked the time. "You should go. I'll need you more later, okay?"

Greg nodded. "We'll see you back at the house."

Other patients seemed to be getting settled in. Some were reading, others chatting with each other, one woman was knitting with scarlet yarn. Sonnet felt reluctant to leave. As a kid, she'd never been the clingy type. But then again, she'd never dealt with her mother having a life-threatening disease. She paused at the door and looked back at the chemo room. The morning light flowing in through a high window illuminated everything with a dreamlike glow. Her mother's oversized chair resembled a throne, and all the tubes, keypads, poles and bags were some kind of weird frame around her. She seemed like a fragile, magical creature, easily broken.

"Okay," Sonnet said, forcing steadiness in her voice. "See you tonight."

CHAPTER
10

Sonnet hurried from the hospital to Camp Kioga where the day's filming was taking place. Certain she was late, she drove too fast along Lakeshore Drive. She hated being late, a propensity that dated back to the fourth grade, when the first class of the day happened to be PE. At the age of ten, she'd been good enough at sports to get picked for the team early on, rather than standing around like a geek, wishing the painted gym floor would swallow her up. However, the rotation she remembered the best, and with the most pain, was the square dancing rotation—six endless weeks of swing your partner and do-si-dos, a discipline tailor-made for social humiliation.

She was almost never late for school, but one drippy autumn day, her mom had forgotten to set the alarm and they'd both overslept. As if responding to a fire drill, they'd thrown on their clothes and bolted for the door. Nina had made Sonnet choke down a container of yogurt in a nod toward breakfast, and Sonnet had yanked on her socks—ridiculously mismatched—and shoes in the car. There had been no time to smooth out her Jheri-curled style or to twist it into the usual neat braids.

"I look like a troll doll," she'd yowled, balking as her mom pulled up at the school.

"You look fine, Sonnet. I have bushy hair, too. Part of my Italian-American heritage."

"Your hair looks nice. Mine doesn't. And I hate this sweater." She regretted grabbing the somewhat worn gray hoodie from a hook as she'd raced out the door. "It's a hand-me-down. I hate hand-me-downs."

"It's a good sweater. It's Esprit."

"It has a G on it. Everybody knows I don't have a G in my name." One inside pocket label, someone had written Property of Georgina Wilson, which added insult to injury. Georgina Wilson was two years ahead of Sonnet in school, and she lived up on Oak Hill in an old-fashioned mansion, and she never let anyone forget that her father was the bank president, and that her mother was in charge of the very exclusive Rainbow Girls.

Sonnet's mom was their maid. Well, not really their maid, but she cleaned house for them once a week in order to help pay her tuition. She'd been in school forever, getting ahead a bit at a time, explaining to Sonnet that a college degree was worth every bit of hard work it took to earn it. The Wilsons probably thought they were doing Nina a favor, giving her Georgina's hand-me-downs, but Sonnet didn't see it that way. To Sonnet, wearing castoff clothing was just another way to make her different from the other kids at school. As if she needed one more thing to make her different.

First, her mom was way younger than all the other moms of the kids in her class. Sometimes people mistook her mom for her babysitter, even. And second, her dad was just gone. She never saw him and heard from him only a couple of times a year, if that. Third, she was biracial, which was not supposed to be a big deal in this day and age (she'd heard people whispering that when they thought she couldn't hear), but different was different, period.

The last thing you wanted on square dance day was to be different.

"I feel sick," she'd told her mom as they stopped at the curb in front of the school. "I think I should spend the day at Nonna's."

"You're not sick, just late," her mom had said, scribbling a note. "Give this to the lady at the office and you won't get in trouble."

"I don't want to go," Sonnet said.

"You love school," her mom stated, as if she was in charge of what Sonnet loved and didn't love. "You always make straight As and check-pluses in conduct."

School was easy, Sonnet thought. The learning part, the conduct part. But everything else—like fitting in and making friends—that was the hard part.

"It's square dancing," she confessed in a huff. "I hate square dancing."

Her mom had chuckled. "Everybody hates square dancing. I think it's required."

"Then why do they make us do it?"

"Builds character."

"You always say that. I don't even know what that means."

"When something is hard, but you do it anyway and get stronger because you did it, that's building character."

Sonnet sighed. "Come on, square dancing? We have to find a partner and sort ourselves into sets and hold hands and dance together. It's not hard. It's just…yuck." She cringed and clung to the handle of the car door. "Mrs. Mazza makes us pick partners."

Her mom had nodded in sympathy. "She's old-school, that's for sure. She believes in building character, too. Now, here's your lunch card. You've got three punches left. I have to get to work, and you need to get to class, okay?"

With a glum nod, Sonnet exited the car in slow motion and

entered the school like a condemned prisoner on the way to the gallows. The square dancing lesson was just beginning when she arrived at the gym. She tried slipping in unnoticed, but Mrs. Mazza had a special radar when it came to kids. She could detect movement from a mile away, it seemed.

"Glad you decided to join us," she said. "Now we have an equal number of boys and girls, so we can get started. Over here, Sonnet. Marcus Swoboda needs a partner."

Nobody called Marcus Swoboda Marcus. Everybody knew his nickname was Leaky. And everybody knew why.

Sonnet took a deep breath and held it. She wondered if it was possible to hold her breath through the entire class. She wondered if she could hold her breath until she passed out.

Surveying the other kids in the class, she could see the mocking amusement in their faces. Even her supposed best friend, Zach Alger, was doubled over, shaking with silent laughter.

Traitor, she thought.

From that day onward, she tried her best to be on time. Because tardiness often carried unpleasant consequences.

Spurred by her aversion to being late, she now arrived at Camp Kioga only to discover she had plenty of time to spare. Very quickly, she was learning that video production involved long stretches of standing around and getting organized. Jezebel was nowhere in sight; someone said she was being primped for her first encounter with the kids she'd be working with—or rather, performing with—for the production. Judging by the production notes Sonnet had hastily studied, the show's purpose was to entertain. Assuring that the visiting children learned anything or benefited from the experience was not the concern of Mickey Flick.

We'll just see about that, Sonnet thought. She had read the dossiers on the participating children, and each one was legitimately in need. Nearly all of them came from a nontraditional household, being raised by single parents or grandparents or even single grandparents, living below the poverty level, surrounded by the noise and chaos of the inner city. A stay at Camp Kioga could do wonders for kids like this, and the notion brought out Sonnet's best instincts and intentions. Her work at UNESCO had been with children's agencies; she was passionate about advocating for kids who had no voice of their own. Even kids involved in a reality show.

She spotted Zach hunched over a laptop, conferring with the director and a couple of others. They were looking at some footage from the day before.

Standing behind the group, she caught a glimpse of the monitor and nearly gagged. It was yesterday's van ride, the part when Sonnet and Jezebel were talking about Nina's cancer.

"That's an outtake, right?" she asked, feeling slightly nauseous as she gave Zach a nudge. "You won't air that."

"Are you kidding?" asked a woman, one of the director's assistants named Cinda. "This is good stuff. A good start, anyway. People like to watch celebrity driven shows to see the celebrity on a human level. You brought that out in Jezebel in a big way."

"It was a private conversation." Sonnet glared at Zach.

"You knew I was filming," he said, glaring back.

"Yes, but I—" All right, she was sputtering now. "This is a show about Jezebel. It has nothing to do with me."

"It's a show about how Jezebel relates to the people around her," Cinda said, shrugging off Sonnet's sputtering. "That's the appeal of this kind of show. People either want to be the talent, or they want to watch the talent from afar and thank their lucky stars they aren't her."

Sonnet grabbed Zach's sleeve and pulled him away from the group. "New rule," she said. "No more filming me."

"You'd better read the fine print in the release you signed," he said.

"I'm not asking you as the videographer. I'm asking you as a friend. Damn it, Zach. This morning I was thinking we could be friends again."

"You're assuming I'd want that," he shot back.

"Don't you?" She felt a chill, and her stomach tightened.

"Okay, everybody, time to get going," Cinda called out to everyone. "The rest of the cast is arriving. We're going to need all hands on deck."

Sonnet's gaze stayed locked with Zach's for maybe a heartbeat. Then he pivoted away and went to work.

"You two fighting again?"

Sonnet gasped and turned around. "Oh, er, hey Jezebel. I didn't realize you were here."

"All miked up and ready to go." She looked even more formidable than she had the day before, in a flowy black top over ripped jeans, black high-top sneakers and plenty of jewelry. "How's your momma?"

"She seemed okay when I left her," Sonnet said. "Thanks for asking. It was strange and scary, but good, in a way. It felt like we were actually doing something about it. But I wonder—"

She stopped herself and glanced around in suspicion. She wasn't going to let down her guard a second time.

"What's the matter?" Jezebel asked. Someone came and touched up her makeup; she barely seemed to notice.

"I don't want to be on camera." She gestured toward the approaching van. "Besides, you've got company."

Just for a moment, something flashed in Jezebel's eyes—fear. She took a step back and drew her arms protectively around herself.

"Are you all right?" asked Sonnet.

"It's a bunch of kids. What the hell do I know about kids?"

Sonnet studied her for a moment, bemused. Jezebel had fought her way up from the projects, she'd stood up to an abusive boyfriend and endured a stay in prison. Yet she was worried about meeting a group of children?

Personally, Sonnet related to children better than she did to adults. "Kids will tell you everything you need to know. You just have to find the right way to listen."

Jezebel scowled at her. "How'd you get so smart about kids?"

Sonnet shrugged. "There's a part of me that never stopped being one. I used to work directly with children a lot when I was getting started at UNESCO. I miss working with them, and I miss that part of myself."

"Then why not go back to working with kids?" Jezebel asked bluntly.

The woman had a point. All through her march along her chosen career path, Sonnet had moved farther and farther away from her passion for being with kids. However, as her father often stated, she did more good for the world's children by heading up an agency and setting policy than she did working with them on an individual basis.

"We're ready for you, Jezebel," called Cinda as a flurry of activity erupted around the approaching van.

Sonnet stepped aside to watch the filming. Everything was so much more technical and involved than she'd realized. Zach was in charge of the shoot, directing two guys with shoulder cams and coordinating an amazing array of lights the viewer would never see. She bit her lip, suddenly nervous for the children. They might take one look at all the gear aimed at them like weapons of siege warfare, and want to hide.

She needn't have worried. A pack of kids of all shapes, sizes and colors spilled from the van, looking around as though they'd just landed on a new planet. She recognized them from their profiles—scruffy and scrappy, all with loads of personality, which was why they'd been selected in the first place.

There was a boy named Darnell, tall and lanky, carrying himself like a long question mark in jeans that sagged precariously on his bony hips. A pudgy girl named Anita stood nearby, her jaw thrust forward in combative fashion. Next to her was another girl, Bitsy, who was even bigger than Anita, herding the twins—Rhonda and Shawna—ahead of her. Other boys— Andre, Quincy, Marley and Jaden. The rest followed in a blur, a small army in scuffed sneakers and sagging socks, some with chalky scabs on their knees and elbows, all heading for the lawn, where Jezebel awaited.

Sonnet clutched her clipboard to her chest and silently prayed Jezebel wouldn't fall apart. She needn't have worried. Jezebel was the consummate performer. With the cameras closing in, she came to life as if an invisible muse had entered her bloodstream, and she offered the kids a smile. "Welcome, my homeskillets," she said. "I got some big plans for you kids this summer."

"Yeah?" said one of the boys. "What kinda plans?"

"What're we gonna do?" asked someone else.

"What do you like to do?" Jezebel asked.

"Hang out." "Play video games." "Sleep." "Watch TV." "Play basketball." The suggestions exploded from the kids.

"We'll do a crapload more than that. Each day, we'll have a theme. Y'all know what a theme is?"

Some of the kids nodded; others looked blank.

"It's like figuring out the idea behind a song you're making up."

"I never made up a song."

"Bet you did," Jezebel shot back. "You just didn't know it was a song." She pattered out a rhythm with her hand on his head. "Don't get me wrong/I can't be makin' up no song…"

He jerked away, his cheeks scarlet. "I don't hear no theme."

"You will. A theme is the one thing you're talking about even when you're not talking. Like, finding happiness. And all the activities of the day will be about finding happiness. Or honoring a hero in our lives, or what friendship means. Come on, it's not rocket science."

The kids looked skeptical, but Jezebel forged ahead, showing no sign of her earlier apprehension. "We're gonna do sports and games and campfires. Art projects. Music. Shit like that. You're gonna love it," she assured them.

A few of the younger ones looked cautiously optimistic.

"What kinda music?" asked Quincy. "Hip-hop?"

"Of course," said Jezebel. "I gotta warn you guys—no TV. No video games. No internet or cell phones. Starting now, we're unplugged."

"No way!"

"Way. What else do you guys like to do? Play cards? Cook?"

"They like to eat," Jaden said, jerking a thumb at Anita and Bitsy. The others snickered.

In one swift movement, Jezebel took him by the skinny arms and lifted him off the ground. Sonnet expected someone to rush to the rescue, but instead, the cameras never wavered. Jezebel lifted the boy so they were nose to nose. His skinny legs dangled helplessly.

"You are not gonna go there," she said, a soft threat in her voice. "You got that?"

Jaden nodded his head, widening his eyes until the whites showed.

"I don't hear you." Jezebel's voice was even softer.

"I got it. Yeah. I got it."

Cinda leaned over to the director. "Now that," she said, "is the money shot."

CHAPTER
11

The filming went on in fits and starts throughout the day, and then they called it a wrap. Sonnet was torn between feeling amazed by the sheer contrivance of the situation, and the authentic moments of drama that emerged from the various setups. By the day's end, everyone had a keen sense of the kids. Like children everywhere, they were annoying, endearing, brash, insecure and endlessly inquisitive. And despite her stated discomfort about being around them, Jezebel took command of every scene and setup.

Every few minutes, Sonnet checked her messages. Greg kept her updated on her mom's chemo day. Things were going well, everything proceeding as expected. They'd be home sometime after dinner. It all sounded so…routine. How quickly they were getting used to her mother having cancer.

As she headed for her car, Sonnet spotted Zach in the parking lot.

"You weren't in any of the shots today, so you don't need to yell at me," he said when she approached him.

"I wasn't going to yell at you. I wanted—" She broke off. What did she want with him? "We didn't finish our conversation this morning."

"Maybe you didn't."

"I don't understand why you're so annoyed at me. I said I want us to go back to being friends."

"And you maintain it's possible to go back after a night like that."

"Why not?"

"You can't unring that bell, Sonnet. Or I can't, anyway."

"Then I'm in trouble," she said.

"What the hell is that supposed to mean?"

"I don't want to lose my best friend."

He offered a short laugh. "News flash. You've already lost him. You threw him out when you decided he wasn't going to fit into your grand scheme."

"I don't have a grand scheme. God, if I've learned anything from my mom's illness, it's that you never know what's around the next corner, so what's the point of planning?"

He unlocked his van and threw his backpack in. "Look, I'd love to stay and debate this with you all day, but I need to be somewhere."

"Oh." A terrible thought struck her. "Zach, are you seeing someone? Is that why you're so ticked off at me?"

"What if I was?"

"I…well…" *That would suck for me.*

"For the record, I'm not seeing anybody. Not a girl, anyway."

"Then who?" She couldn't help it; she was impossibly nosy when it came to him.

"Not that it's any of your business, but I've got a hot date with an inmate up at Indian Wells."

She melted a little inside. His dad was incarcerated at the

minimum-security facility there. Ever since the sentencing, Zach had visited Matthew Alger faithfully, week in and week out, and apparently the pattern still held. "Ah, Zach. I'm sorry. I've been acting as if I'm the only one with troubles. Really, I apologize."

"Don't." He leaned against the van, propping his foot on the side. "I'm not looking for an apology from you."

"Let's not do this," she said. "Let's not fight."

"But it's so entertaining when we fight."

"I'd rather just talk."

He checked his watch. "Go for it, then. Let's talk. How's your mom doing?"

"All right. Greg's been texting updates. They're still at the clinic." She paused, noting how his jaw tightened. He always did that when he was tense. Of course he was tense. No matter how many times he visited his father in prison, it was bound to be stressful. "For what it's worth," she said, "I've got dad problems, too."

"Seriously? He's running for the freaking Senate. How is that a problem?"

"My relationship with him is…confusing. And I can't believe I just said that. God, Zach, I always do this with you. I always say too much."

"Could be there's a reason for that."

He had a point. Sonnet trusted him; she always had. He knew what her past had been like, which meant he understood her in ways few others could. The things she told Zach remained in a safe place. It had always been that way with them.

She'd once tried to explain her relationship with her father to Orlando, but he'd brushed her off. It was a relief to have Zach to talk to. "My father and I…we love and respect each other. I really believe that. I'm proud of who he is and what he's achieved."

"But…?"

"But at the same time, I wish he'd figured out a way to be my dad when I was growing up."

"He's an idiot," Zach said matter-of-factly. "He missed an opportunity to know an amazing person."

She laughed. "Yeah, what's up with that?"

"It's like some guys suffer instant brain damage when it comes to their kids."

"Ours did, anyway. It took me forever to figure out what to call him. I mean, Dad? Really? Dad is someone who teaches you to fast pitch. Who takes you to the movies and coaches your soccer team. And Daddy? Please. That's even more intimate...."

"I never knew you missed him like that," Zach said. "You never said anything."

"No, I didn't. I didn't want to seem disloyal to my mom, as if she wasn't enough. But when I was little, I'd see kids with their daddies, and I'd wonder where mine was. And why wasn't he with me and my mom. I was lucky enough to have all the Romano uncles in my life, but I always wanted a daddy. So when we connected when I was in college, I was so ready. It was like I was starved for him. I wanted to be the best daughter I could for him."

His gaze lightly touched her from head to toe and up again. Somehow, that gaze felt as intimate as a caress. "Mission accomplished."

She felt a flurry of attraction, but instantly stuffed it away somewhere. Her goal was to recapture her friendship with Zach, minus the attraction element. She wasn't there yet. She hoped he couldn't tell.

Zach knew the layout of the Indian Wells Correctional Facility by heart, though he still remembered his first visit there, right after his father had been sent up. Zach had been a senior in high school, just a kid still, filled with so much fear, hurt and humiliation that some days, he thought he might explode. If not for the compassion of his employer—Jenny Majesky of the Sky

River Bakery—and Nina Romano, he might not have made it through that year.

He'd always understood that what had happened was not his fault. His father had a gambling addiction. He would have sold his own grandmother just to place another bet, certain that a big payoff was right around the corner. But Matthew Alger didn't have to sell his grandmother. As town treasurer of Avalon, he found a way to systematically defraud the taxpayers, even though it meant running the town finances to the brink of ruin.

Everyone—Matthew included—would have understood if Zach had chosen to simply write him off, a man who let addiction consume him and left his son holding the bag. Yet despite his anger and shame, Zach couldn't bring himself to do that.

By now, the habit was ingrained. It was what he did, nearly every single Monday. He usually had a light workload on Mondays, a typical day off for people who worked in the wedding industry. No one got married on a Monday. At least, no one who wanted the proceedings documented. Now that he was working on the reality show, Mondays were as busy as any other day, but he still made time for the visit.

As he drove through town en route to Indian Wells, he took his time past the pretty wood-frame houses in the Oak Hill area and around Avalon Meadows, the older areas of town. Massive chestnut and oaks and maples shaded the boulevards, and the gardens were bright with summer color. The director had asked for some footage of this area to show the contrast between Avalon and the city. When Zach was younger, he used to look longingly at the pretty houses with swing sets in their yards and maybe a barbecue on the back patio. He imagined families living there and how secure it must feel, to have a love like that. As he grew up, he came to understand that the house with the white picket fence was a myth, for the most part. But there was a stubborn part of him that continued to believe that inner kid.

There were some illusions that couldn't be shattered, no matter how many times they were hit.

Even smaller than Avalon, Indian Wells consisted of a mini-mart and gas station, a retirement community, and a cluster of low-profile buildings and yards surrounded by razor-wire. He went through the familiar routine—metal detector, check-in at the reception area, name tag. Even though most of the staff knew his name, he still had to state his relationship to the inmate. He didn't cringe anymore when he said, "I'm his son."

He was accustomed to the big, drafty common room where the visiting took place, too. His father was waiting, seated on a bolted-down stool next to a bolted-down table. He greeted Zach with a warm smile and a handshake. Ironically, their relationship had improved since Matthew had been behind bars. When he was on the outside, Zach had been a hindrance and an unwanted expense; now he was the highlight of his father's week.

"How's that production going?" Matthew asked. Now that the production was underway, Zach had told him all about it.

"It's good. I thought it would make me mental to be working in Avalon, but work is work."

"That's the attitude. I bet you're doing a fine job and making a bundle at it, too."

The old man was all about money, even now. "How about you?" Zach asked. "Staying out of trouble?" Matthew Alger had never lost his predilection for gambling, even in prison, although the currency he used wasn't money. He'd been known to wager everything from deodorant sticks to goldfish crackers from the commissary, just for the sport of it.

"You betcha," he assured Zach. "I got another parole hearing coming up in the fall and I aim to be ready this time."

Zach said nothing. His father couldn't seem to keep from committing infractions that kept him stuck here. He had a habit of sabotaging himself.

"I know what you're thinking," Matthew said. "I'm not gonna blow it this time."

"That'd be good," Zach said.

"How about a game of crib?"

Zach took out the board, the cards and the pegs he brought to each visit. Cribbage was their thing. It had started when Zach was very young. His dad had taught him to play this crazy, fast-paced card game with colored pegs being moved around a racetrack-shaped board. The two of them spent hours carefully discarding into the crib, trying not to give away any points. His dad was notorious for stealing points if Zach counted his points wrong. The man was very serious about cribbage. Zach made it his mission to surpass his father. He had no problem stealing points if his dad left them behind. Both snarled at terrible hands and gave whoops of joy when the cards were good.

The current game went swiftly, the two of them squaring off across the board, the cards rippling as they shuffled and discarded.

"Done," said Matthew, making his final move with a flourish.

"Good game," said Zach. "At least you didn't skunk me."

"I'll keep trying."

"See you next time." Zach put away the board.

"Sure," said his father. "We'll have another game of crib."

CHAPTER
12

Nina woke with a start, bathed in sweat. Her heart beat with the latent panic of some unremembered dream. Automatically, she reached for Greg, snuggling up against his reassuring bulk. He made what she'd always considered the bear sound—a contented grumble from deep in his chest—and drew her closer.

She could tell the moment reality awakened him. The grumbling turned to a sharp inhalation. "Hey," he said. "You okay?"

"Yes. I am."

"You sure?"

"I'm sure, and it's a huge relief. I guess the anti-nausea meds are working fine for now." She lay flat on her back, her hands cupping her growing belly as she stared into the half dark. "We came through my first round of chemo, Greg."

Yes, she was completely freaked out and exhausted. Yes, she was worried about the cocktail that had been pumped into her. But she was determined to stay positive.

"You were awesome."

"*We* were awesome. Every one of us—you, the baby and me, the crew at the clinic, and Sonnet, too. That was really nice of her to have dinner ready when we got home."

"You raised a good daughter," Greg said.

"Indeed I did. And now we get to do it all over again, with a boy this time. Think we can handle it?"

He chuckled. "We're old pros."

"Don't say old. I don't need any reminders."

"He's going to keep us young, this little dude." Greg laid his hand on hers.

She rested her cheek against his shoulder, savoring the firmness and the warmth of him. "I'm so excited to be having your baby. I'm so excited that most of the time I'm not scared about the cancer."

"Ah, sweetheart. We'll get through this. Everybody's pulling for you."

"I know. I'm a lucky woman." It was a miracle she could say so with utter sincerity. It wasn't even a lie; it was the truest thing she knew. She had so very much—her husband and their blended families, the baby on the way, her big Romano clan and the Inn at Willow Lake. Since marrying Greg, she had so many blessings in her life that it seemed ungrateful to give in to her cancer fears.

They lay in the quiet night, listening to the creaking of the old house and the breeze outside the window.

"Can I get you anything?" Greg asked.

"No, thanks." She had a collection of water bottles and meds on the nightstand, alongside a stack of books and snacks. There was a basin close at hand just in case the nausea kicked in. "I had a message from Orlando in my email today," she said. "He was thanking us for having him here."

"He didn't stay long."

"No. He seems nice enough, don't you think?"

"Nice enough for what?"

"Touché," she said, propping herself up on one elbow. "I want Sonnet to be with someone who adores her. Who cherishes her. Do you think he's the one?"

"Too soon to tell."

"Yes, all right. I'll give him a chance. But…"

"But what?"

"He said something weird in the email. Well, not weird, but he mentioned that upcoming campaign event again. Like I needed a reminder or a heads-up or something."

"He works for a politician," Greg said reasonably. "He's always looking and thinking ahead."

"I suppose. And I bet I know what he's thinking—that I had Laurence's child out of wedlock, and the opposition is going to try to make something of that."

Greg tightened his arm around her. "There's no way in hell I'm letting anyone near you. No way. That's the last thing you need to worry about."

"I like being near you," she whispered, snuggling even closer. I have to get better, she thought. I have to get better, because I can't bear to be apart from him.

"I'm a lucky guy, then, because I like it, too." He turned his head and pressed a gentle kiss to her temple. "I ran into Sophie today," he said. "She wanted me to let you know she's thinking of you."

"Nice of her." Greg and his ex-wife Sophie, the mother of Daisy and Max, did a pretty good job getting along. Every once in a while, though—like now—Nina faltered and insecurity took hold. "Sometimes I have this negative fantasy that you look at Sophie—perfectly healthy Sophie—and wish the two of you had stayed together after all."

"That's a fantasy, all right."

"I know. But she used to be your whole world."

"Okay, listen. To be honest, there was a time, before I fell in love with you, when I wanted my marriage back. Sophie and I both did, and we gave it our best shot. I wanted to be a family again, to fix whatever the hell went wrong. It didn't work, though. And then you came along…" His voice broke, and his arm tightened around her.

"What, Greg? Tell me."

"Now I can't thank her enough." He propped himself on one elbow and gazed down at her, his face only a shadow in the darkness. "If she hadn't left me, I wouldn't have found you. I've never loved anyone as much as I love you, Nina, and so even though I'll never actually thank my ex, I'm grateful every day for the way things worked out."

"Ah, Greg." She wound her arms around his neck and arched upward, knowing his rhythm so well now, knowing he wanted to make love.

"Really?" he asked.

"Ahem. Yes, Mr. Bellamy, your wife is horny."

"Then I'd better get busy."

She surrendered to his tender, erotic touch, reveling in the closeness, the intimacy, the safety of his embrace. He touched and kissed her breasts, just as he had when she was healthy and there was no bandage where the drain had been removed, no shunt for the drugs. She caught her breath. "I love when you kiss me like that," she said.

"I love kissing you like that."

"It's going to be weird for you after the mastectomy," she said.

He never even paused in his lovemaking. "Maybe. Might be weird for you, too. Nothing we can't handle. I love you, Nina. I love *you*. We'll deal."

"I'm going to be bald soon."

"Okay, now *that* turns me on."

He kissed away all her insecurities and worries. He kissed her until she couldn't think anymore. He kissed her until she surrendered, wrapping her legs around him and splaying her hands over his back. As always, he took his time with her, but tonight it wasn't necessary. "Greg," she whispered, "ah, the fireworks are starting early...."

He gave a soft, sexy laugh and then shuddered against her. She kept her arms twined around him, wishing she could hold onto this moment forever.

Cancer changed a person. Sonnet could see it happening day by day to her mother. Though Nina struggled to keep her spirits up, she couldn't stop herself from looking wan and exhausted. "I'm tired of the fight," she confessed to Sonnet one day. "And it's just getting started."

"Remember what they told us in the support group. It's not a sprint. It's a marathon."

"And that's supposed to make me feel better?"

"Guess not. But I've got an idea. I have the day off from shooting. Let's go shopping. There's a sale at Zuzu's Petals." She loved the quirky indie boutique in town. Suzanne, the owner, always found fun, colorful things created by off-the-beaten-path designers.

"I'm still in my bathrobe." Nina folded her arms on the table.

"I rest my case. You need something great to wear."

"I don't feel like shopping."

"Well, I do. Come on, Mom. We both need to get out. Hanging around and worrying isn't doing anyone any good, and yes, I'm starting to sound exactly like my mother."

"I'm good, aren't I?"

"We both need a little retail therapy. Please."

"Okay. I can see that resistance is futile. Let's do it."

Avalon was alive with a Saturday-morning vibe, people out doing errands or window-shopping, tourists armed with cameras, weekenders strolling along, nursing cups of coffee. The air was sweet with the promise of a pretty day. Suzanne was in the process of rolling a rack of sale items out to the sidewalk beside a table displaying candles and soaps.

"Hey, Nina," she said. "Sonnet. Good to see you."

"My daughter says we need some retail therapy," Nina said, picking up a scented candle and holding it to her nose.

"You came to the right place." Suzanne gave Nina a look full of sympathy. "How are you doing?"

"Gestating. Doing chemotherapy. You know, the same old, same old."

"I wish I could do something to help. My cousin Sarah went through breast cancer, and I remember she was always cold. I gave her a pink pashmina and she took it everywhere with her." Suzanne gestured at a rack of scarves inside the door.

"That's nice," said Nina. "How's she doing?"

Suzanne blanched as she fumbled through an explanation. "She, oh, she passed away. She was a lot older than me. Way older. And it was a long time ago. Gosh, I'm sorry. I shouldn't have brought it up."

Nina shrugged. "It's hard to figure out what to say. Until a few weeks ago, I would have been wondering, too."

Sonnet yearned for it to be a few weeks ago. Before...everything. She tucked her hand into Nina's arm. "Let's go find something pretty."

The shop smelled of soaps and scented candles and potpourri. There was a samovar filled with herbal tea, and a tray of mints. "Everybody always wants to mention their friend or relative who had cancer," Nina murmured. "I hate that. I know people are only trying to help, but I really hate that."

"Just remind yourself people love you and are pulling for you," Sonnet said.

"You're right, Miss Smarty-Pants. I stand corrected."

"I wasn't correcting you. Just reminding you. Whoa. Check out these earrings." She directed her mother to a display of artfully mismatched chandelier earrings.

"*Love.*" Nina lifted her hair and held an earring to one of her ears. "You were right about getting out, too. I feel better already."

"You'll feel like a million bucks if you get those earrings." Sonnet was drawn to a Victorian-inspired jacket fabricated from a vintage fabric. She tried it on, smoothing her hands down the sides. It felt wonderful, the brocaded velvet hugging her hips, the pockets lined with smooth satin.

"That looks fantastic on you," said Nina. "You should get it."

Sonnet checked herself out in the three-way mirror, picking up her long curls to see the detailing on the back. There was corset-style lacing with satin ribbon over a panel of rich, lime-green brocade. "This is fantastic. Totally fun," she said, regretfully taking off the jacket and putting it back on the hanger. "But I can't imagine where I'd wear it."

"Anywhere you need to look fabulous," her mother said.

"It's a little on the indie-chic side. Not quite the look I'm going for these days."

"Oh? And what look is that?" With a grin, Nina held up a tailored white blouse displayed with a tasteful scarf and matching brooch. "Urban chic? Boardroom-meeting chic?"

"Orlando would prefer that," Sonnet said. "He hasn't yet embraced my funky side."

"Then he's missing out. I love your funky side." Nina picked up a wonderful shawl of loose-knit angora. "So…Orlando. Tell me how that's going. It must be hard on the two of you, being apart."

"Yes, and no. He's so busy with the campaign ramping up that even if I was in the city, we'd be like two ships passing in the night."

"You're okay with that?"

"I don't have a choice. Why do I get the idea you're trying to tell me something?"

"Because I'm trying to tell you something. Or ask you something. Baby, he seems like an amazing guy. And I know for a fact that *you're* amazing. What I'm not hearing from you is where you think this relationship is going, or where you want it to go, or even if you want it at all."

Ouch. Her mother had never shrunk from asking difficult questions. "Of course I want it. Like you said, he's amazing. I know it's ridiculously idealistic, but I think we're going to be amazing together some day."

"Why is that ridiculous? I want that for you, too."

Sonnet held up a pair of fabulous distressed leather boots that would look great with the Victorian jacket. "I just don't know if we're getting there. I look at Daisy and you, and I know that's the kind of love I want in my life."

"Sure you do. And Lord knows, I want that for you. I want it for everybody. If we all had that, there would be world peace, I swear."

Sonnet laughed. "Did you suddenly take a happy pill when I wasn't looking?"

"This conversation just reminded me to show a little gratitude for what I have."

And that, thought Sonnet, feeling a lump in her throat, pretty much said it all. Her mother was dealing with a risky pregnancy and breast cancer, yet she could still be grateful for her friends and family, her husband. This was the kind of love Sonnet knew she was looking for, the kind she dreamed of finding with Orlando. Yet deep down, she knew they weren't there yet. And deeper down, she feared they'd never get to that place.

She wondered how a person found the kind of love that could survive anything. Did you find it by looking, or did it find you? And how did you know it for sure when love walked in? It was the kind of question that drove her crazy.

"I *need* this bag." Nina held up a vintage-inspired tapestry satchel. "If I get it, and the worst happens, I can honestly say I don't have a single regret."

"Mom—"

"Kidding. Not about the bag, though. What do you think?"

"Nice," said Sonnet, "but it's huge."

"I need to practice carrying a big bag again. Because when the baby comes, I'll be carrying a giant bag like an extra appendage." She turned, rippling her hand through a display of hanging scarves. "Those are pretty, too," she said.

"They are."

Sonnet plucked a nice one from the display. "This looks great with those earrings you picked out."

"You think?" A single line of worry formed between Nina's brows.

"Did the happy pill wear off already?"

Nina sighed. "No, but…okay, I'll just say it and get it out of me. The idea of shopping for a scarf to hide my bald head is depressing."

Sonnet caught her breath. "Oh, God. *Mom.*"

"I know, it's vain and it's the last thing I should worry about—"

"That's not true. I don't blame you one bit and nobody else would, either." She tried to picture her mother, bald as a just-hatched bird, but simply couldn't get the picture to form in her mind. Nina had wavy dark hair that perfectly complemented her olive-toned skin. She'd been growing it long the past few years, which made her look young; she still got carded in bars. Her hair—any woman's hair—was part of her identity. Losing it to the chemo was going to be traumatic.

"Just know it's part of the process, okay?" Sonnet said.

"You're right. Thanks for the reminder."

"And I think you should get this one *and* the earrings. Because with or without hair, you would totally rock that scarf."

The worried frown eased a bit. "All right. But you have to buy something too. If you don't get that jacket and those boots, you're not the daughter I raised."

★ ★ ★

The days fell into a routine of sorts, although with a group of kids and a hip-hop star who had a mouth like a longshoreman when provoked, the routine was anything but predictable. Some of the filmed sequences, when edited, would have more bleeps than dialogue in them. Yet to Sonnet's surprise, the production was beginning to feel like more than a job to her, like more than a way to pass the time while she was in Avalon. Yes, there was a lot of waiting around, a lot of conferring and planning, but her favorite moments were exactly what made an unscripted show so weirdly compelling.

The youngsters revealed themselves bit by bit, often without meaning to. She learned that Darnell dreamed of taking piano lessons, and Anita had the ability to read a whole chapter book in a couple of hours. Jaden had a knack for dreaming up crazy inventions involving ropes and pulleys. The twins sometimes communicated with made-up words and gestures only they could understand. Each child had gifts and flaws and quirks— sometimes endearing, sometimes annoying, always compelling.

On a soft, misty morning, they gathered in the dining hall to talk about the day's theme and activities. Today's theme was "facing our fears."

"Why we got to face our fears?" asked Andre, never shy about speaking his mind.

"So people don't call you a wuss," Darnell pointed out.

"S'pose I don't care if somebody call me a wuss?" asked Andre.

"What're you afraid of, anyway?" Jezebel asked him. "Be honest."

"Nothin'," the boy said. "Except stuff everybody's scared of, like snakes and bad guys."

"I used to get stage fright real bad," Jezebel said.

That got the kids' attention. "You?" asked one of the girls. "You told us you been performing since you were a kid."

"I have been. Was in the church choir, and the director

wanted me to sing a solo. And I wanted to, in the worst way. But I was scared. And the director told me if I ever wanted to lift my voice up for the Lord, I'd have to start by lifting it up for the people in the church. I told him I didn't know about the Lord, but I wanted the whole world to hear me."

"So did you sing the solo?" Quincy demanded.

"Yeah, I did. I almost peed my pants before the performance, but I did it. Again and again, until I wasn't scared anymore."

"You still sing in church?" he wanted to know.

She shook her head. "I still like gospel music, but my audience has changed."

"My momma doesn't let me listen to your music."

"My music isn't for kids, that's why. You should listen to your momma," Jezebel said.

"That what we're gonna do today?" asked Rhonda, one of the twins. "Sing for people?"

"Maybe later. Is singing for people something that scares you?"

"Heck, no," said Shawna, the other twin. "It scares other people."

"Nice." Jezebel offered her a high five. "Let's go around and say something that's scary."

"Crocodiles!" "Math tests." "Clowns." "Bridges that hang over deep, deep canyons." "Goosebumps books." "Worms."

"Worms?" Andre snorted at Rhonda's contribution. "How can anybody be afraid of worms?"

"They're slimy and you don't know which end is which."

"Then don't touch them. Don't look at them. You think they're gonna chase you down or something?"

A squabble erupted, and it was allowed to go on for a bit while the cameras rolled. Jezebel grabbed Andre by the back of the collar and pulled him out of the fray. "Is this an elimination-type show? Because if it is, I know some kids who're gonna get sent home."

"Nuh-uh. You can't send nobody home."

"Quit picking fights, or I'll change the rules."

"But come on. Worms?"

"Look, y'all," Jezebel said, "a fear is a fear. It doesn't have to make sense."

Sonnet grinned, wishing she could laugh aloud. "How about you?" she whispered to Zach, who was directing the sequence rather than filming today. "What are you afraid of?"

"Personal questions," he whispered back.

The kids were debating the comparative horrors of spiders versus salamanders, but all agreed a trip to the principal's office trumped them all.

During a break in the filming, Zach said, "You're enjoying this, aren't you?"

"I'm falling in love with these kids. They remind me of how much I liked working with children. And how much I miss it."

"Then why'd you quit?"

"I didn't quit. I moved on to an agency directorship. It's a way to help thousands of children, not just a few." So she'd told herself. She'd spent the entire past year rationalizing her career path, each time she got stuck in a meeting, or encountered some kind of frustrating bureaucratic situation. Her father had taught her that leadership was the way to change the world, and she clung to that advice.

Cold logic didn't keep her from missing what she really liked to do, though.

She shot Zach a resentful look, but he was already busy with something else. It was just as well that the conversation had been abandoned. He tended to ask her hard questions, the kind she didn't have the answers to.

A short time later, they were filming at a zip line that stretched from the top of Meerskill Falls, a cataract that thundered down a gorge, ending in the lake. Some of the kids were only too happy to leap into the adventure, screaming with laughter and exhilaration as they rode the cable down to the water's edge.

For all his brash talk, Andre refused to budge from the platform above the falls. Everyone else—including Jezebel herself—had gone, but Andre had managed to hang back until a crew member noticed him at the bottom of the ladder to mounting platform, being uncharacteristically quiet. They managed to cajole him up to the platform, but he refused to take a step farther.

"We need the kid whisperer," said one of the cameramen.

That was the nickname they'd given Sonnet, because she'd proven to be remarkably persuasive when it came to getting the kids to cooperate on set.

Time was wasting, and she didn't have the luxury of a lengthy shrink session. Much as she hated to be on camera, she moved in close to Andre, went down on one knee and looked him in the eye.

"Tell you what," she said to the shaking boy. "Let's go together. You and me. What do you say?"

"What good's that gonna do? Then we'll both die."

"Nobody's going to die. You saw everybody take a turn and they loved it. Come on, I'm scared, too, but I still want to do it."

"You're not scared. I heard you telling Salt over there that you couldn't wait to take a turn."

"Salt?"

"That's what we call him." Andre jerked a thumb in Zach's direction. "'Cause the two of you are salt and pepper."

She felt her cheeks heat up. She didn't want to be pepper to Zach's salt. "Never mind that. Let's do this thing."

"Tell me what you're scared of," Andre said. "Then maybe I'll think about it."

"I'm...well, there are lots of things that scare me," she admitted.

"That's not an answer. Tell me one thing, just one thing you're afraid of."

"Riding horseback. And I'm sorry to say, that activity is on the agenda this afternoon."

"You ain't acting scared," Andre said.

"Just because I'm not acting that way doesn't mean I'm not scared."

"You gotta tell me something real."

"Okay, get into your harness and helmet, and I'll tell you something real." She had no idea what she was going to say, but she was not going to feed the kid a line of bull. Like all children, Andre had a highly sensitive bullshit meter, and he was sure to call her on it.

He negotiated a little further, demanding a milk shake as a reward for bravery.

"You got it," she promised. "With whipped cream and a cherry on top."

Boys were so simple. You could buy their cooperation with so little. It was only when they turned into grown men that they became complicated.

While she and Andre geared up with the help of the crew, she tried to think about what to tell him. The thing about kids was that they could spot a phony a mile away. Andre was not going to relent until she leveled with him and confessed a real fear. There were so many to choose from, it was ridiculous. Yet she'd always been pretty good at dealing with her fears. She was rational in the extreme, and could usually simply explain them away.

Once they were both in their harnesses, she felt a shot of exhilaration. The perspective was amazing, the slender cable arcing gracefully down the gorge, topping the trees that sloped down to the lake. The morning mist swirled on the water, adding a hint of magic to the scene.

"It's going to be great, Andre," she said. "You're going to love it."

"Okay, so now you have to tell me what scares you."

She bridled at his tone. "Andre, I really don't appreciate being quizzed by you."

"You said you'd tell me. You promised."

"But—"

"You promised!"

"I'm afraid of lots of things."

"Then just tell me one. Just one."

"Fine," she retorted, the words coming out ahead of her common sense. "I'm afraid of what my mother's going to look like when she loses all her hair to chemo." The pain in her voice seemed to echo through the empty woods.

Everyone went still for a moment, although she was certain the camera kept rolling. Even Andre stopped struggling. Young as he was, he seemed to understand how deeply personal the matter was, how painful to reveal. Sonnet's own pounding heart told her that it wasn't really her mom's imminent baldness that frightened her, per se. Hair would grow back. What she truly feared was that the chemo wasn't working.

"Happy now?" she said to Andre, and stepped off the platform.

CHAPTER
13

The night before her mother's mastectomy, Sonnet barely slept. In the window seat of her room, with its view of the darkened grounds of the Inn at Willow Lake, she sat in the predawn light and battled a worry so acute it struck her like nausea. The sheer, wafting curtains smelled of fresh air and lavender, and the sound of crickets filled the air.

She felt a million miles away from her old life in the city. The goals she'd once pursued so relentlessly seemed far away, too, mattering so little now.

She tried to soothe herself with the reminder that so far, the treatment program was going according to plan. The initial chemo treatments Nina had undergone would make surgery easier to perform. They'd met with the surgeon twice, and he was reassuringly confident of a positive outcome. And if that wasn't enough, Orlando had made good on his promise to involve his aunt, a highly regarded oncologist with the Krokower Clinic in the city. Dr. Rivera had familiarized herself with the case, going over the physical examinations, breast ultrasound, core biopsy, CT scan and MRI. She had done several phone consultations with Nina's team.

Orlando's aunt had advocated a combination of very new "smart drugs" that would be filtered by the placental wall, keeping the baby safe. She'd even taken the time to speak with Sonnet personally, and her confident professionalism was reassuring to hear. Still, Sonnet worried. People suffered from cancer. They *died*.

Restless, she paced over to her laptop and checked her email. There was nothing new since the last time she'd checked. She sighed and leaned back, cautioning herself not to go trolling the internet for information about breast cancer. There was too much out there. She'd catch herself reading a blog by some kindly woman documenting her breast cancer "journey," only to see the blog abruptly end, leaving her hanging. Had the woman survived? Or had the narrative ended because she hadn't made it?

A chat window popped onto the screen. What are you doing up? Orlando typed.

She smiled, surprised to see the message. Worrying about my mom's surgery. What are YOU doing up?

Thinking about you. I knew you'd be worried. Hang in there.

That's nice. Thanks, Orlando.

Give her my best. And get some sleep. You're not going to be much help if you're exhausted.

OK, she typed. I'll try.

Call me later.

OK. Orlando—

The chat window informed her the user orivera47 was unavailable. Like a computer-generated image, he'd disappeared into the digital ether. But the fact that he'd checked in with her made her feel a little less alone.

She tried to take his advice, getting back into bed and doing the breathing exercises she'd been working on with her mom. Sleep was far away, though, held at bay by the persistent worry of all that could go wrong. Her mom, her beautiful mom, was about to have one of her breasts cut off.

Sonnet shut her eyes and sent out a wordless, fervent little prayer that all would go well.

Gathering her things for the trip to the hospital, Nina felt like a warrior girding for battle. She knew a struggle was imminent, she knew she would come home wounded and that there would be pain, but she was ready. Even with an empty stomach and her head buzzing with fear, she made herself put one foot in front of the other.

Sonnet and Greg were waiting in the car. Nina stood in the foyer of the house where she'd lived since her marriage to Greg. Last night in front of the camera Zach had installed on her computer, she had spoken of her fears and her determination.

Then, on impulse, she had peeled off her shirt and bra, taking the last pictures of her intact breasts. It was the last time her body would look this way, unmarked, as nature had made her. Soon, her hair would be gone as well, and she would look as strange to herself as an alien from another planet.

She'd broken down then, wept and raged while her husband and daughter slumbered, and then pulled herself together. Then she had shut off the camera and saved the file. She would not be giving that sequence to Zach for editing. She might never look at it again. But she felt compelled to keep it, the way she'd kept her seventh-grade diary and the love notes she'd sent to Shane Gilmore when she was fourteen. It was a private part of her, something she would keep…at least until she didn't need it anymore.

Now she turned back and looked at the furnishings they'd picked out together, the lace curtains wafting in the breeze, the frieze of family pictures in the hallway. She saw all the smiling faces of the people she loved, so many of them. The sight gave her strength. This was her home, a place of joy and safety, and she was determined to come back and get better.

Her hand came up and touched her right breast. Not all of her would be coming back. It was hard to think about how radically different her body would look, but she reminded herself that the breast was diseased; it had to be excised to save her life. There was nothing more precious, not a body part, not vanity, but life, and those she held dear. "We're going to be okay," she said to the little stranger inside her. She refused to think about the alternative.

Sonnet and Greg were chatty as they drove, but Nina couldn't focus on their words. She wore a small smile, listening to their nervous chatter but not really hearing what they said.

In the first waiting room, they stuck to her like glue. She paged through a magazine, browsing through recipes for braised chicken and frosted cupcakes. Every time she glanced up at Greg, he was watching her, his expression both earnest and helpless. Sonnet, too, wore that face, desperate to help, but there wasn't anything they could give her, not a glass of water, a cookie, a word of encouragement that hadn't already been said.

"I don't need anything more," she told them softly. "You two have already given me everything I need."

Greg took her hand. Sonnet said, "Oh, Mom. You've been through everything with me. I wish I could give you even a fraction of what you've given me."

Nina's heart swelled. Yes, she was afraid, but the love she felt from her daughter and husband wrapped around her like a cloak. She felt worse for them than she did for herself, knowing that soon she'd be unconscious while they worried and waited.

Time dragged, and then sped up when a nurse came to take her into the next room. "Patients only," the nurse said, holding the door for Nina. She paused and turned back with a smile and a wave. Then the door hissed shut behind her.

She took a few steps into the next waiting room. Then a flash of panic shot through her. "I forgot to kiss them goodbye," she whispered. Oh, God. What if something went wrong? What if she never saw them again?

"You'll be with them soon," the nurse assured her.

Nina caught the unspoken message—don't add to the drama with a long, panicked goodbye. She nodded and took a seat in an oversized lounge chair. There were four other women having either a mastectomy or a lumpectomy that day. The wait dragged on, there in that windowless room, with only a few tattered magazines and a droning television for company. After a while, Nina was taken to change her clothes for a robe and thick compression socks. Her breast and underarm were marked with a black marker to specify the surgery site and what had to be done. She regarded the proceedings with a curious detachment, until the anaesthesiologist came in to talk to each patient. Then the fear rolled back in like a wave.

One by one, each woman went into surgery, like virgins to sacrifice, solemn and silently fearful. Then only Nina remained. When her turn came up, she paused for a moment, frozen by the knowledge that her body was about to be forever transformed. She was losing her breast willingly, but it was still a loss to be acknowledged. She smoothed her hand over herself, silently sending a message of gratitude that she'd nursed her baby daughter with it twenty-eight years ago.

Now she was impatient to get it done. She paced back and forth, restless as a caged animal, hunger gnawing inside her, as she hadn't eaten a bite since the night before. Finally a nurse escorted her to the pre-op room. By now she was used to the procedure—the high gurney, the IVs, the monitors. A chill hummed in the air, and even the thick blanket they gave her failed to keep the shivers at bay. One of the nurses held her hand and they chatted. Nina knew she wouldn't remember anything they talked about.

In the operating room, which was even colder, she was lifted onto the table. Someone told her she'd be feeling very sleepy.

"Nothing's happening," she murmured, feeling a resurgence of panic. There were things she had left undone. There were things she'd forgotten to say to people. She hadn't thanked her parents for loving and supporting her. She'd forgotten to kiss Greg one last time. She should have reassured Sonnet more, told her how proud she was of her and how much she loved her. She should have put that all on the video in her last session with Zach, but she'd neglected to do that. If something happened and she never woke up, would her family know how very much she loved them, how very sorry she was that she had to go?

Sonnet thought she was prepared for the sight of her mother shortly after the surgery. Even so, the gray tone of her skin, the tubes and drips, the streaks of amber disinfectant and the slack exhaustion in Nina's eyes shocked her. There was a drain leading down to a clear pouch of blood on the floor.

Greg seemed wrung out by worry as he bent and gingerly placed a kiss on Nina's forehead.

"I don't exactly look minty fresh, do I?" Nina asked with a glimmer of a smile.

"Nope," Sonnet said, "and we don't care. How do you feel?"

"Other than starving to death, surprisingly good, I guess thanks to this delicious cocktail of painkillers. I might be less happy when they wear off."

"The surgeon already spoke to us," Greg said, "and he'll be in to see you soon. It's good news."

Her mom glanced down at her chest, the right side covered by layers of bandaging. "It's gone."

"Yes," said Greg, "and that's the good news. I wrote it down—complete surgical excision and negative axillary nodes."

Nina seemed to go limp on the pillow. "Wow. Good riddance to bad rubbish."

"In other news, you get to eat," Sonnet said. "We brought you a milk shake—banana mango. That's still your favorite, right?"

"I didn't know she had a favorite milk shake," Greg said.

"When I was little, we used to get a milk shake every Friday after Mom got off work. We ordered every flavor on the menu until we figured out our favorites."

Nina sipped from the straw. "That's delicious. I thought I was going to pass out from hunger before the surgery."

Sonnet's phone vibrated with an incoming text message. "Orlando," she said. "He wants to know how you're doing."

"Better now," Nina said.

"I owe Orlando a big thank you," Sonnet said. "It was nice of him, right? Bringing in his aunt for a consult?"

"Very nice, Sonnet. He's very…nice."

"Why do I get the feeling 'nice' is a code word for something you're not saying?"

"Maybe because there's something she's not saying," Greg suggested.

Nina sipped her milk shake. "Okay, I'll just say it. I wish I sensed more passion in this relationship, Sonnet. The two of you seem so…nice together. I want so much for you, and know you have to find it on your own. I want you to love him, if that's what will make you happy. I want you to be in love with him, head over heels, and I want that love to make you so happy you might just burst."

"Whoa. Those are some drugs you're on," said Greg.

"Maybe I am that happy," Sonnet said. How could she not be? Orlando really was everything her father had told her—smart, helpful, professional. She felt guilty for wishing exactly what her mother had voiced—that he was just a tad more romantic. Or—she might as well be honest with herself—a lot more romantic. She reminded herself that romance was fleeting; there were more important things than that. Orlando was the person she should be with. In the midst of the fear and uncertainty, he was nothing but helpful.

"Are you?" her mother asked.

"You're supposed to be resting."

"I'm resting. If I rest any more, I'll be a corpse."

"Don't be morbid." Sonnet handed her a water bottle with a straw. "Hydrate."

There was no let-up in Nina's battle. The chemo treatments continued, now with the added challenge of recovering from surgery. This was when the friends and family kicked in. Sonnet had never seen anything like it.

People came to the house with offerings like pilgrims to Lourdes. There were casseroles from Greg's mother Jane and a tagine from his brother, Philip, who had just taken a class in Moroccan cooking. Jenny Majesky McKnight, the owner of Sky River Bakery, arrived with her signature Irish Cream Cake and a new indulgence, Pavlova with fresh fruit. Olivia Bellamy Davis, manager of Camp Kioga, took time every other day to do a power walk with Nina, and worked through the recommended range-of-motion exercises to help with the healing.

But the irony was, with all the outpouring of generosity from friends and family, Nina got sicker.

In a silent state of terror, Sonnet found herself staying up late at night browsing the web for information, and nagging the medical team by phone for ways to make things better.

The biggest issue was that Nina couldn't stand to eat, particularly right after chemo. Sonnet tried not to fret, but it was impossible to watch her mother pick at her food, or stare out the window, her brain fuzzy from fatigue and the poisonous cocktail of drugs.

She seemed exhausted all the time, though she insisted her spirits were good. Sonnet recognized the anxiety and discomfort in the twingey expression on her face, and her slow movements. "They say my hair's going to start falling out in a week or two," Nina said.

Sonnet still cringed when she thought of what she'd blurted on set about being fearful about her mother losing her hair. It seemed so petty to worry about her mom's hair in the face of everything else. But she knew why she was afraid. A bald woman might as well walk around with a sandwich board on her chest, announcing, "Cancer Patient." She knew her mom would hate that. Worst of all, she might be one of the unlucky ones, the ones who lost the battle.

She tried to shrug off a sick fear. "Nonna brought over your favorite," she said, setting a platter on the table with a flourish. "Caprese salad and pasta with butter tomato sauce. With salted rosemary focaccia bread."

With an expression of sheer determination, Nina took a seat. "That's pretty much everyone's favorite. I'm getting extremely spoiled. The whole town is spoiling me."

"Same as you would do for anyone else," Sonnet pointed out.

"She did the same thing for my uncle," Greg reminded her, offering a tender smile. His most adventurous relative, the elderly George Bellamy, had returned to Willow Lake, gravely ill, for his final adventure—to make amends for the past and to be with his family one last time. "She made him her mind-blowing lasagna once a week for a whole summer."

"The kind with the bechamel sauce?" asked Sonnet. "We should make some, Mom. If that doesn't give you a craving, I don't know what will."

Nina picked at her salad. Sonnet could tell she was trying not to worry her and Greg, which only worried her more.

"Lasagna sounds good. Oh, and I made *you* something." She handed Sonnet a gift bag.

"What's this? Besides a way to avoid the topic of eating."

"Just a little something, Miss Smarty-Pants. I took up embroidery to give my hands something to do during chemo."

Sonnet reached into the bag and pulled out a decorative pillow. The face of it was embroidered in fancy lettering. "'Don't get so busy you forget to fall in love,'" she read aloud. "I can't believe you remembered saying that to me right before Daisy's wedding."

"I don't say profound things very often," Nina admitted. "This one stuck with me. Seemed like a good reminder for anyone."

"But especially me," Sonnet said, slowly putting the pillow back in the bag. "I'll keep it in mind, Mom."

"Tell me about your week. I feel as if I've been to another planet and back. What did you do on the show?"

"We faced our fears," said Sonnet. "Film at eleven."

"Really? How'd that go?" Nina asked.

"All right, I assume. It's all in the editing. We've got footage of kids going off the high dive, doing the zip line, eating mushrooms, talking in front of an audience, you name it. It's still hard to imagine what the finished show will be like, but sometimes I think I can see it taking shape."

"What fear do you have to face?" Nina asked, looking at Greg.

"Having Max quit school and move back home," he said instantly.

He spoke so quickly, Sonnet knew he must have been thinking about Max before he spoke. Daisy's younger brother was a rogue of the charming variety, taking his time getting through college as he focused on girls and fun.

"What about you?" Greg asked Sonnet. "Your turn."

"Oh, I have a list," Sonnet said, wishing she could forget

what she'd blurted out at the zip line. "Last time I found myself paralyzed with fear, it was over hemming a good pair of jeans."

"I hear you," Nina said. "It's a dilemma, figuring out what heel height to match."

"Heel height." Greg shook his head sadly.

"I'm scared of parallel parking," Nina continued. "Especially having to do it with someone watching. And it's so silly, isn't it? People don't judge you for your parking ability."

Sonnet felt a surge of love and admiration for her mom. Pregnant and dealing with cancer, she had any number of fears to choose from.

"I'm afraid of yoga," Greg said. "Especially the kind where they play gong music."

Sonnet laughed. "Good one. And how about black-diamond ski runs?" She shuddered. "They always look like they could be the death of me. Plus I'm scared of wine lists. No matter how hard I try, I can't pretend to know what I'm doing, and I always end up picking the Malbec."

"Playing Scrabble with my daughter," Nina said. "Now, that's scary."

"You're not scared of Scrabble with me." Sonnet hesitated. "Are you?"

"You didn't say it has to make sense. And yes, if you must know, you are a horror on the Scrabble board. You out-strategize me every time."

"Electrical wires," Greg added. "Hole number four at Avalon Meadows Golf Course. Small dogs."

"I never knew you were scared of small dogs," Nina said.

"I'm not. I just threw that in to make sure you're listening."

"I always listen to you, even when you aren't making sense," she said. "Why don't we have a dog, anyway? I love dogs."

"Let's focus on having a baby, for the time being," he said.

"I'm scared of my wicked stepfather," Sonnet said.

He lifted his water goblet and they clinked glasses. Nina cupped her chin in the palm of her hand and poked at her salad.

Sonnet couldn't help but notice that Nina had barely touched her dinner. "Mom—"

"I know. I'll eat. I'm just… Okay, here's something I'm afraid of. I'm afraid there were too many days I coasted through on autopilot. I'm afraid I didn't cherish them enough, but only let them slip by." She shivered a little. "That's more of a regret than a fear, I suppose. We can't do anything about regrets, can we? Fears are more manageable."

Her mother was rambling. Chemo brain, she sometimes called it, a mental fuzziness caused by her meds.

"Mom, please eat." It was all Sonnet could say. She didn't trust herself to go on, and that ticked her off. She wanted to be strong for her mother. She wanted to have all the answers, but she simply didn't.

"Yeah, don't let this amazing meal slip by," Greg said.

"Very funny." Nina took a bite of pasta. An extremely small bite, after which she set down her fork. "It's delicious. I need to remember to send a thank-you note. But lately, I can't even remember my own name, so I'll probably forget to do it. I already feel guilty."

The doorbell rang, and Greg pushed back from the table. "Let's hope that's not a cranky guest. I'm scared of cranky guests."

A few minutes later, Zach and Jezebel appeared. Sonnet felt an unbidden and undeniably pleasant surge at the sight of Zach. Because they were becoming friends again, she told herself. They also had a young woman in tow. She wore a gauzy black sundress and gold gladiator sandals, which could have looked ridiculous, but instead, made her seem cutting-edge stylish.

"Sorry, we're interrupting your dinner," Zach said. He had one of his bigger camera bags with him. Lately, they were practically appendages.

"Not at all," Nina assured them. "We were just finishing."

It didn't take long to finish three bites of food, Sonnet thought.

"Let's go into the living room," Nina suggested. "I've been wanting to meet you."

"Likewise," Jezebel said. "You got a super nice daughter. I guess you know that."

Greg stayed behind to clear the table.

"We were just hearing about how the day went," Nina said. "I have to say, this show is definitely one of the most interesting things to happen in Avalon."

"Come by when we're shooting," Zach said. "Sonnet can let you know a good day for that. Tonight, Jezebel wanted to introduce you to Paige."

Sonnet regarded him with silent suspicion. What were they up to?

"Paige was my stylist in New York up until a couple years ago," Jezebel said. "She used to give me the most wicked weaves. My hair was totally fly when she was doing it."

"I got out of the business in order to pursue something else," Paige explained. "My grandmother got sick and I found a new passion—I became a wig maker."

"Whoa," said Nina, pulling back. "I think I can guess where this is going."

Sonnet felt queasy. Like an idiot, she'd blurted out her fear of Nina losing her hair, thus putting a crazy idea into someone's head—Zach or Jezebel; she couldn't be sure. She turned to glare at Zach. He stared back, unapologetic.

"Is this some kind of hair intervention?" Nina asked. "Because if it is—"

"I wanted you to meet Paige, see what she can do for you," Jezebel said.

"Sorry, I don't mean to sound ungrateful. This is... It's difficult for me."

"It's hard for every cancer patient," Paige said. "Believe me, you are not alone."

"You're very kind to stop by," Nina said. "Something I've found since getting sick is that I have a lot of angels in my life. A lot more than I ever knew." She offered a smile that was soft with relief. "Thank you for showing up out of the blue like this."

Sonnet let out the breath she didn't know she'd been holding. Despite the illness, her mom was still her mom, gracious and open-minded. "Did you drive all the way up from the city?" she asked.

Paige nodded. "Jezebel's been wanting me to see this place. It's beautiful here. And the inn is incredible. They gave me a room with a balcony." She turned to Nina. "I'm here to help, or just to pay a visit. Up to you."

Nina put a hand up to her head. Her arm looked thin—not slender, but genuinely thin. "I brought a wig catalog home from the clinic but I'm not quite ready to look at it. Supposedly I get to keep my hair for a few more weeks. And then...I guess I'd better have a plan B."

"That's why I'm here. I'm your plan B," said Paige.

"Honey, you want to see this," Jezebel said, motioning Paige over to Nina's side. "Take a look at her pictures."

"Here's my grandmother before she lost her hair," Paige said, offering a photo of a middle-aged woman with a nice head of nut-brown hair. "And here she is with her wig."

Nina frowned and motioned Sonnet closer. "She looks virtually the same, just shorter. You do beautiful work."

"Thanks. Gran was my first client." She showed them a few more pictures of women and men. "You can see I got even better with practice."

"Check this one out." Jezebel handed over another before-and-after shot of herself.

Sonnet frowned at her. "I don't understand."

"I'm a cancer survivor, Creampuff," said Jezebel. "Couple of years ago."

"Jezebel, really? I had no idea."

"I kept it quiet. The tabloids put it out that I was in rehab or some nonsense like that."

Sonnet readjusted her thinking. Jezebel…a cancer survivor. It explained so much—Jezebel's knowledge and compassion, her interest in Nina.

"Thanks for sharing that," Nina said. "You're very inspirational. And the wig looks incredible. When the time comes—"

"That's why we're here tonight," Jezebel said. "It's time now. See, the reason Paige's clients look so good is that she makes the wigs out of the patient's own hair. That's the good news. The bad news is—"

"You need the hair now," Nina said, comprehension etched starkly on her face.

Sonnet gaped, looking from Zach to Jezebel to Paige. "Seriously?"

Paige explained the process. They'd take Nina's hair tonight, leaving only enough to cover her scalp—the k.d. lang look, Jezebel explained. Paige would weave the hair, strand by strand, into a wig modeled after Nina's natural look. Sonnet nearly forgot to breathe, listening to Paige, whose eyes lit as she talked about her work.

"Anyway," she concluded, "it's an option. Would you like some time to think about it? There's a gel on the market now that sometimes prevents hair loss. Maybe your doctor told you about it?"

"Yes, but it hasn't been approved for use in pregnant women, and it's not always effective." Nina pressed her hands to her face. Sonnet rushed over to the sofa and put her arms around her. Since she'd been back, she hadn't seen her mother shrink with terror, not even before the surgery. It felt as though someone had snatched a rug out from under her, and she was unsteady, disoriented. Yet at the same time, it felt right to put her arms around her mother and simply hold her close. "Mom, you don't have to do this at all—"

"I know." Nina brushed her sleeve across her face. "I could always just let my hair fall out in tufts and throw it away, right?" She smiled through her tears. "But what good would that do? I say we get started, if that's okay."

"It's great," Jezebel said.

"On one condition. I want Zach to film the proceedings."

"Really, Mom?" Sonnet squeezed her hand.

"Someday I'm going to look back and say, 'I can't believe I did that.' Zach?"

"Sure, no problem. I had a feeling you'd want to."

It seemed so natural for Zach to be present for this very personal matter. He was far more than a friend, Sonnet reflected. He was family.

"I brought all my gear with me. Maybe on the back porch?" Paige suggested. "It's a nice night, and being outside makes cleanup easy."

Nina nodded in agreement. "Let's do this thing." Despite the brave words, her voice wavered.

Now it was Sonnet's turn to tear up. She caught Jezebel's eye. "Thanks," she whispered.

Greg was tidying up the kitchen when they all trooped through en route to the back porch.

"Brace yourself," Nina said, a glow of excitement in her eyes. "I'm about to get all my hair cut off."

"Um, okay. Mind if I watch?"

"Of course not."

"Mind if I drink while I watch?"

"That's fine," Nina said. "By now, I'm used to you drinking without me."

He took out a six-pack of India Pale Ale and offered them around.

"Thanks, I'll wait until I'm done here," Paige said, and Nina looked relieved.

"One more request," said Greg, and he took Nina in his arms, burying his face in her hair. He whispered something and she lifted her hand to his cheek.

I'm so glad she has you, Sonnet thought. She wondered if she'd ever find a love like that, and the notion startled her. She was supposed to be finding exactly that with Orlando. Under the current circumstances, however, they were in a holding pattern and not likely to find anything together other than higher mobile phone bills. There was something wrong with that picture, she realized, but now was not the time to think about that.

She hadn't had a beer in ages, and the cold IPA tasted like heaven. Zach set up his video and still camera equipment. Paige explained the shots she needed, pictures from every angle, so she could replicate the look as closely as possible. She even requested some video shots, so she could study the way Nina's hair moved.

With a flourish, she fastened a drape around Nina and took out a pair of wicked-looking scissors. "I've got a mirror if you'd like to watch," she said.

"No, thanks," said Nina. "I'd rather be surprised." She took a deep breath, then let it out. "I have no idea what my scalp looks like. It might be gnarly."

"You're beautiful, Mom. That's not going to change. You know that, right?" Sonnet wasn't just saying it.

"I can get your hairpiece done in a couple of days." Paige gently lifted a lock of hair. The scissors made a crisp snipping sound, and the strand came away in her hand. She laid it on a sheet of plastic and moved on to the next one. The process seemed oddly ritualistic, with an air of gravitas. Zach recorded the proceedings, and Sonnet felt grateful for him, because she knew he would capture her mother's sweetly tentative smile, and Greg's indulgent regard.

"You're going to look fine," Paige said. "I think you'll be happy with your wig."

"I'm sure I will," Nina said. "This is an incredible opportunity." She seemed relaxed as Paige finished with the haircut, leaving maybe an inch of length all around. She shaped Nina's remaining hair into an extremely short bob.

"You look like a kid," Greg said. "I like it."

"The piece might look slightly shorter and thinner than you're used to," Paige explained, brushing off Nina's neck. "I have to use quite a bit of the length and volume of the hair in the weave, and there's only so much of it. It's best if I have extra hair to work with. Do you mind if I make use of donor hair?"

"No," Nina said. "Of course not."

Paige aimed a meaningful look straight at Sonnet.

Sonnet put a hand to her head, startled. "Seriously? Can you use mine?"

"No," said Nina quickly. "No way. I'm not letting you—"

"I was asking Paige."

"I could make it work," Paige said picking up a curly lock of Sonnet's hair. "I work with donated hair all the time. You and your mom are a pretty close match, even though you're different races. The color matches, and your hair's pretty similar in texture."

"Fine," said Sonnet. "It's all yours, then."

"You've never had short hair," her mother pointed out.

"Neither have you." Sonnet wanted to get it over with before she lost her nerve. "We'll look like sisters."

It was remarkably hard to sit still while Paige methodically cut off her long, curly hair. "Remember when I was little, how much I hated my hair?" Sonnet asked her mom.

"All girls hate their hair," Jezebel said. "If it's straight, they wish it was curly. If it's curly, they want it straight. And if it's *nappy...*" She twirled a lock of her own hair around her finger. "Then you know you're hot."

Nina looked mystified.

"It's a line from one of her songs," Sonnet explained.

"You used to put that goopy stuff in your hair," Zach said.

"Hey, that goopy stuff kept me from setting my head on fire out of sheer frustration," Sonnet said. She tried not to wince as the scissors clipped close to her ear.

After what felt like an eternity, her mother handed her the mirror. "There. You're Halle Berry."

Sonnet stared at the stranger in the mirror. The breeze whispered across her neck and throat, and she felt as light as a feather, as if she might fly away. The transformation was startling and dramatic. She had no idea if she looked good or not. But when she saw the expression on Zach's face, she knew for sure she didn't look bad.

CHAPTER 14

"What the devil did you do to your hair?" Orlando exited the campaign bus, scolding her before both feet reached the pavement.

Sonnet patted her short curls. "I gave it to my mother. And if you're going to yell at me for that, we've got a serious problem."

"Ah, sorry. I'm being an ass." Flashing his irresistible smile, as if delighted to call himself an ass, he strode over to her and gave her a hug. "Stressed out, and that's no excuse. But...what are you wearing?"

She looked down at the vintage jacket and boots she'd bought at Zuzu's Petals. "My new look. You like?"

"Cute. It's kind of Bohemian."

"That's what I'm aiming for."

His jaw hardened, but then he smiled. "You look fantastic, and I've missed you."

Behind him, campaign staffers poured from the bus, which was painted with a flowing banner and "Laurence Jeffries: Leadership for Tomorrow." It was still surreal to Sonnet that her father had a campaign bus. Or that he had a campaign at all.

"Has anyone from the Delvecchio camp come around?" Orlando asked.

"No. Why would they— Oh." Her heart sank. Of course— the election. Orlando ate, slept and breathed the campaign, sensitive to every nuance in the press or on the internet. The process actually made Jezebel's show seem sane. "They're not seriously going to make an issue of the fact that my parents were never married."

"I warned you, they might."

"Is my father with you?" She craned her neck to see what was going on. More aides and volunteers came out, swarming around the bus. A separate truck had pulled up alongside Blanchard Park, where the debate would take place. Already the town was swarming with the press, political bloggers, supporters and detractors from both sides.

"He's flying up by floatplane from Westchester in about an hour."

"Oh, good. Then there'll be time to have a visit—"

"Not hardly. He's got to prep for the event, and the press conference afterward, and then he needs to get back to the city for a fundraiser breakfast in the morning."

She swallowed her disappointment. "He really wants this. He's determined."

"You're right. He's a good man, Sonnet, and he'll be good for this state—for the country. But getting there means he's got to sacrifice a lot of personal time."

"I understand. Really, I do."

"He wanted me to ask you if you'd find him in the greenroom before the debate. He really wants to see you."

"Of course. I'll make sure I find him." She felt herself visibly brightening up. "What about you? Are you staying overnight?"

"I wish. Your mom's place is incredible. But I've got to be

at the breakfast." He hesitated, then said, "I'd love to see your mom, if she's up to it."

"Thanks." She took his hand and gave it a squeeze. "And I've missed you, too."

They drove to the inn, where they found Nina and Greg busily whitewashing a set of Adirondack chairs. It was good to see her mom going about her life, doing everyday things. Yes, she moved slower. She had to force herself to eat, and her chemo brain made her forgetful. But she was committed to her treatment. So far, it was too soon for the docs to say for certain the drugs were working, but there would be news soon.

As Sonnet and Orlando approached, Nina straightened, took off her hat and waved them over.

"She looks good," Orlando said.

Sonnet felt a rush of gratitude. The wig created from her mother's and her hair was a remarkable match for Nina's natural look. Her own was completely gone by now, but thanks to the wig, she still looked much like herself. Only much too thin, her gauntness accentuated by the advancing pregnancy.

"Welcome back," she said, extending her hands to Orlando. There was a brief hug, made awkward by the fact that they barely knew each other. Orlando smoothed things over by turning to Greg for a handshake.

"You must be here for the big campaign debate," Greg said.

"That's right. Unfortunately, I can't stay long, but I definitely wanted to drop by, see how things are going."

"Well enough, all things considered," Nina said. "Do you have time for a lemonade, or maybe something stronger?"

"I wish," Orlando said. "Things are already getting set up in town, and the press is arriving. You, ah…were you planning to attend?"

"Wouldn't miss it," Nina said.

Orlando's shoulders stiffened and his eyes narrowed. Sonnet wondered if his tight, stressed expression was noticeable.

"I already know who I'm voting for," Greg said. "A debate's not going to change my mind. Laurence is the right man for the job."

Orlando grinned, his natural charm emanating from him like a halo. Sonnet suspected she was the only one who could read the tension in his eyes. "Everyone on the campaign thinks so. We all appreciate your support." He handed her a shopping bag. "I brought you an e-reader. Sonnet mentioned you're a big reader, so I thought you might want to try one out."

"That's really nice of you, Orlando. Thanks. I'm spending a lot of time in waiting rooms these days, so I'm sure I'll put it to use."

"I loaded it with books I thought you might be interested in."

"You're thoughtful," Sonnet said, turning on the reader. "Let's see what you've picked for my mom." The screen filled with an array of nonfiction books—*Nutrition for the Cancer Patient, The World According to Cancer, Knowledge is Power.…* Okay, her mom was going to hate these books. Certainly she was committed to learning about her disease, but reading was her escape. Of course, Orlando couldn't have known that. "What's nice is all the variety that's out there. I can get you the new Robert Dugoni novel, if you like."

"Thank you again," Nina said to Orlando. "I'm going to enjoy it a lot, I'm sure."

"You're more than welcome." His phone buzzed, and he checked it. "Sure wish I could stay longer, but duty calls."

"I'm going to head over to the venue with Orlando," Sonnet said. "I'll see you there, Mom."

"You sure she's up to it?" he asked, once they were out of earshot.

"She's sick, not brain dead," Sonnet said. "It's good for her to get out. For me, too. I haven't seen my dad in a long time. I know he doesn't have much time, but let's hope he can spare a little."

A beat passed. Then Orlando said, "Yes, sure. I know he'd love to see you."

She stopped in her tracks. "You cannot be serious. You're worried about the press."

"You know me. I worry about everything."

"I'm not exactly a deep, dark secret. I've been front and center in lots of his bios."

"Yes, but that was when—"

"When what? Oh, I see. When I had a prestigious job with UNESCO. Now I'm just a slacker, right?"

"You never know how they're going to spin things."

"But you know, right?"

"It's my job to know."

"And how are they going to spin things?"

"Delvecchio will put forth something to cast you in the least flattering light—maybe trying to get people to speculate on why you turned down the most prestigious fellowship in your field."

"No speculation needed. I'll simply say I'm attending to a family matter. If they need more detail, well, I'll deal." She hated the idea of bringing up her mother's condition.

"Sonnet, I'm really sorry. I'd protect you from all of this if I could."

"News flash. I don't need protecting."

"That's admirable of you, even brave, but is it going to help your father for you to march out in public just to show how brave you are?"

"It's not going to hurt him."

"We can't be sure of that."

She glared out the window, reminding herself that Orlando was a professional, a campaign operative. Her father had a reputation for surrounding himself with the best possible people. Orlando was at the core of Laurence Jeffries's inner circle, and if she wanted to belong there, too, she had to play along.

They got out near the campaign bus. The area swarmed like

a kicked anthill. News vans disgorged coils of thick cables, camera and sound equipment. Orlando stopped amid some stacks of campaign placards and took both of Sonnet's hands. "Honey, I wish we had more time. I miss you. I do. More than I ever thought I would."

"I miss you, too," she said, softening toward him. "Think how much worse it would be if I'd taken the fellowship. I'd be overseas, not just a few hours from the city."

"Sure, but at least if you'd taken the fellowship, you'd be getting ahead in your career."

"And being here for my mother just doesn't rate with you." She felt a fresh twinge of annoyance.

He chuckled. "I think you're determined to pick a fight with me just so we can kiss and make up."

"Right. That's exactly what I'm thinking."

"Tell you what. I'll come back for the weekend if I can get away. Or you could come down to the city."

"I'd like that. Maybe—"

His phone buzzed again. "Your father's here. Let's go say hello."

The venue for the debate was the auditorium of the public library. The venerable old building, made of blocky Gothic gray stone, now swarmed with inquisitive voters, high school civics students, and of course the ever-present media, dragging their cables and equipment over the flower beds in the front, the on-camera reporters earnest and self-important as they blocked out the broadcasts that would air on the evening news. The debate itself would be televised and no doubt analyzed and parsed through, each word and gesture weighed and discussed by commentators.

"You look amazed," said Orlando.

"I think I'm finally starting to get the gravity of the situation," she said, recognizing Rachel Maddow, perfectly made up and looking sharp as a treble hook. Behind her came more familiar faces from rival networks—CNN, Fox, and talent from the local affiliates of the other big networks.

"This particular Senate seat matters more than most people realize," Orlando agreed. "The outcome will likely tip the numbers to give us a guaranteed majority—but only if your father wins."

They found General Jeffries in a side office of the library, which was serving as a greenroom before the debate. He was surrounded by people doing his makeup and sound check, but when he saw Sonnet, he held up a hand to put a halt to the proceedings.

"Hi Dad," she said, giving him a hug.

"What do you think?" he asked, spreading his hands. "Am I going to do all right in your hometown?"

He looked dazzling as always, in an impeccably tailored suit cut to accentuate his imposing height, polished shoes, a burgundy silk tie. Every hair was in place and even the anti-shine makeup didn't look strange on him. She knew that each detail, from his West Point class ring to the tiny pin in his lapel, had been carefully chosen for him based on feedback from focus groups. And as always, his attention made her feel like the only person in the room.

"You look like the perfect candidate."

"I'd rather look like the perfect senator. The problem is, so would my opponent."

"The best man will win," she assured him. "And you're the best."

"Thank you, Sonnet. Wish I had more time to spend with you," he said.

"My mom needs me now," Sonnet said, remembering how upset he'd been with her at their last meeting. She hated the idea of disappointing him. "You understand, right?"

"Of course." His eyes narrowed. "What did you do to your hair?"

"I had it cut off for a wig for my mom."

He gave a little laugh of disbelief and set his hands on his hips. "You don't say."

"It's no joke," she assured him.

"That's very generous of you, Sonnet."

"Not really. There's nothing I wouldn't do for my mom. Same goes for you, too," she added. "Just so you know."

"And I'm sure your mother appreciates that as much as I do." He touched her hand briefly. "We didn't raise you together, I know. But she raised a good daughter. I hope she knows I'm grateful for that."

You could tell her, thought Sonnet. Then she tucked the thought away. Even now, she sometimes fantasized—if only for a blink of time—about what it would be like to have her parents together, a traditional family. However, her father would not be telling her mother anything personal so long as it was campaign season. According to Orlando, he couldn't even risk sending a get-well note to what the opposition termed a former flame.

"I'll make sure to tell her," she said, trying to sound upbeat.

"Excuse me," said Orlando, who was standing by the door. "I think you're in the wrong place."

"Not," said Jezebel, striding into the room. She was dressed in bright yellow silk and snug jeans covered in zippers, and a pair of platform sandals that made her seem even taller than usual. She grinned at Sonnet. "Hey, baby girl," she said. "I came to meet your daddy."

Startled but pleased, Sonnet turned to her dad. "This is Jezebel," she said. "Jezebel, my father, Laurence Jeffries."

"Pleasure to meet you." Jezebel stuck out her hand.

"Likewise," Laurence said, exuding poise.

Sonnet suspected she was the only one who could tell her father was less than pleased. Although he smiled and offered a powerful candidate's handshake, there was a distinct chill in his eyes.

"Looking forward to the debate," Jezebel said. "I'd say you got my vote, but I'm one of those nonvoters." With a slightly mischievous smile, she added, "If you get what I mean."

"I get it," Laurence said, his stiff demeanor betraying his discomfort. Other than race, these two had absolutely nothing in common. And Jezebel seemed completely amused by that fact.

"I'll be rooting for you. I'll be holding up a sign."

Sonnet glanced over at Orlando. He was far less practiced than her father at concealing his disapproval. *You don't know her,* Sonnet wanted to yell at them both. *You don't know her, and you're already judging her.*

"Thank you. And now, duty calls. I need to get ready for the debate."

Sonnet tamped down her frustration. It was hard being the daughter of a public figure, even here in Avalon. Maybe especially here in Avalon. She left the greenroom, followed by Orlando and Jezebel. "Come on," she said, "I'll give you a nickel tour of the library."

"That's all we're worth to you?" Maureen Haven, the town librarian, was putting out a sign that read Closed for Special Event on the circulation desk. "A lousy nickel?"

"You're priceless," said Sonnet. "Maureen, I'd like you to meet Orlando Rivera and Jezebel."

"Welcome to my domain." Maureen beamed. Unlike Sonnet's father and Orlando, she was completely sincere as she greeted Jezebel. "I'm a fan," she added. "My husband's in the music business, and he introduced me to your music."

"No shit?" Jezebel stood even taller. "Thanks."

"Your music circulates like crazy here," Maureen told her. "Especially since you came to town."

"I appreciate that," Jezebel said.

"I hope you'll come back during regular hours," said Maureen. "I have to go help out in the auditorium now."

"Can I take them up to the children's collection?" Sonnet asked.

"Sure. I'll see you later."

"This place was my home away from home when I was growing up in Avalon," Sonnet said to Orlando and Jezebel, leading the way up the white marble stairs that flanked the atrium. "I came here nearly every day after school or sports practice to read and do homework until my mom finished work." She stopped at the top step. "My friends and I used to play wedding on these stairs. They're so curvy and dramatic. We'd parade up and down them, humming the wedding march."

Orlando chuckled. "Were you the bridesmaid, or the bride?"

"Do you even have to ask? The bride, of course, even if it meant knocking Georgina Wilson down off her pedestal."

"And you didn't get shushed by the librarian?" Jezebel asked.

"Yes, but in a nice way. It was…perfect for me here." She continued to the mezzanine level and they looked down at the marble atrium of the building with the two-story foyer clock in the middle. The black-and-white floor tiles resembled pictures she'd seen of the Alhambra in Spain, a graphic kaleidoscope like something out of a dream. "I loved coming here. It always felt so…safe. I was allowed to read any book I wanted. No one interrupted me, or if they did, it was done gently and with respect. I always wished the rest of the world would be run like a library." She smiled up at him. "I still think that."

He didn't see the smile; he was leaning over the iron railing, perusing the gathering crowd of media.

Jezebel was paging through a book on Neapolitan art. "I agree with Sonnet. Run the world like a library, and we got nothing to fight about."

Orlando ignored her, too. "Check it out—that's Courtney Procter," he said, indicating a reporter in a melon-colored suit. Her blond hair was as solid as a helmet and she carried herself with the poise of a prom queen. "She's in Delvecchio's camp, although she'd never admit it. And she likes to go for the cheap shot."

"By cheap shot you mean...?"

"Personal stuff. She'll find a way to bring up the breach of security at NATO headquarters when your father was in charge, or his daughter Layla's suspension from boarding school."

"There was a breach of security?" Sonnet was flabbergasted. "And Layla was suspended from school?" She couldn't believe her perfect half-sister could have done something to get herself suspended.

"No, and no. That's what makes it so insidious. Just by mentioning these things, she plants a seed of doubt. That's her M.O., anyway." He patted Sonnet's hand. "I need to head down to the auditorium, make sure the general's final briefing is going okay."

"Tell him to break a leg."

"Jezebel, it was nice meeting you." Orlando leaned down and brushed a kiss on Sonnet's forehead. "See you after the show."

CHAPTER
15

Sonnet watched Orlando go, carrying himself with smooth confidence as he went to the crowded foyer of the library. His sense of purpose when he was in work mode never failed to impress.

"So that's Orlando," she said to Jezebel.

"He's like you said he'd be," Jezebel said, "only even prettier."

"You noticed." Sonnet smoothed the front of her jacket, observing Orlando as he wove his way through the crowd. He was exactly the kind of person to run a high-stakes political campaign. From the very start, her father had told her Orlando would go far. Once the election was won, he'd stay on, crafting fundraisers and perhaps a campaign for an even higher office.

"Pretty is as pretty does," Jezebel said. "So you really think he's the one?"

Sonnet hesitated, wishing she didn't feel so confused. Back in the city, she'd liked being part of that world, the whirlwind that surrounded her father. Yet the longer she stayed in Avalon, the farther away that world seemed. "We're great together," she said finally.

"I ain't convinced," said Jezebel, watching him go into the auditorium.

"Convinced of what?"

Jezebel showed Sonnet a photo on her phone. "You want to know what being with the wrong man can do to you? That's what it can do to you."

Sonnet winced at the graphic shot. Jezebel was barely recognizable in the mug shot, her cheeks and lips battered and split, one eye swollen shut and bleeding from a cut on the brow. "That's how I looked the night of my arrest. The son of a bitch beat the crap out of me so I left him a little message spray painted on his dog. Wrecked his prized possession, too—his BMW Roadster."

"God, I'm sorry, Jezebel. I'm so sorry you had to go through that. But my situation with Orlando is nothing like this. We get along fine. He'd never, ever lay a hand on me."

"I'm sure he wouldn't. But there are a lot of ways loving the wrong man can crush you."

"Orlando and I…we're…trying to make this work."

"Girl, you tie yourself in knots over that dude. You're trying too hard. I've seen it. Look at you, with your fine education and fierce smarts. You're not cut out to be any man's trained lapdog."

Sonnet made her way down the stairs, checking the VIP ticket Orlando had given her. Row Q. That was the closest he could get her to her own father?

Her phone vibrated, signaling a text message. Her mom had just arrived and was waiting under the big clock.

For a moment, Sonnet couldn't pick her out of the crowd. Then she spotted her and was struck by how lovely her mother was, standing there with the golden light of early evening slanting through the oriel windows high above the atrium. She wore a loose silk top that flowed gracefully over her baby bump, skinny jeans and nice wedge sandals. With a pair of shades perched atop the handmade wig, and the bag they'd picked out together at the boutique, she looked stylish, hardly a cancer victim. But Sonnet could see the fatigue around her eyes and the hollow spots in her cheeks. The illness lay over every moment, like a cloud that wouldn't go away.

"You're by yourself," she said, crossing the foyer to Nina. "Greg didn't come?"

"He can't get too excited about seeing Laurence." Nina gave a wry smile.

"I understand." Even though Nina and Laurence were ancient history, Sonnet's very existence was proof that the two of them had once been young and foolish—and, happily for Sonnet, productive—together. "You look fantastic, by the way."

"Thanks. Not feeling so hot, though."

Sonnet's stomach clenched. "Can I get you something? Water, or…?"

"I've got a bottle of water in my bag," Nina said. "I need to eat more but my appetite is completely shot."

"Aw, Mom. Remember what the doc told you. You're not just eating for two. You're eating to survive."

"I know. I'll try. Greg brought home a bacon and cheese quiche from Sky River Bakery. If I can't eat that, I'm doomed."

"Don't say doomed."

Nina chuckled. "Done for, then. Dead meat."

"Stop it." Sonnet felt a cold rock of dread in her stomach. She tried to ignore it as she nudged her mother. "Want to meet Angela Jeffries?"

"Laurence's wife?" Nina raised her brushed-on eyebrows. "I won't pretend I'm not burning up with curiosity."

"She just walked in. This way." Sonnet tried to imagine how this would feel to her mother, meeting a woman with whom she had nothing in common, except that they'd both had Laurence Jeffries's children.

Angela seemed to revel in her role. She was the ideal wife of a candidate to the last inch of her shadow, in a St. John Knits suit and low-heeled shoes, her hair and makeup flawless. As she approached Angela, Sonnet wished she was wearing something more conservative than the vintage jacket and boots.

"Sonnet, I was hoping I'd see you here. How are you?" Angela gave a warm smile. She was well-mannered and had always treated Sonnet with a peculiar aloof kindness. She took Sonnet's hand. "And look at your hair. It's so…short."

"Thanks. I think."

"I love it," Angela scolded her. "It's a big change for you, that's all. And Sonnet, I'm so sorry to hear about your mother. If there's anything I can do—"

"Angela, this is my mom, Nina Bellamy." Sonnet spoke up quickly, before things got too awkward.

She shouldn't have worried about awkwardness. Angela Jeffries was the soul of tact, having long experience as a high-ranking officer's wife. Nina had been in local politics, and her natural warmth and charm served her well.

"It's a pleasure to meet you," she said, shaking hands with Angela. "I hope you're enjoying Avalon and Willow Lake."

"Beautiful town," Angela assured her. "Unfortunately, Laurence's schedule doesn't leave much leeway for tourism."

"Maybe you'll visit when you've got a bit more time."

"I'd like that." Angela paused, and took Nina's hand again. "I mean it. I really would like that."

"I'm glad we're finally getting to meet," Nina said. "I wanted to thank you for your hospitality to Sonnet when she was studying abroad."

Angela sent Sonnet a gracious smile. "It was my pleasure. How lucky that we were stationed at NATO headquarters when she was doing her internship in Germany."

Sonnet wondered if she really believed she was lucky to have met her husband's child by another woman. Angela had never been anything but accepting, though she'd kept her barriers up. Sonnet hadn't minded. Her focus had been to find her way to her father, and the fact that Angela had opened her home meant the world to her.

While Angela and Nina chatted, Sonnet saw a flash of coral in her peripheral vision—Courtney Proctor. Across the room, she was having an animated discussion with a crew member. Several cameras lenses pointed in her direction. Sonnet felt a twist of nausea in her gut.

"Mom—"

"Mrs. Jeffries, it's time to take a seat," someone said, ushering Angela away.

She offered Sonnet an apologetic look. "Let's try to catch up later," she said.

"Of course." Sonnet watched her go, knowing neither of them would try very hard.

Taking her mother's arm, she moved toward the auditorium, hoping the interest from the reporter didn't amount to anything. How could it, she wondered, when the issues of the day were so pressing? Her father wanted to work on jobs, education, the environment and crime; that was where the focus needed to be.

"So that's Angela," Nina mused. "She seems like the ideal candidate's wife."

"Somehow I sense that's not a compliment."

"I'm not trying to be mean. I just don't get a sense of her as a separate entity from Laurence."

"I know exactly what you mean." Angela was a hard woman to know, seeming comfortable in her role as an adjunct to her husband's career. Sometimes Sonnet wondered if Mrs. Jeffries ever wanted anything for herself, something separate from Laurence and their two daughters. The idea of giving herself com-

pletely to the career of a husband was a foreign concept to
Sonnet.

She found their seats in the auditorium, now swarming with
observers and press. "Feeling okay?" she asked her mom.

"I'm fine."

Sonnet had taken to carrying granola bars wherever she went
in case her mom needed something. "Hungry?" she asked, offering a lemon coconut bar to Nina.

"Not right now, thanks."

Sonnet heard this far too much from her mother. She bit her
lip, knowing it was not the time to argue.

The president of the local chapter of the League of Women
Voters came up to the center podium to introduce the candidates. Sonnet could not deny a surge of pride as Laurence Jeffries came out, looking larger than life and supremely confident
as he took his place at another podium. The moderator read a
brief bio that touched on the high points of his career—West
Point graduate, theater commander in the first Gulf War, head
of security at NATO, Undersecretary General for UN Peace-
keeping Operations, advisor to the governor's economic devel-
opment council. His opponent, Johnny Delvecchio, came from
the world of commerce, having made a fortune in meatpacking
and having served in city and then state governments for the past
decade. Both men were very different, yet equally determined
to capture the Senate seat in the fall.

It felt so strange to Sonnet, having her father in town. Her
two worlds had always been entirely separate—Avalon was the
home of her heart, small and protected, insulated by its remote
location on Willow Lake. The campaign felt weirdly invasive
now, as though a boundary had been breached.

The opening statements were fairly bland declarations from
both men. Sonnet gave the edge to her father, who had a better
stage presence and voice. Delvecchio was a bit of a drone. Nina
leaned over to Sonnet. "My eyes are glazing over," she confessed.

"Pretty boring stuff," Sonnet agreed.

They sat through discourses on improving the economy and creating jobs, the candidates' past performance in their respective fields. Then toward the end of the hour, came the question Sonnet had been dreading, the one she'd been praying would not surface.

"General Jeffries," said Courtney Proctor in her well-modulated voice, "given your stated commitment to conduct in the military, how do you reconcile your personal indiscretions with your current views? I'm referring specifically to the fact that while you were at West Point, you fathered an illegitimate child with a local girl right here in the town of Avalon."

Sonnet forgot to breathe. Her mother grabbed her hand and held on tight. "Here we go," she murmured. Sonnet looked around wildly for Orlando but couldn't see him.

General Jeffries seemed to grow taller at the podium. "It's disappointing that a private matter that was resolved decades ago would enter into a serious discussion of today's issues. I would respectfully request that we return the debate to the matters at hand."

Ms. Proctor seemed unfazed. "It's not private if the issue speaks to a candidate's conduct in—"

A squeal of electronic feedback shrieked through the auditorium. Then the sound system failed, leaving the reporter mouthing words no one could hear. There was a scramble of activity around the sound console at the back of the auditorium. Meanwhile, the audience moved restlessly and people started to leave.

"This might be a good time to make our exit," Sonnet murmured, and led the way out. As they passed the sound console, she noticed a pale flash—Zach, dealing with equipment. What was he doing here? The feedback squealed again as she and her mom moved past. They made their way to the foyer.

"Are you all right?" she asked her mom.

"Fine. What about you?"

"It's just so…awkward. I'm sorry, Mom. This shouldn't have come up."

Zach appeared, burdened with some video gear. "Guess they're wrapping up," he said easily. "Party's over."

"What just happened?" Sonnet asked him.

He shrugged, all innocence. "Technical difficulties. It happens. What're you gonna do?"

"Zach, did you—"

"Ms. Bellamy, do you have any comment on the general's sex scandal?" asked Courtney Proctor, pushing forward with a microphone angled toward Nina.

"I beg your pardon?" said Nina.

"And Ms. Romano," the reporter continued, "as the illegitimate child of General Jeffries, do you have any comment?"

"No, she doesn't," Zach said with calm intensity. "So back off. Go find some relevant news to report."

"It's certainly relevant that General Jeffries has a troubled past. And isn't it true, Ms. Romano, that you were forced to leave your post at UNESCO due to—"

"Lady, what part of 'back off' do you not understand?" Zach took Nina gently by the elbow and steered her toward the exit. Sonnet followed, her face burning, and she clenched her teeth to keep from saying something she'd regret.

Nina's cheeks looked hollowed and pale, and her hands shook visibly. Sonnet was incredibly grateful for Zach. She hadn't seen him arrive, but as so often was the case, he showed up right when she needed him. He handled the situation with calm aplomb, accompanying them to the parking lot.

Maybe, thought Sonnet, just maybe, they were getting back to the friendship that had faltered because they'd slept together. The idea should have brought a sense of relief, but instead, she caught herself thinking of that night, and wondering if friendship would ever be enough.

CHAPTER
16

"Sonnet!" Orlando hurried over, for once looking harried, his shirttail out and his briefcase about to spill over. "Wait up."

"Friend of yours?" Zach asked Sonnet, sizing up Orlando.

"Orlando, this is Zach Alger," Sonnet said.

Zach greeted him with a brief handshake. "I think the ladies would like to leave right about now."

"Of course." Orlando took a breath. "Nina, I'm sorry about that. Live events like this can be pretty unpredictable."

"I'll be all right," Nina said. "Zach, would you mind walking me to my car?"

"Of course."

"Unpredictable?" Sonnet asked Orlando. "You knew this was going to come up."

"I was hoping it wouldn't." He watched Zach go. "Who the hell is that and how are you his business?"

"He's my oldest and best friend and…" She stopped, remembering her earlier thoughts about sleeping with Zach. "I don't really need to explain him to you."

"You don't need to, but I want to know all the people in your life. And with all due respect, he didn't seem all that friendly."

"We've had our ups and downs. Zach and I—"

"Wait a second. Zach Alger. Why do I know that name?"

"You're looking at me funny. Why are you looking at me funny?"

"Your father mentioned him. Said he was trouble."

She recalled confessing Zach's troubles to her father, back when Matthew Alger was arrested and Zach declared himself an emancipated minor. Her dad had seemed sympathetic at the time. "Like I said, I've known Zach forever, and I'm sure I've spoken to my father about him. He's a good guy. He's gone through some rough times and his own father is no prize, but Zach is definitely *not* trouble. If anything, he made the situation in there a lot more tolerable." She felt a fresh rush of gratitude for what Zach had done with the sound system.

"What's he do around here?"

"He's an award-winning filmmaker."

"Ah."

"Why 'ah'? Why do you say it like that?"

"'Award-winning filmmaker' is usually a euphemism for 'My day job requires me to wear a white paper hat.'"

"Very funny. Zach's working on the Flick production. He's actually the chief videographer."

"So you work with him."

"Every day. And excuse me for pointing this out, but you've changed the subject. My mom and I were just ambushed by some stupid, ignorant political operatives, so I don't really need the twenty questions right now."

"I'm sorry about that. I am. I wish that hadn't happened."

"But you knew it was going to. Or something like it. Couldn't you have stopped it, or at least moved the event to another town?"

"That would have made us seem afraid to make an appearance. We needed to prove to the opposition that we don't have anything to hide. We had to show that your father's willing to face up to his past mistakes."

"Ah, that word. Love that, Orlando. Love being called a mistake."

"It's not my word. Good God, if you were a mistake, let's hope people will make more of them."

She could still picture the expression on her mother's face, still feel the pounding of her own heart when they were confronted. She was horrified by the encounter and the questions and innuendo. "What's next?" she asked him. "Should my mom and I brace ourselves for more attacks?"

He touched her shoulder. "I don't have a crystal ball, but I'm guessing this will blow over. Nina is dealing with cancer. And is expecting a baby to boot. I'm sorry they harassed her, but now we can make them look like the anti-Christ for intruding in her private life."

"My God, you sound glad my mom's sick."

"Come on, Sonnet. What do you take me for?"

"All right, that wasn't fair. I'm just so creeped out by all of this…attention. I do want my father to reach his goal, but I hate the fact that my mom was thrown under the bus."

"I'm sorry. Really. Let's hope we've heard the last of it. We're going to focus on keeping the media on message and getting your father elected. It's his dream, Sonnet, and it's a big one, but it could be the start of something amazing, not just for him, but for everyone. He needs our full support."

"Why do people have to get stepped on in order for him to reach his dream?"

"I didn't create the system." He gave her a hug. All around

them, crews were rolling up and preparing to leave town. "I have to get going," he added. "Call you later?"

"Sure, of course."

"I'd like to talk about us," he said.

"What about us?"

"Not here, though," he said. "And not now. But soon. The two of us are really good together, and I miss you."

"I miss you, too," she said quietly, and watched him head toward the campaign bus. She felt a niggling confusion, not knowing if it was Orlando she missed, or their life in the city—the bustle and excitement surrounding her father. For now, though, she belonged here.

She saw Orlando stop and talk to Shane Gilmore, who was carrying a Delvecchio for Senate sign. He set down his sign and handed something to Orlando. Sonnet felt a chill of premonition. When Gilmore walked away, she hurried over to Orlando.

"What was that about?" she asked him.

He hesitated, just for a second, which wasn't like him. Orlando never hesitated; he was always decisive. "Some local guy—do you know him?"

"Kind of. He's the bank president. He once dated my mom, but it didn't work out. He has a habit of making trouble for people who trouble him." *And he saw Zach and me the morning after the boathouse.* She didn't say so aloud, but even now, as she stood here with the man she was supposed to be making a future with, she felt a powerful yearning—for Zach. "What did he want?"

"He… Nothing. Just wanted to remind me that your father is slipping in the polls. Don't worry, it's nothing. A head game, that's all." Orlando checked his watch. "Listen, I can't stay. I really need to go."

"You do," she said, and a very strange sense of clarity swept through her, like the sunlight slicing through the clouds. She thought about the conversation she'd had earlier with Jezebel, and she thought about Orlando's words. *I really need to go.*

"Before you take off," she said, "there's something I have to say. You've been really great, but…you and I…it's not working."

He scowled at her. "What's that supposed to mean? Look, I realize your mom's illness has been hard on you, and your decision to give up on your career is hard on us, but—"

"There is no 'us,'" she said, and a wave of regret came over her. "I wanted there to be. I tried my best. But things between us haven't felt right in a long time. Maybe they were never right, and we just didn't want to admit it."

"Oh, come on, Sonnet. Who the hell have you been talking to? Your friend Zach? He looks at you like you're a lamb chop. Jezebel? What, are you starstruck by a woman under house arrest? *Nice*, Sonnet."

She let him fume, resisting her old habit of mollifying him and telling him what he wanted to hear. "I feel as if I don't even know why we're together," she said quietly, though she wasn't sure he was even listening. "Maybe I never did." The admission was painful. The most important thing about Orlando had not been her feelings for him. The most important thing about Orlando had been that her father approved of him. "I feel terrible about this, because I thought I knew what I wanted—from myself, and from us, but I didn't, not until now. I finally know my own mind," she added. "I know what my heart is telling me to do."

"Oh, that's cute." His face, so handsome, hardened into a mask of contempt. "So you've decided all of a sudden to get in touch with your feelings?"

"I'm sorry. I don't mean to hurt you—"

"You're hurting yourself, Sonnet. Will you listen to what you're saying? What the hell do you plan on doing? Launching a new career as a script girl? Settling down in this place in the middle of nowhere and doing…what?"

"I've always had a plan. But lately the plans I've made haven't worked out for me, because I haven't been listening to myself."

"You had an incredible career. You had a once-in-a-lifetime opportunity with the fellowship. If you're going to turn your back on those things and pass up a chance to truly make a difference in the world, then you're not the person I thought you were."

His words cut deep, yet at the same time, she felt cleansed, the sharp clarity still shining inside her. "Or maybe I'm exactly the person you think I am," she told him.

PART
4

Must-Do List (revised, round 4)

- ✔ expect a miracle

- ✔ count blessings

- ✔ learn to let go

- ✔ breathe

- _ really fall in love

  (once mom gets better)

A sudden bold and unexpected question
doth many times surprise a man and lay him open.

—Sir Francis Bacon, 1561-1626

CHAPTER
17

Needing to decompress, Sonnet walked. She didn't have a destination in mind; she simply needed to move, to clear her mind, to get her head around what had just happened. She found herself on the lakefront trail at Blanchard Park, as familiar to her as her childhood memories. In the early twilight, joggers and dog walkers moved along the pathways, and the occasional family or a couple hand-in-hand strolled by. People laughed and talked together, and everyone seemed so… normal. She envied them. Her life didn't feel normal at all. She was dealing with a sick mother, a father who took no prisoners on his run for national office, a boyfriend who never should have been her boyfriend, and an uncertain future in her job.

Stress broke over her in a wave, and Sonnet did something she rarely allowed herself to do—she crumbled. She was very deliberate about it; she sat on a bench facing the lake, drew her knees up to her chest and silently sobbed. Emotions came up through her like a fountain—fear and uncertainty, helplessness and loneliness—causing her shoulders to shake and her chest to burn. Crying was supposed to be good, wasn't it? Cathartic and cleansing. But she didn't feel cleansed at all, only exhausted and sad, which made her cry more. She hoped none of the passersby would notice.

"Um, hey, I couldn't help but notice you're upset," said someone behind her.

Zach. She paused midsob and tried to choke it back down. *Zach.*

She was glad that he had found her. She was mortified that he had found her. "I'm a mess," she said. How many times through the years had she made just that confession to him, over issues large and small—a failing grade, a stray cat, a lost locker key, a quarrel with her mom.

"Yeah," he agreed, taking a seat beside her. "You're a mess."

"Thanks."

"I'm not gonna lie. I've seen you better."

She brushed at her cheeks with the back of her hand. "Got a Kleenex?"

"Nope, sorry. Here." He dug in his pocket and took out a packet of lens cleaning papers. "This will do in a pinch."

She blotted her face. "I'm being a big baby."

"You're being human."

She was tempted to blurt out her news about Orlando, but in fact, that was not the worst thing that had happened to her all evening. Which said a lot about the quality of her relationship with Orlando Rivera, she reflected. How depressing, to spend her time and effort on a guy who would walk away rather than fight for her.

"You're being nice to me," she said to Zach. "Why are you being so nice?"

"I'm always nice. You just don't always notice."

"Ah, Zach. I don't know what I would have done without you today."

He turned toward her, rested his elbow on the back of the bench. "Yeah?"

"Well, I suppose I would have muddled through, but you... thank you. That's what I really need to say. Thanks for being there, and for knowing how to disable the sound system, and for walking my mom to her car."

"No problem."

"Speaking of my mom, I should go make sure she's all right."

"Hey. She's got a husband. I bet he's doing just fine, looking after her."

"You might be right. Maybe my mom doesn't need me here, not really. In fact, she might be better off if I wasn't around.

"Tonight was awful for her. She acted fine, but I know she was hurt. In the press, they're going to focus on the fact that she was an unwed teenage mom, not on everything she's accomplished in her life. And my father's chance at a seat in the Senate might have been compromised. Who knows how the public will react?"

"And how is any of this your fault?"

"I'm not saying it's my fault. But I feel as though I'm at the root of it all."

"Get out," he said. "You didn't cause any of this."

"Maybe not, but...sometimes I think I should have gone away, just like I'd planned."

He took her hands. She felt his warm grip wrapping around her fingers. "You came back here for a reason," he said.

"But—"

"You're *staying* for a reason. Christ, don't go second-guessing yourself."

"I have no idea how to help her. It's the worst feeling in the world. Sometimes I just lie awake at night and beg for this thing to go away and leave her alone." Her voice broke. "She's not eating. I don't know how to get her to eat."

"What does the doc say?"

"Loss of appetite is the most common side effect in cancer patients, so this is not unexpected. She's supposed to eat well or she'll get too weak to tolerate chemotherapy. It'll help her feel and look better, too. And my mom has the baby to think about, too. She has to get enough nutrients for both of them. If she doesn't, she'll just get weaker and weaker. The baby absorbs the nutrients first, taking what it needs, and—oh, Zach. Sometimes...sometimes..." She lowered her voice, scarcely able to speak the unspeakable. "Sometimes I hate the baby."

His arm moved from the back of the bench to around her shoulders. "You don't hate the baby."

"Yes, I do. I'm terrible."

"So go ahead and hate the baby, but it's not going to do your mom any good."

"I can't help thinking she could get better treatment if it wasn't for the pregnancy. And I know I shouldn't think like that, but my thoughts keep going there. Oh, God, Zach. I'm so worried about her."

"I know," he said quietly. "I know." Ever so gently, his hand stroked her shoulder.

"Thanks for not telling me not to worry."

"That never works."

She tried not to lean into his stroking hand, but it felt so comforting just then, with a mesmeric effect she couldn't deny. "Nothing works," she said faintly.

They sat together, staring outward at the dark glassy surface of the water. She kept remembering times spent with Zach, making snowball forts in the winter, skipping stones from the shore on the way home from school, daring each other to swim longer and longer distances in the summer. Willow Lake was a backdrop for their childhood and their coming-of-age, as omnipresent as music drifting from a radio. Just being back here made her think about matters that lay far out of range when she was in the city.

"What are you doing tonight?" Zach asked after a long silence.

All of its own accord, her heart sped up. She was glad they were both facing the view, not each other. "Besides attending my own pity party?"

"Seriously. What are your plans?"

"I have no plans. Actually, I need to get hammered," said Sonnet. "Getting hammered as a form of therapy is underrated."

"I like the way you think." He took his arm away and turned toward her on the bench. "You don't have some hot date with your boyfriend?"

She tried not to miss the feel of his arm. "He had to go back to the city tonight." She could have explained more, but the change was so new and so raw, she needed some time to think about it, to reimagine her life without Orlando.

"Excellent."

"Why is that excellent?"

"Because three's a crowd."

"Zach—"

"I'll pick you up at seven."

"But—"

"See you then."

CHAPTER
18

"*owling?* I thought we were going to get hammered."

"What, we can't do both? Bowling's more fun when you drink, anyway. When was the last time you had a little fun, Sonnet?"

"I..." She paused, thought for a bit. "I always have fun," she said, miffed.

"Right."

"I mean, life itself is fun." Yet when she thought about it, really thought about it, she realized her days were made up of work and social obligations. Things had been that way for quite a while. Doing something purely for the fun of it had become an alien concept. Suddenly she felt far older than her age.

"Life is life," Zach said. "Bowling is fun. It's impossible to have a bad time bowling."

"I haven't done this since I was in sixth grade, at Leaky Swoboda's birthday party."

"Did you have fun at that party?"

"You ought to know. You were there."

"It was awesome." She remembered bits and pieces—the Go-Gos on the stereo, giggling over nothing, speculating over who liked who. It wasn't so much the things they did or said, but the feeling of being with friends, the kind of friends who didn't expect you to be a certain way, other than yourself.

She checked out the sign, a flashing neon monstrosity with the name King's Cross Lanes. Then she caught herself checking *him* out, and it struck her that after the exchange with Orlando, she was free to check out anyone she wanted. She reminded herself that it was too soon to be thinking of *any* guy. "So this is what you do for fun in Avalon?"

"What do you do for fun in the city, smartass?" He held the door and she stepped inside. To her surprise, it lacked the harsh lighting, noise and gym-locker smell she remembered. Instead, there was a sleek bar with ambient lighting, sculptural stools, good music drifting from unseen speakers. An upholstered console landscaped with plants divided the bar from the lanes.

Sonnet paused to take it all in. "Whoa. This is really something, Zach. I don't remember it being so cool."

"It's under new management." He waved to a broad-shouldered guy stationed near the bar. "You remember Marc, right? Marc Swoboda."

She hoped her expression wasn't too surprised. *That* was Leaky Swoboda? He'd turned into Captain America, complete with biceps the size of a normal man's thighs, a head full of glossy dark waves and an easy smile, underscored by a dimple in his chin.

She waved at him, too, unsure whether or not he recognized her.

"You're staring," Zach observed, sliding into an upholstered booth.

"Oh. Oops. It's just that he's changed a lot."

"Don't act so shocked. Not everybody has to travel the world in order to change." He touched her chin. "I think you might be drooling."

She jerked her head away. "You're funny. I wasn't staring at him like that. He's not my type."

"That's for sure." Zach grinned and flipped through the bar menu.

"Is he single?"

"Nope. He has a boyfriend."

"*Oh.* Well."

"I stared at him, too," said Maureen Haven, arriving with her husband, Eddie, and another couple, Bo and Kim Crutcher. "We all do. I think he likes it."

"What if I don't like it?" Eddie complained.

"Then I'll stare at you," said Maureen.

"Can we all play the same lane, or should we get a second one?" asked Bo, ever the competitor.

"We can all play here." Kimberly sat down at the scoring desk. "This is going to wreak havoc on my manicure."

Sonnet sidled over to Zach. "A couples date? Really, Zach?"

He shrugged, unapologetic. "You can use the distraction."

Sonnet watched Bo hefting a bowling ball, trying to find the perfect one for Kim. Eddie knelt at Maureen's feet, tying her bowling shoes for her. Watching functional couples, so at ease with one another, made her glad she'd told Orlando goodbye. She knew that no matter how hard she tried, she would never have reached that point with him. Truth be told, he'd been exhausting. She used to have to think everything through, even something like what to order from takeout. It was all strategy with Orlando. He was hard work, she admitted to herself. And he wasn't worth it. Sometimes it was better to just go bowling with friends.

Still, she didn't know how she felt about this couples date, mainly because she and Zach weren't a couple. Nor should they be, she reminded herself.

The waitress came for their order, and Sonnet asked for a Long Island iced tea.

"You don't mess around," Bo observed. He ordered a pitcher of beer and some soft drinks.

"It's been a tough day," she said.

For the next couple of hours, they bowled. No one was very good at it, but that wasn't the point. In that span of time, Sonnet forgot to worry about her mom's illness and her dad's campaign, her disintegrating relationship with Orlando and her job. Instead, she simply sipped her drink, ordered another and enjoyed the supremely silly situation with friends who let her be herself. She felt like a kid again, and it felt good. Except unlike a kid, she had one drink too many. As the second round of bowling came to an end, she knew she'd reached that goofy, clumsy, happy stage of inebriation.

"You guys are so good together," she said to Kim, who had just scored a nice spare, earning a high five and a kiss from her husband.

"Thanks. We work at it. Sometimes it doesn't come easy."

"Really? You make it look easy."

"With the right person, it is," Kim said. "Eventually."

Zach, she thought. The easiest thing in the world had been to fall into his arms. "Everything looks easy after a couple of Long Island iced teas," she said.

"Bowling is never easy," Maureen said, flopping down beside them, "no matter how much I drink. So I don't bother drinking. I don't need the calories."

"But Eddie's easy, right? Why do other relationships look so good to me? What's up with that?" Sonnet finished the last of her drink and sucked on the ice.

"Yeah, I'm easy," Eddie said. "She can't keep her hands off me. Damn, I love eavesdropping on girls." He elbowed Bo. "They're talking about relationships."

"We're experts," Bo said to Sonnet. "What can we help you with?"

"My love life's in the toilet," Sonnet said. "Can you help with that, or am I beyond hope?" As she spoke, she dropped the bowling ball she was holding, and it nearly crunched Zach's foot.

"That's it," he said, steering her away from the bowling lane. "I'm cutting you off."

"Good idea. I should get back to my mom's, anyway. Good night, you guys. Let's do it again sometime." Sonnet changed her shoes, swaying a little as she straightened up. "I'm not that good at drinking, remember?"

"I wouldn't say that. Last time we drank together, it worked out well for us. I thought so, anyway."

She felt vulnerable, her emotions softened by spiked iced tea and memories. "Zach, if the two of us are going to try to be friends again, we need to move on from that night."

"And that's what you want," he said. "To move on." He steered her toward the exit by the bar.

"I want us to be friends, the way we were before. The way we've always been."

"News flash," he said. "I've got all the friends I need."

"What's that supposed to mean? We've been friends since the beginning of time."

"You know, I was watching this documentary about the relationship of hyperbole in speech to alcohol consumed—"

"God, you always do this. You always bring up the most arbitrary things to make a point. It's so…so oblique."

He laughed. "Ouch."

"Hey there, my homeskillets." Jezebel came into the bar, trailed by Cinda and a couple of others from the production. "Fancy meeting the lovebirds here."

Sonnet nearly choked. "We're not—"

"Join us for a game," Jezebel said, jerking her head toward the lanes.

"We were just going," said Zach.

"He cut me off," Sonnet explained. "I didn't know you were a fan of bowling."

"I am, lately. Under the terms of my parole, I'm not supposed to be in a bar," Jezebel said. "But I'm allowed to bowl." They went to the counter to trade their street shoes for bowling shoes. She fanned her face at the imaginary fumes from Sonnet. "Hoo-whee."

"Two drinks," Sonnet protested. "That's all I had."

"They were doubles," Zach said.

"Guess you got spun out by that campaign debate," Jezebel said.

"Did you stay for the whole thing?"

"Yeah, I saw."

"I can't believe it was brought up by someone who's supposed to be a bona fide member of the media."

"What, you want fair and balanced? From the media?" She laughed loudly, attracting stares.

"It was really just to make my father look bad. You saw, the whole thing was just so…pointless but humiliating, for everyone involved."

Jezebel nodded in sympathy, inspecting one of her long, polished nails. "Welcome to the world of the tabloids."

"I need a ride home," she said, groping in her purse.

"You're barking up the wrong tree, girl," said Jezebel. "My license is still suspended on account of me having a little too much fun with my ex's Z4."

"I've got this," Zach said easily.

"'Course you do," Jezebel said. "One of these days, the two of you are gonna get over whatever it is that's holding you back and go for it."

"We're just friends," Sonnet said, her voice a little too loud.

"Uh-huh." Jezebel's eyes narrowed skeptically.

Sonnet lifted her chin and tried to walk away with steady
dignity. "I'll see you at work tomorrow."

"Thanks," she said, getting into the passenger side of Zach's car.

"No problem."

"I am," she said. "I am a problem. Can't help it, I was born
that way."

"Right."

"No, you're not listening. I'm a problem because my parents
were never married. If it wasn't for me, my dad wouldn't be in
this stupid fight about his reputation."

"Ah, I got it," he said with a chuckle. "You wish you'd never
been born. Like the guy in that movie *It's a Wonderful Life*. Get
over yourself, Sonnet."

"Hey, I warned you it was going to be a pity party tonight.
If you can't handle that, you'd better let me call a taxi."

"In Avalon? There's still just the one taxi, Maxine's. Do you
really want to get her out of bed just to pour you home?"

"Fine, then take me home."

"Fine."

They drove along in silence, the streetlamps from the main
part of town giving way to long stretches of unrelieved darkness. He parked in front of the house. "You need me to walk
you to the door?"

"I'm tipsy, not hammered," she said. "I was trying to get
hammered but then I realized I have to get up in the morning.
We've got the cooking segment first thing." She turned to face
him on the seat. "Thank you, Zach."

"For taking you out drinking?"

"For everything today." She felt a surge of emotion, and knew
it wasn't coming from the Long Island iced teas she'd consumed.
"It would have been a lot more awful if you hadn't been there."

"I've always been there for you," he said. "It's about time you
noticed."

He got out and came around to the passenger side to open her door. She stood up and found herself impossibly close to him, looking up at his face.

"Something the matter?" he asked in a low voice.

"I'm just tipsy enough to want to kiss you," she said, her mouth working several beats ahead of her brain.

"And I'm just sober enough to say no."

"I thought you said... Sorry. I misunderstood."

"No, you didn't." He leaned down slightly so their faces were very close, their lips almost touching. "I said I was attracted to you. And hell, yes, I want to kiss you and I intend to do just that. Not now, though. When you're clearheaded and you're over your so-called boyfriend and the time is right. *Then* I'll kiss you."

Oh, boy, she thought.

"See you tomorrow," she said, then fled in confusion.

Jane Bellamy was the kind of old lady you saw on denture commercials, the kind who was pretty enough to make you practically want to have dentures. As he was directing the lighting of the set, Zach didn't need nearly as many diffusers as he normally used on women of a certain age.

Mrs. Bellamy, whose parents had founded Camp Kioga back in the 1920s, had agreed to make an appearance on the show once the network promised to fund the education of the participating kids. The kitchen was set up for a cooking lesson, and her husband, Charles, was on set, beaming with pride as he watched her.

They'd been married almost sixty years, longer than anybody else in the room had been alive. According to the director's notes, this was something that Jezebel was going to talk with her about while they showed the kids how to cook something.

Jezebel arrived, and next to the neatly done-up Mrs. Bellamy, she looked more imposing than ever. They were the ultimate mismatch, the old lady in her pearls and the hip-hop star with the ankle bracelet, but Mrs. Bellamy acted as though she had company like this every day. The prep area was set up with a ceiling mirror and lighting, and the kids gathered around on bar stools. Each one wore an apron embroidered with their name.

"Before Camp Kioga was a summer camp, it was a farm," she told everyone. "It's still surrounded by gardens and orchards, and summer is the best possible time for rhubarb pie. Ever tried rhubarb pie?"

A few blank stares, shrugs. One camera got a reaction shot from one of the younger boys; Andre narrowed his eyes and gestured at a pile of dark green leaves. "We picked a bunch in the garden this morning."

"For pie, you use only the stalks," said Mrs. B. "Jezebel's going to show you how to cut off the leaves and slice the red stalks."

A boy named Russell grabbed a chunk of rhubarb and popped it in his mouth, giving them the first money shot for the day. "Yuck," he said, spitting into a wastebasket. "That tastes terrible."

"Rule Number One of rhubarb is that it should never be eaten raw," Mrs. Bellamy said. "It's terribly bitter and sour, isn't it, Russell?"

"Yes, ma'am."

Zach glanced over at Sonnet, who was conferencing with the production coordinator. As always, she looked supremely self-possessed, in jeans and sandals and a fluttery top, her short hair tucked behind her ears to reveal oversized hoop earrings. Just the sight of her got his motor running. Since the bowling alley the night before, they hadn't talked much. There simply wasn't much to say. He wasn't sure about her status with the boyfriend who was never around, and Zach had vowed to wait until she was ready to talk. Bo and Eddie had advised him to take his time or—more importantly, give *her* time. It had taken all his self-restraint to keep his distance, but he hadn't wanted to blow it. She was too important to him.

It was hard to keep his mouth shut about the boyfriend,

though. She never talked about him anymore, which gave Zach hope that maybe she'd come to her senses. Yet when it came to stuff like this, she'd never shown a lot of sense. She had no idea how much better off she'd be without that Rivera guy and Zach was hardly the one to tell her. He totally got why she stuck around Rivera, though. The dude was her father's right-hand man, and she'd always placed her father on a pedestal. There was this loyalty thing that happened with fathers; Zach knew just what that felt like. You had to be loyal to the guy, whether he was an SOB or not.

Zach got skeezed out, imagining what Sonnet's dad thought of *him*. He was the son of a felon, still struggling to make a living despite the awards and accolades he'd won. Not exactly the kind of boyfriend you want for your daughter if you were running for Senate. Or even if you weren't, he thought, clenching his jaw.

He was still helping Nina with her video diary. Unlike Sonnet's father, Nina didn't judge; she never had. Sometimes he was even tempted to level with her about his feelings for Sonnet. He probably would one day, but not now. Nina had enough going on in her life. He wished he didn't understand so well why she was recording her thoughts and observations on video. He did, though, because the memories of his own mother's struggle were still vivid, no matter how much time had passed. A person facing this kind of crisis wanted to make sure she didn't leave things unsaid.

Zach's mother had left him some letters, and in those letters, she'd told him the things she feared she wouldn't be around to say—things like, whatever you choose to do in your life, choose it because you love it, not because you think it's something you should be doing. It was no coincidence that he'd been doing just that—or at least, trying to. He struggled to balance his love for the art with his need to make a living. Once this production was done, then he'd really be on his way. That was the plan, anyhow.

Probably the letter from his mom that haunted him the most

was something she'd sent him toward the end. She'd written about how much it had torn her up to leave him, but how much worse the damage would be if she'd stayed. As a kid, he hadn't understood that at all, but now that he was older, he was starting to get it. His mother's final words in that letter had stayed with him through the years, and lately he'd been thinking about them a lot: "My wish for you is that you find the kind of love that grows and expands and is solid enough to last a lifetime."

Mrs. Bellamy demonstrated the proper way to roll out pie dough, with a chilled marble rolling pin. The kids were delighted when they each got one of their own. "You folks been married more than fifty years," Jezebel said as they worked with dough. "What's your secret?"

"Keep an open mind and a closed mouth." Mrs. Bellamy grinned and the camera's captured Jezebel's reaction. "That's oversimplifying things, of course. A marriage is a long journey, and there are bound to be detours, peaks and valleys along the way. People change, circumstances change, the world around us changes. It's no wonder some marriages don't survive. It's a lot of work sometimes, and it involves some luck, too. Finding the kind of love that lasts forever is like finding a stranger in a crowded subway. You never know what he's going to look like. He might be the man who helps you onto the train with your suitcase. Or he might be the one you've seen on your commute every day for ten years."

There was something riveting in her delivery. The others, Jezebel and the kids, sensed it, too. They fell quiet and stopped what they were doing while she spoke. Zach couldn't put his finger on it, and he only hoped the taping captured it.

"And now," said the old lady, not missing a beat, "for the secret ingredient. What do you suppose this is?" She held up a small bowl.

"Sugar?"

"No, although you do need plenty of sugar in the filling. It's tapioca. You sprinkle it over the rhubarb to make it turn thick as it bakes. How about you do the honors, Rhonda?"

The rest of the morning was spent finishing up the tarts, then filming the kids eating their wares, which they did with plenty of enthusiasm. The director declared it a wrap, and Zach planned to spend the afternoon editing.

He watched Charles and Jane Bellamy take their leave. The old man gently rested his hand at his wife's waist, and she looked up at him with a soft smile as she spoke. They had the kind of love his mother had written of in her final letter to him, the kind Zach went looking for each time he dated a girl, the kind that seemed so impossible when a relationship didn't work out. Until recently, that steady, enduring love had seemed out of reach, something he could never have, but sometimes these days, he could picture it.

Sometimes when he thought about Sonnet Romano, he could picture it.

CHAPTER
19

S onnet immersed herself in work, and in helping her mother. Her days melded together, a sequence of production, her mom's appointments and avoiding her growing feelings for Zach. Somehow she made it work, getting through each day as she adjusted to the slow, steady rhythm of life in Avalon. She came to believe that there was something special about the small town where she'd grown up, the place she'd always viewed as limiting. Now that she was back, she was starting to appreciate the fact that a small community offered things she had never found in the city.

People came to see Nina. Claire Bellamy, a nurse at the hospital, brought a neck roll pillow, special Popsicles and tea, and some heavy-duty hand cream. Kim and Bo had to go back to the city, but they sent a massage therapist to the house to treat Nina to some pampering. Eddie and Maureen showed up with an mp3 player loaded with music. Suzanne from the boutique arrived with scarves in the softest of fabrics. The manicurist from the Twisted Scissors Salon, owned by three sisters, did a weekly pedicure. Friends and neighbors showed up with food and good wishes, books to read and handcrafted objects. It seemed most of the town rallied around her, and the attention and caring seemed to boost Nina's spirits. It gave Sonnet hope, too. There was something powerful in the energy that came from friends and neighbors and family.

But sometimes it wasn't enough. She got home from work one evening to find Nina and Greg locked in a staredown over a wedge of quiche.

"I can't get her to eat," said Greg.

Nina sighed, the breath rattling unsteadily out of her. "I can't even lift a fork."

"I'll lift the fork for you," Greg said reasonably.

"It's going to make me gag." Nina looked pale, her cheeks hollowed out. Everything about her was hollowed out except the growing mound of her stomach.

"Mom, please. You have to eat," Sonnet said. "What about one of those Queasy Pops Claire brought over?"

"Maybe later." She swayed a little with weakness and fatigue.

Sonnet literally bit her tongue to keep from nagging. It was hard not to wheedle and cajole, though. Eating seemed so simple. Put the food in your mouth, chew and swallow. Yet her mother was looking at the quiche as if it was a plate of poison.

She glanced at Greg, whose face was a mask of tension, his jaw tight and his eyes dark with worry. An unspoken message passed between them, and he stood up. "I'm going outside for a bit," he said. "I need some air."

"That's fine," Nina said, her eyes filling. "I'm sorry, Greg. Just give me a few minutes."

After he left, Sonnet said, "You married a good guy."

"The best. I hate myself for worrying him."

"Don't hate yourself. Just eat the damn quiche."

Nina glared down at the plate. With a will, she picked up a

forkful and put it in her mouth. Almost instantly, she gagged into her napkin. "I can't," she said.

"Mom—"

"I'll try later. I just need to rest. Can you let me rest?"

Sonnet totally got why Greg needed some air. Sitting here and arguing with her mother wasn't going anywhere. "I'll be back," she said, and headed outside to find Greg. The two of them had joined a cancer support group for families, and one of the key things they'd learned was to talk things out, to feel their feelings instead of holding everything in.

She found him alone on the porch steps, facing the lawn and pathways that led to the inn. The historic building looked beautiful in the evening, with lights glowing in the windows and along the walkways. The inn was full to capacity with vacationers. Nina and Greg had refurbished the place together, and Sonnet had watched with gladness as the shared enterprise drew the two of them closer. Nina had always been a happy person, but once she was with Greg, she had blossomed in a way Sonnet had never seen before.

"She's still not eating," Sonnet said. "She told me she's sorry. She hates worrying us."

"Then why the hell doesn't she just eat?" He raked a hand through his hair. "She's wasting away to nothing."

Sonnet felt a frisson of fear. Greg had been a rock through all of this. She'd never seen him break down. "I feel really helpless. I guess we both do."

He nodded. "Your mother and I are glad you're here. I don't think I've told you that."

"Thanks."

"I know you made a lot of sacrifices to be here."

"It's not a sacrifice. Being here with Mom is a complete privilege." She truly believed that now. Helping her mother was rewarding in a way her career had never been. "Nice night," she commented, taking a seat on the steps beside him. "The air feels just about perfect."

"Yep," he said.

"You and Mom made the inn really beautiful. When I was a kid, she always told me she thought it would be amazing. You're a good team."

"Thanks." He let out a shuddering sigh. "I love our life here. I don't want it to end."

"It's not going to end."

"I know. I just... Tonight feels like a low spot."

"Then there's only one direction to go from here. It's a law of physics."

"How'd you get so smart?"

"I'm not so smart. Sometimes I think I'm a total mess."

"Come on."

"I mean it. I want to be able to say what you just said, that I love my life—because what you said, that's everything. And to be brutally honest, I'm not there yet. It's kind of freaking me out. What if the future you thought you'd mapped out for yourself turned out to be the wrong thing?"

"Is that what you think, that you've been on the wrong path?"

"I never used to think that, never used to question myself. I simply put one foot in front of the other and stayed busy with work. But lately, being here, I've had a lot of time to think and reassess."

"And?"

"And I'm as confused as ever. I'm not complaining, Greg. I have an amazing family and friends, but...okay, I'll just say it. I want to be in love. The kind of love you and Mom have."

"Everybody wants that. Hell, I want that for everybody. And you'll find it. Maybe with Orlando, maybe with somebody else."

"Definitely not with Orlando." She tried to picture herself having a conversation like this with her father. The picture wouldn't form. Her father would simply tell her to march ahead toward a goal and everything would fall into place.

"Why do you say definitely?"

"Because that's something I'm completely sure of. Orlando isn't the one." She hadn't told anyone about her last conversation with Orlando. She wasn't sure why she hadn't; perhaps because she didn't want to seem vulnerable, didn't want people hovering over her, worrying about how she was handling the breakup.

And yes, it was a breakup. There hadn't been a fight; recriminations had not been flung back and forth. She and Orlando had never been that way. Still, the relationship, such as it was, had flamed out. She was not inclined to revive it. Maybe she didn't talk about what had happened because she didn't want people to urge her to make up with him. She could hear people now: What's wrong with you? He's gorgeous and educated, he's your dad's right-hand man...what more do you want?

She knew, now. She looked at couples like Greg and her mom, Maureen and Eddie, Kim and Bo...and she knew what she wanted.

"That's nothing to be afraid of," Greg said. "It takes time, but you'll figure it out."

"But what if I don't? Suppose I'm the problem, not him? Suppose I just don't know how to sustain a relationship?"

"Believe me, you're not the problem. Don't think that way. You're an incredible young woman, Sonnet. I've always thought that. Just...take your time. Live each day, isn't that what they told us in the support group? Sure, some days—like today—are going to suck. But something else is going to be right around the corner."

"Here's something I know," Sonnet said. "Daisy is lucky to have you for a dad."

"Thanks." He stood up and brushed off his pants. "I'm going back in. I'll see if I can coax her into eating."

"I think I'll sit out here for a bit." She wrapped her arms

around her knees and breathed deeply, savoring the sweetness of the air. She thought about her own question, whether she was on the right path and what it would mean if she discovered she wasn't. No, that was crazy. The day she'd graduated high school, she had set out to see the world, to help the children of the world. She'd been driving toward that goal ever since, yet now she was plagued by questions. The prospect of losing her mother haunted her, and though she tried to stay positive, it was hard to do when Nina was wasting away and the tumor markers weren't budging. It made Sonnet wonder if she was focusing on the right things in her life. Her mom had said, "If the worst happens, I can honestly say I don't have a single regret."

Headlights swung into the driveway, and she recognized the lumbering bulk of Zach's van.

She stood up and shivered a little in the evening chill as he walked toward her. "Hey."

"Hey, yourself."

"I wasn't expecting you."

"Nope." He came over to the porch. Sonnet could barely look at him. She was still confused by their last conversation. Were they friends? Enemies? Frenemies? They just didn't seem to want the same thing. "So," she said. "What's up?"

"Nina called. Said she was having a hard time eating tonight."

"Why'd she call you?" Sonnet asked, frowning.

"I, uh, I've got something that might help." He took a small plastic bag out of his pocket.

"Oh, my God." Sonnet took a step back. "Is that pot? Where in the world did you get pot?"

"It's good stuff. Don't worry."

"That's not what I asked."

"Let's see if it'll help your mom."

She had joked with Orlando over the matter, but this was clearly no joke. "Don't you dare."

"You got a better idea?"

"Did she *ask* for weed? She can get a prescription from her doctor."

"True, but she called me."

"And why would she ask you? Are you a stoner and I'm the only one who doesn't know about it?"

"Give me a break," he said. "You know me better than that, and so does your mom."

"Then what are you doing with a bag of weed?"

"I know people."

"This is ridiculous."

"She's nauseous and she can't eat. Even one of her doctors thought marijuana might help. Nina didn't want to go there but now she's ready to try anything as long as it won't harm the baby. So, excuse me, I don't want to keep her waiting." He brushed past her and went to the door.

"I'm not having any part of this," Sonnet said, fuming. She stormed away, hiking toward the lake with no idea where she was going. Just…away, into the dark night. In the back of her mind she wondered why she was so freaked out by this. And she had to admit, it might be because of her father. His campaign. His reputation. If it was somehow revealed that she was involved in her mother using pot, his chance at getting elected could be seriously compromised.

This thought caused Sonnet to stop in her tracks. There was no way she was putting her father's ambitions above her mother's health. She turned on her heel and went back to the house. She walked in, hearing an old Rush song on the stereo. In the living room, Greg was dozing in a chair. Zach was fiddling with a camera.

And her mom was on the sofa, giggling and eating Cheetos from a big shiny bag.

Zach was alone in the meeting hall at Camp Kioga, which the production company had taken over for storage and edit-

ing. It was long after the day's shoot had ended and everyone
had gone home, but he'd stuck around to do some rough editing. That was pretty much what he did with his free time—he
worked. Lately there was plenty to do, because each day yielded
more and more footage of the show. Later in the process, there
would be story line editors and final cut editors, but the initial
decisions were up to Zach.

Despite his reservations about working on this project, he
could see a story taking shape. The kids were great; they had
no filters and had no trouble being themselves despite the constant, invasive presence of the cameras. Jezebel owned every
shot she was in, but Zach could see her shifting and changing
in subtle ways. She was forming relationships with the kids, real
relationships despite the artificial setup. Some of them brought
out her anger, while others seemed to touch on an almost-hid-
den nurturing side.

He watched an exchange with her and one of the girls, Anita,
who was heavyset and shy and always trying to please others.
"Don't be running yourself down," Jezebel was saying to her
during a sequence at the archery range. "You got a lot more
skill than you're showing us. Now, you aim at that target, and
you nail it."

There were some outtakes from the archery range; he watched
one with Sonnet and her ever-present clipboard trying to shoo
a couple of grazing deer out of the background. The deer were
a little too used to human presence; they sidled away but didn't
run for cover. Zach grinned as Sonnet waved the clipboard. She
was so damn cute, in her cutoff jeans and tank top and short
haircut. She looked as young as some of the kids.

His phone signaled a text message, and his grin faded. Jenna
Munson, the reverend's daughter, was inviting him to Hilltop
Tavern and pushing him for an answer. He sent back a note saying he was busy with work, which was true. But the truth was,
he didn't want to see Jenna, or Glynnis, or Viv, or Shakti, or

any of the women he used to hook up with. Since the production had started, he had been as cloistered as a monk.

"Hey," said Jezebel, coming into the hall. "Looking at footage of your girlfriend?"

"She's not my girlfriend," he said.

"Uh-huh." It was one of her signature phrases, that canny "uh-huh" speaking volumes of skepticism.

"We go way back, Sonnet and I," he explained. "We're friends, that's all."

"Yeah, she told me. Best friends, right? Then you should have no problem explaining to her that you're falling in love with her."

He laughed, though hearing the words made his heart speed up. "No way. That's not what's happening. She's got a boyfriend anyway. Or she did, last time I checked."

"Maybe you should check again."

He ignored a surge of excitement. "I'm not interested in getting involved with Sonnet even if she did break up with her boyfriend," he insisted, "and I'm sure as hell not going to push her into something with me. She and I are...we're not right together. She's only here for her mother. And I'm only here until..." He let his voice trail off. He was here. He'd always been here. It was home.

"You waiting for a better offer? What's better than this? What's out in the world that you can't find right here?" She gestured at the bank of windows facing the lake. It was too dark to see outside, but the various computer monitors showed Willow Lake in all its beauty.

"I haven't been anywhere," he said. "How would I know?"

"You're a small-town guy at heart," Jezebel said. "I can tell. You might think you want to escape, but look what you're doing with your life. Every choice you've made has kept you here— your jobs, your friends. Your crazy notion of making up for what your father did."

He swallowed, half wishing he hadn't told her about that.

"You could walk away at any time," Jezebel continued, "but I don't think you want to do that. I think you want to live in Avalon in a nice house, with a white picket fence and kids everywhere. You want the family you never had growing up."

He felt a twist of yearning in his gut. The damn woman was right. This was his world, it was where he'd always wanted to be. He just didn't want to be alone here.

She went over to one of the computers and opened a music program. "I've been working on a new song, just for you. I call it 'Don't Make Me Wait to Tell You.'"

"You're a secret romantic," Zach said, flushing. "Who knew?"

"Don't let on you know that about me. It'd ruin my bad-ass image."

"Is that what it is? An image? All an act?"

She shrugged. "I'm an entertainer. It's my job. For a while, I got all caught up in some persona that wasn't me. It was the public me. I was confused and it got me in trouble. Here's what prison did for me. It let me figure out who I was out of the limelight. Now I'm not confused anymore. I know what I'm doing. It's a good feeling. You should try it sometime."

"I'm not confused. I know what I'm doing, too."

"Uh-huh." She eyed him skeptically.

CHAPTER
20

"I brought something for your mother," Zach said, coming up the walk to Greg and Nina's house.

Sonnet put aside her laptop. She'd been sitting at her favorite spot on the porch swing, putting together some information for the PR firm engaged by Mickey Flick Productions. It was strange to think the production was winding down. The long hours and weeks of filming had yielded a huge archive. From that, the series would be created.

She stood and folded her arms. "More pot?"

"Not today," he said simply.

In his skinny jeans and sneakers, his black T-shirt and shaggy hair, he looked ridiculously sexy. No matter how hard she tried to view him as the old Zach, the kid she'd grown up with, she couldn't deny that he'd changed.

"What, then?"

"C'mere." He held out his hand.

She hesitated, then took it and followed him to the van. Their hands linked together with startling ease. She felt a shiver of tenderness mingled with confusion. Zach opened the door and took out a small molded crate. "I found something," he said.

"A wild animal? What—"

"A dog. She was wandering around on a back road between here and Camp Kioga." He opened the crate and lifted out a squirming, silver-gray bundle. "I dropped her off at the Humane Society, but no one claimed her. So I picked her up today." The dog scrambled out of his arms and danced around their feet.

In spite of herself, Sonnet laughed at its antics. "And you're bringing this to my mom...why?"

"To see if she wants to adopt her. I can't keep a dog at my place; it's a rental. So I thought maybe your mom and Greg—"

"Zach, that's awesome. What a fantastic idea."

"Really?"

"Don't look so surprised."

"I thought you'd yell at me."

"I never yell at you."

"You yell all the time."

"I do not." She caught herself raising her voice, and spun on her heel. "Come on. Let's see if Mom wants to adopt her. She and Greg just finished dinner."

The little dog skittered up the walkway as if she already owned the place, and ran through the door when Sonnet opened it. Her mom and Greg were in the TV room, settling in for the evening. Nina had removed her wig for the day. Sonnet was used to seeing her without hair, and in fact, she thought Nina looked kind of cool, her head as smooth and pale as a new moon. She quickly glanced at Zach and put up a hand. "Oh, hey," she said, then noticed the dog. "Who's this?"

"She's a stray," said Zach. "I just got her from the Humane Society. She's all fixed, shots, housebroken. You interested?"

"You brought us a dog?" Greg asked.

"He brought *me* a dog," Nina said. "I mentioned that I wanted to get one. And yes, I'm totally interested." Leaning down, she patted her thigh. The dog jumped lithely into her lap, clambering over the mound of her belly, put her paws on Nina's shoulders and seemed to grin straight up at her.

"I'm going to call her Jolie," Nina said decisively.

"As in Angelina Jolie?" asked Zach.

"*Please.* As in Jolie Madame. It was my mother's favorite perfume. Jolie is French for pretty. Oh, Greg. Look how pretty she is."

Greg wore a pained but indulgent expression as he watched the little stray snuggle up to her. It was a dog only a smitten mother could love. There was poodle in the mix; Sonnet could tell by her curling silver fur. Yet she also had the short legs of a dachshund as well as a mysterious combination of other breeds.

"I think she's a hit," Sonnet said to Zach.

"I *know* she's a hit," Nina said. "Thanks, Zach."

"It's not going to be too much, with the baby coming?" asked Greg.

Nina laughed. "You can't handle us?"

"Hey. I'm just worried about *you.*"

"After this summer, I can handle anything," Nina said.

"Great." Zach stuck his thumbs in his back pockets, looking on like a proud uncle, then turned to Sonnet. "Give me a hand bringing her things in?"

"Sure." Sonnet followed him outside. "So I was talking to Jezebel on set earlier," she said, her nerves fluttering, "and she said I should tell you I broke up with Orlando."

His shoulders stiffened. "Why should you tell me?"

"Because we're friends, right? We tell each other stuff. So I'm telling you. If you want more detail—"

"Nope. Not too interested in the details of your breakup with a guy who was never right for you to begin with."

"You're being annoying. I'm telling you something very personal, and you're being annoying," she said.

"Are you devastated? Brokenhearted? Or are you over the guy?"

"No. Just…disappointed in myself."

"So is this an opening?" he asked bluntly.

"Zach!" Her cheeks felt hot. "I can't deal with another relationship in the middle of what's happening to my mom."

"Sure you can. It's all in the motivation."

"I'll take it under advisement." As they went to the van together, she said, "This is really nice of you."

"I'm nice," he said matter-of-factly. "I've always been nice."

"Agreed."

"Then why are you having such a hard time falling in love with me?"

"I'm not."

"Not what? Not having a hard time, or not falling in love?"

"Neither. Zach—"

"*Sonnet.*" Greg came out onto the porch.

She froze. There was something in his voice and in his stance that galvanized every cell in her body. Zach was standing very close. In a split second, she took in everything—the way the wind lifted his hair and the ropy muscles of his arms relaxing as he stopped with the box of pet supplies. The sound of her own intake of breath and the crunch of gravel underfoot as she turned to face him, telling him what his face already told her he knew:

"Something's wrong."

The hospital waiting room overflowed. Between the Romanos and the Bellamys, visitors filled every available chair and bench, though most milled around, walking up and down the hallway, talking in low voices as they waited for news.

Sonnet felt nauseous with terror. Everyone clustered around her, offering words of comfort and reassurance, but nothing penetrated. Nina was beloved, that was why everyone had come, but there was no one in the world who knew what Sonnet was feeling. This was her mom—her *mom*.

Nonna Romano sat amidst Sonnet's aunts and uncles, her rosary beads moving slowly, steadily and silently through her shaking fingers. On the Bellamy side, Greg's parents, Charles and Jane, were there, looking desperate and exhausted. Like Nonna, they'd been ecstatic at the prospect of a new grandbaby, though consumed by worry.

The tension and dread in the waiting room felt like a crushing vise around Sonnet's chest. She stood gazing out a window, her hands gripping the sill. The hospital was located at the confluence of the Schuyler River with the Hudson, with the Catskills rising in the distance. Sonnet could only stare down at the parking lot, watching people come and go—workers in their scrubs, visitors, patients, EMTs on call, hanging around the ambulance bay.

When Zach's van turned into the parking lot, Sonnet felt a slight easing of tension. She wasn't released from her worry but a tiny bit of the stress unfurled. It made no sense, but just the sight of him calmed her.

"I'm going to step out for some fresh air," she said to no one in particular, and walked over to the elevator.

She met up with Zach in the parking lot. He held out both arms and she stepped into his embrace. They didn't have to say anything; she could feel his concern, and she knew he could feel her worry. They stood that way for several beats, and then he stepped back.

"Tell me," he said.

"Her water broke. The baby's not due for another five weeks, so his lungs are underdeveloped. The latest plan is to pump her full of antibiotics and steroids to help the baby's lungs, and hope she carries him a bit longer." Sonnet could honestly say she no longer hated the baby. It was nobody's fault, least of all the baby's, that Nina had gotten sick.

Greg came out of the unit wearing wrinkled scrubs and paper booties, a stunned expression on his face. No, she thought. Please God, no no no no...

He leaned against the wall. The floor was so shiny, his reflection shone in it. He took a breath and encompassed everyone in the waiting room with a glance.

"It's a boy," he said. "Lucas Romano Bellamy and his mom are both all right."

There was a moment of breath-held silence. Then the waiting room erupted with questions and congratulations, expressions of relief, laughter and tears. Sonnet pushed her way toward Greg. "Can I see Mom?"

"Soon," he said. "And you're first in line. Where the hell is Max? He finally has the brother he's been wanting since he was little."

"I'll see if I can find him." She took out her phone. Damn Max. He was as unreliable as ever, thought Sonnet, probably taking his time getting here in hopes of missing the drama.

Max picked up on the third ring. "Yo."

"Where are you?"

"How's Nina?"

"She's okay. The baby, too."

"Jesus. That's a relief."

"Where are you?" she repeated.

"Just getting here. Come down to the parking lot."

"Max—" The call ended.

"Everything okay?" asked Zach, joining her in the elevator.

Before she could stop herself, Sonnet sagged against him, overwhelmed by relief.

He didn't say anything. Neither of them did while the elevator whooshed to the ground floor. As the doors parted, she moved away from him, trying to compose herself.

They stepped out of the elevator. At the same time, her stepsister Daisy came through the revolving door. Squealing, they ran toward each other and hugged.

"Oh, my gosh, it's so good to see you again," Sonnet said, stepping back, studying her—blonde, smiling, her blue eyes shining.

"I've missed you so much," Daisy said. "So Max told me your mom and the baby are okay."

"Yes. Let's go right up. Did you come by yourself?"

"Uh-huh. First time leaving the kid home with their dad. It had to happen sometime." Daisy noticed Zach by the elevator. "Hey, you. Long time no see." She gave him a hug, too.

"It's good to see you, Daze," he said. "Hey, Max."

As the four of them stepped back into the elevator, Sonnet was overcome by the most amazing feeling. When friends and family pulled together to support each other, some kind of magic happened.

"That shot is genius," Sonnet said, looking over Daisy's shoulder at the computer screen. The two of them were going over raw files of the photos Daisy had taken.

"Thanks. Although it's not a stretch to do a good job on a picture of a mother and her newborn."

"My mom has a newborn," Sonnet said. "That's so…strange. In a good way."

Daisy had outdone herself, documenting the baby's birth day. Photography was not just her job, but her passion. Sometimes Sonnet envied her the intensity of that passion. Unlike Sonnet, Daisy never questioned her own career path. She just *knew*.

"You look pretty happy in this shot." Daisy clicked on a photo of Sonnet holding the baby, a six-pound armful who had only spent a short time in the NICU before being pronounced healthy despite being premature. "My lord, that short hair looks incredible on you."

"Think so?" Sonnet studied the screen. "Do you think I should keep it short?"

Daisy clicked to a candid shot of her showing off the baby to Zach. "*He's* pretty crazy about it. He's pretty crazy about you."

Sonnet flushed and looked away.

"What's up?" Daisy asked. "The two of you…I mean, you've always been close, but something else is going on now. I can tell. And you know what they say—the camera doesn't lie."

"I can't lie to you, either. I'm in trouble, Daze. Man trouble. I broke up with Orlando."

"Really? Ah, Sonnet. I'm sorry. I thought things were going well for you two."

"They were…but they weren't. Things haven't felt right in a while. Still, you're right. We were compatible. So even now, I don't know if it was the right thing to do."

"Don't second-guess yourself," Daisy advised. "Do what your heart's telling you to do."

"Zach and I are… I can't stop thinking about him and it's bad. It's messing with my head."

"I think you're not in trouble at all," Daisy said.

"It's not that simple. We don't… We can't…"

"Or maybe you can. Ask yourself—not me."

"Zach brings my mom pot and puppies. He makes me laugh and isn't always rushing around, busy all the time." She hesitated, rubbed her hands up and down her arms. "He holds me when there are no words. But Orlando got her a consultation with one of the best oncologists in the country. Am I an idiot for not choosing him?"

"How about you choose based on how you feel about the guy, not how much he's helped your mom?" Daisy asked reasonably.

"Sure. But at the moment, I really can't separate the two. Ah, Daisy. I don't know what to do."

"Don't rely on my advice. When it comes to choosing between two guys, I'm no expert. Took me forever to figure it out."

"I don't have forever."

"Slow down. Relax. Don't make any big decisions until you finish up here in Avalon."

"That's the thing. I'm pretty much done. I'll stick around a while longer to help Mom, of course, but both she and Greg are adamant that they want their privacy back. And here's the scary part. I have no idea what I'm going to do next."

Though on the small side, the baby had a loud, lusty cry and a voracious appetite, with the face of a wizened apple. He had dark hair and adorable elfin features, and a deep, dark-eyed stare that was strangely mesmeric.

Seeing the start of a new life up close and personal had a deep and resounding impact on Sonnet. This was the essence of life at its most elemental, made more precious by the risks and pain Nina had endured. Sonnet's heart swelled with gratitude. She viewed everything—her mother, the world, herself, this town, through new eyes. She used to think Avalon was the smallest, most insignificant town in the world, but she no longer felt that way. The outpouring of strength that came from the community gathering around her mother was amazing to Sonnet—the tenderness in a man's eyes when he smiles at his wife, the smells of fresh baked goods brought by a friend, the sounds so often drowned out in the city—barking dogs, laughing children, the burble of a running creek. She wondered why she'd been so eager to leave, growing up.

CHAPTER 21

Zach brought his smallest camera—the latest version of the GoPro—to the wrap party for the series. Camp Kioga had always been known as a place for celebrations of all kinds—anniversaries, reunions, weddings, family gatherings—but it had never hosted an event quite like the *Big Girl, Small Town* farewell party. A local band called Inner Child had been hired to provide the entertainment, but Jezebel herself was inspired to join in. While their usual repertoire consisted of '80s and '90s cover music, the band members were only too happy to change things up. An urban beat thumped from the speakers, and the kids and crew filled the plank dance floor to celebrate the conclusion of shooting.

Eddie Haven, the singer/songwriter at the heart of Inner Child, seemed gleeful as he performed with Jezebel, backed by his bandmates Noah Shepherd, Ray Tolley and a bass player named Brandi in a purple plaid miniskirt. There had been a time when a girl in a miniskirt would cause Zach's entire prefrontal cortex to shut down, but instead of gawking, he found himself scanning the crowd for Sonnet. It was weird, how even a pretty girl failed to attract him now. He could appreciate a woman's looks, but the pull was gone. Sonnet had ruined him for other women, and she didn't even know it. It was a crazy position to find himself in. This person he'd known all his life, the proverbial girl next door, had suddenly become his whole world.

Not seeing her, he went over to the refreshments table and grabbed a beer. Jezebel took a break from the band and joined him. "Beer?" He offered her the bottle.

"I'll stick with water," she said. "Saving my celebrating for when I lose this piece of bling for real." She lifted up her ankle with the security bracelet. They'd filmed a ceremonial removal for the series, even though it wouldn't be official for a few more months.

"You made something great here," he said. "That's something to celebrate. At least eat something."

The food looked fantastic, including some of the stuff the kids had learned to make alongside Jezebel—the rhubarb pie, buttermilk fried chicken, a salad made of greens they'd grown themselves. There was a giant sheet cake from the Sky River Bakery decorated with a ribbon of film wrapped around a heart, not that film was in use anymore.

She grabbed a stuffed celery stick and lifted it in a toast. "*We* made something great here," she corrected him. "Yeah, we did."

He nodded, surveying the milling crowd. Shooting for the series (they were already calling it Season One on the assumption that it would be renewed) was done. Now the work would shift to studio editors, continuity specialists, sound technicians and other techs to put the story together out of the raw material created at Camp Kioga. Sonnet was nowhere in sight. Maybe she was going to skip the wrap party. His hand went to his phone; maybe he'd send her a quick text.

Then he took a swig of his beer. Maybe not.

"Call her," Jezebel said. "What you waiting for?"

He didn't even pretend ignorance. Jezebel had a freakish ability to read his mind. "I'm going to take a few pictures of the kids," he said. "They look so different from the kids who showed up here at the beginning of summer."

"Yep, that's plain to see. I swear, some of the boys are inches taller," she said.

They were so used to cameras and mics, they didn't even seem to notice when Zach turned his viewfinder in their direction. Today in particular, the kids looked vibrant and relaxed. Friendships and alliances had formed between them; time would tell which ones would withstand time.

"Don't you forget that number, now," Darnell was telling Anita. "That's how we're gonna stay in touch."

"Okay," she said. "I still think Facebook is easier."

"Facebook's lame. I don't want to be telling everybody in the world my business."

"I don't think the world cares about your business," she said in her matter-of-fact way. "But I get what you're saying."

Zach moved on to the twins and Jaden, who were tying colorful handmade friendship bracelets on everyone, cast and crew alike. Whether the series ever made it to a network or not, this experience had meant something to the inner-city kids. Each one had planted a maple seedling, marking the site with a rock etched with their name and the year.

Mr. and Mrs. Bellamy arrived to see everyone off. Out of instinct, Zach filmed the significant details—their aged hands, tightly clasped as they walked together. The subtle way Charles slowed his pace to match Jane's. The shine in her eyes as they stepped up to the mic, where the band had paused.

"I hope you'll come back often and see them," said Mrs. Bellamy, beaming with pride. "There will always be a place here for you."

"Serious?" one of the kids piped up.

"Word," said old Mr. Bellamy. Only on a reality TV show would the old married couple find themselves hanging out with kids like this.

In the background, he could see Sonnet arriving from the main pavilion, and it was all Zach could do to keep the camera trained on the Bellamys. She looked fantastic in tight faded jeans, sandals and a white top with a wide gold belt and gold hoop earrings. When the kids spotted her, they swarmed her; they always did, and his viewfinder followed. After Jezebel, Sonnet was their favorite.

With the kids, she wasn't cautious or tentative at all. She hugged them and laughed with them, and insisted on having several friendship bracelets for each arm. This was Sonnet in her element, not in some cubicle in a New York high-rise. He wondered if she realized that.

Jezebel finished her water. "I'm gonna do a few more numbers," she said. She stepped up and rejoined the band. "This is for my boy Zach," she said. "Mr. Camera Man."

He was chagrined, but not surprised, when she launched into "Don't Make Me Wait to Tell You." Glancing over at Sonnet, he saw her tilt her head to listen, and he set down the camera. Her gaze connected with his and he didn't blink. He had plenty he wanted to tell her. She looked completely vulnerable, though she offered him the tiniest of smiles. It wasn't even a smile, but a softening of the eyes. Then, with unhurried deliberation, she turned away and started dancing with some of the kids.

After a few more numbers, it was time to go. The van was waiting to drive them home. Everyone trooped over to the parking lot to see them off.

"Doing okay?" Zach asked Sonnet. He recognized the tremor of emotion in her chin.

"It's just really hard to see them go. This show was a lot of hard work, but I never wanted it to end."

"It doesn't have to end," Jane Bellamy said, joining them for a final round of hugs. "Certainly, we won't miss the cameras and the commotion, but children are always welcome. We've long wanted a program for children from the city, but still haven't found the right person to make it happen. Unless you're interested in organizing something..."

"This was a temporary situation for me," Sonnet said.

"I understand. Still, if you'd like to discuss it further, come see me and Olivia anytime."

Sonnet changed her outfit at least four times, getting ready for a date with Zach. No, she told herself. It wasn't a date. She simply wanted to see him. She'd sent him a text: Meet me at the Hilltop Tavern. I have something to celebrate.

Now she wondered if the cool jacket and cowboy boots were a bit much. Did she look as if she was trying too hard? Primping too much?

"You're overthinking again," she reminded herself as she parked and headed into the tavern. "It's not a date."

Yet it felt like a date. She had the butterflies, the sense of anticipation, the sweet tug of yearning deep inside, just at the prospect of seeing him. Maybe it *was* a date. They were getting together like two grown-ups getting to know each other, maybe even like two grown-ups falling in love.

His work van rumbled to a stop in the parking lot, so she stopped to wait for him. He got out, and he looked wonderful, his long hair shining, his shirt pressed. *Pressed.* The butterflies intensified, and she felt a little silly. She'd been on plenty of dates; she'd met guys who arrived in limos and sports cars, but she'd never felt this crazy melting sensation inside when she saw them.

"Hey," he said, then stooped and gave her an awkward hug. Yes, it was awkward. "What's up? You're celebrating?"

"Yes, oh, Zach, yes. It's the best news ever."

He held the door for her. "You gonna clue me in?"

"Order me a drink first." She took a seat in a booth. The bar was dim and familiar, yeasty-smelling, music drifting from unseen speakers.

"Oh, I like drinking with you. Beer?"

"Please. This is champagne news."

"Let's make it a kir royale," he said to the waitress who approached. "Utica Club for me."

"I'm impressed that you know what a kir royale is," she said.

"It's a way to make average champagne taste better."

"I heard that," said the waitress, serving their drinks.

"All right," said Sonnet. "A toast."

"Sure." He clinked glasses with her. "What are we toasting?"

"My mom." To her surprise, Sonnet felt a wave of emotion. "Her latest tests came back this afternoon. No further evidence of cancer."

His shoulders sagged and he set down his beer. "Jesus, that's...Christ, that's the best news. I'm happy for her. For all of you."

"It's great. I mean, she's not completely out of the woods. There'll be further tests and checkups, but this is good. *So* good." She studied his face, the face of a guy she'd known forever. Even in the dim light, she could see a sheen of tears in his eyes. "Zach..."

"Yeah, I know." He wiped his eyes, took a quick slug of his beer. "It's such a damn relief. I just...hell." He pushed his glass away. "I just need to kiss you."

Without hesitation, he took her in his arms and kissed her with a fervor that took her breath away. Good grief, it felt amazing. She never wanted it to stop. She kissed him back, moving against him, shamelessly forgetting they were in a public spot. He tasted like heaven, and she was swept back to the night of the wedding, the night that had changed everything between them. How was it that he had been in her life for so long, and she'd never realized they could be like this together? Her goals and ambitions had blinded her to the simple power of passion with the right guy. No wonder she hadn't been able to make her heart fit together with Orlando. Her heart was smarter than her head; it was waiting for *this*.

He moved back, smiled down at her. "You're being nice to me tonight."

"I'm always nice to you."

"Right."

"Ah, Zach. What's happening to us? Have we both gone crazy?"

"Maybe. I can't complain, though." He kissed her again, very tenderly. "I want you to come home with me. *Now.*"

"But—"

"And I want to put on some good music and fix you another kir royale, and then I want to take your clothes off, and—"

"Okay," she said in a rush, "that sounds good to me."

He signaled for the tab. While they waited, she got a call from her father. God, the timing. It was as if his disapproval came vibrating through the phone. *Later,* she thought, dismissing the call.

"Everything all right?" Zach asked.

"Everything's fine." She resisted the urge to check her voice mail. Her dad could wait, just this once.

Then a text came in from her mother. Without hesitation, she checked the message. I'm fine, but I need you to come home. I'll explain when you get here.

"That's weird," she said to Zach after he paid the bill. "My mom needs me to come home."

"Hey. *I* need you to come home. *My* home."

"My mom needs me. Tell you what. I'll go check on her, and then I'll meet you at your place."

"Okay, that works."

In the parking lot, he kissed her again. His hands skimmed over her, and it was all she could do not to wrap her legs around him and never let go.

"See you soon," she said.

One more kiss. A soft promise. She drove home, but it felt more like floating.

Sonnet sailed into the house. Her mom and Greg were waiting for her at the kitchen table. Jolie, the little dog, was curled in her nest by the stove. These days the kitchen was perpetually littered with baby things—extra bottles, toys and burp pads. She took one look at their faces and asked, "Who died?"

"Ah, baby." Nina offered a wan smile. "Somebody put a stupid video up on the internet to try to damage your father's reputation."

Her heart sank, but she wasn't surprised. "Johnny Delvecchio's people fight dirty. Dad's known that all along. I'm sure he can handle it. What is it this time?"

"It's…" Nina glanced from side to side, seeming as though she would rather be anywhere but here in her own kitchen.

"Just show her," Greg said.

"Yes," Sonnet said. "Show me."

He turned the laptop toward her. "I'm sorry, honey," he said. "I'm sorry as hell. I wish I could make this go away."

Sonnet stared at the screen. Horror spread over her like a sudden frost, icing every inch of her skin. She blinked at the title of the video on the site: Candidate Jeffries's bastard daughter's sex video.

Her mouth went dry. Despite the cold, her cheeks burned all the way up to her scalp.

"It's staged, of course," Nina said, her voice very faint. "Someone's trying to pull a dirty trick."

Her mother was wrong about that. Perhaps the most shocking thing of all was that the girl in the video really was her. Despite the darkness of the candlelit boathouse, the dashboard camera had picked up telling details of her night with Zach, right down to the whispers and giggles, the bared flesh and hands skimming, the unmistakable sounds of surprised ecstasy.

The number of views on the site was a shocking testament to the speed of the internet. Already, the pro-Delvecchio contingent had disseminated the link through every social network on the web. The scandal had made the local news. With a pinched expression on her face, Courtney Proctor narrated the "Jeffries issue," as she called it. Besides the sex video, she managed to bring up the fact that Sonnet had made a sudden departure from her job at UNESCO and wound up in a menial role with a "shock reality show" production company, working closely with a convicted felon. The ace reporter had pulled together some "man in the street" interviews and aired some of the more incendiary comments: "This makes us wonder what else Laurence Jeffries is hiding." "The video just proves it. If the guy can't raise his own kid, how's he going to represent a whole state?"

Regardless of the inanity of the remark, Sonnet knew the scandal had taken hold. No wonder her unread email queue was full. She dared to glance at it, and could tell just from the subject line that the word was out, far and wide. Senatorial candidate Laurence Jeffries's illegitimate daughter was not only a reject and a slacker, hanging out with unsavory characters—she was a slut. And the damage was already taking its toll, according to the follow-up to the first broadcast. Laurence Jeffries's numbers had slipped below his opponent's.

"Who did this?" Sonnet whispered, horrified. "Who's behind this?"

"The Delvecchio camp, of course," her mother said. "Deep breath, okay?"

Sonnet rose from her chair, unable to look at her mother and Greg. "Excuse me," she mumbled. Somehow she managed to stagger to the bathroom before she threw up.

CHAPTER
22

When she could manage to think straight, Sonnet called her father. "I just saw," she said. "I'm sorry. I'm so sorry."

"I'm not going to lie," he said. "It's very damaging."

"What can be done?"

"Orlando's got somebody on it."

Orlando. She hadn't spoken to him since they'd parted ways. She could feel her father's disappointment coming through the phone. "He'll fix it," she mumbled. That was what he did. He did things right, and he kept his nose clean. No wonder her father counted on him.

"Sonnet, I warned you about the company you keep," he said, "but you didn't listen."

The company she kept. He meant Zach. He couldn't even say the guy's name. Though her father didn't say it, he was ordering her to get back to being the good daughter he knew, or he couldn't associate with her.

"I'm sorry," she said. "I know I sound like a broken record, but it's all I can think of to say."

"There's a glimmer of good news for you," her father said, and now his voice sounded a tiny bit less tight.

"Please, I need some good news."

A pause. Then: "The Hartstone Fellowship is being offered to you again."

"What?" She was dazzled. "Seriously? Dad, what did you do?"

"It's what *you* did. It's your achievement to claim," he said. Now the disapproval was gone, replaced by a note of pride and hope.

"I thought I'd lost my shot at the fellowship."

"You'll get an email explaining everything, probably later today. There's an opening for a directorship in Bhutan."

Bhutan. She nearly reeled with excitement. Bhutan was a tiny, isolated, mountainous kingdom tucked away in the eastern Himalayas, bordered by China and India. Peaceable and impoverished, it had recently adopted a constitution and was ripe for aid. Her work there would help Bhutanese children gain access to quality education.

"That's incredible," she said. "Really?"

"Really. The only contingency is that they need you right away."

"How right away is 'right away'?"

"Does next week work for you?"

Only a couple of hours earlier, Sonnet had envisioned quite a different night with Zach. She'd been thinking about wine and kisses, deep sighs of contentment as he took her in his arms. That was a fantasy; she should have known better. Now she had to force herself to go and see him. She knocked once and let herself into his little bungalow on Spring Street. He was standing at the kitchen bar. He wore the same face as her mom—slightly nauseated, helpless, frustrated.

"You saw," she said.

"I feel lousy about this. I don't know what the hell to do."

"It's too late to do anything. I look like a complete slut, and my dad's opponent is broadcasting it all over the state. He's already slipped below Delvecchio in the polls."

"To be honest, I'm more worried about you." He took a step toward her.

Just a short time ago, she would have fallen into his arms, at his feet, wherever. Now she just felt...violated. Betrayed.

"How could you let this happen?"

"I didn't let anything happen."

"You were supposed to make sure that...that thing on the camera was deleted."

"I thought I had. I took out the SD card. I didn't think about the camera having a memory backup. Jesus, I wasn't thinking of anything that night, Sonnet. Anything but you."

"Oh, God." Her skin crawled, and she wrapped her arms around her middle. Whether or not Zach was to blame wasn't the issue. A wedge had been driven between them—or maybe it had been there all along. Even if he'd made an honest mistake, the damage was done, and it was clear they were on different paths. The scandal had blown through her like a storm, and she was no longer blinded by his kisses and her emotions.

The two of them...she couldn't imagine how they could make it work.

"The Hartstone Fellowship is back on the table for me," she said. "I'm going to Bhutan next week."

"What? Next week? Sonnet—"

"It's for the best. I can't turn it down again." She felt hollow, but determined. She would give up the fellowship to help her mother through cancer. But to give it up because of a wild night of sex...no. That was too transitory.

"I have to go," she told Zach. "I have to go, and you have

to stay, and it's crazy to pretend there's anything in our future together."

His eyes, too blue and too beautiful to look at, turned dark with anger. "I'm not pretending a damn thing, but whatever. Go. Do what you have to do. Marry Rivera. Tell him you want him back. Turn yourself into something respectable so your dad can get elected."

"It's not like that."

"It's exactly like that."

"I'm not going to marry Orlando, which you would know if you'd been listening. I'm not marrying *any*body."

"Fine with me. Look, I'm not going to stand in your way or try to talk you out of anything."

This was what she had asked of him all along, to step aside and let her forge ahead with her plans. Now he was doing just that. He had dreams and plans of his own; he couldn't simply follow her around the globe, carrying her bags for her or taking pictures. And she couldn't bring herself to let this opportunity slip by a second time.

There was a catch, though. She hadn't expected it to hurt so much.

CHAPTER
23

Sonnet returned to the world she knew best, back to Manhattan. Everything about it felt familiar—the traffic sounds, the smells of exhaust and garbage and sizzling street food, the press of crowds, the bustle…yet it was a life that didn't seem to fit her anymore. She couldn't imagine going back to the way she'd been…before. Before her mom got sick, before the baby had been born, before she'd returned to Willow Lake.

Before she'd looked into the face of her best friend and realized she'd fallen in love with him.

She could not deny the power of what had happened there. She was a different person now.

From the bottom of her heart, she believed she had found something rare and special with Zach, a deep and abiding passion fueled by a kind of love she'd never felt before. Yet despite what her heart knew, she questioned whether or not it would endure. She and Zach both understood the price of being together. The cost of being with him was the plan she had for her future. The life she'd always dreamed about beckoned, even though it meant leaving everything, including Zach, behind. For a while, at least.

She found herself completely alone, packing her bags and getting things boxed up for storage or charity. She missed the kids at Camp Kioga and worried about some of them returning to a life full of danger and risk in the city. She missed Jezebel and working with the rest of the crew. She missed her family and couldn't stop thinking about Zach.

Despondent, she went to see her father, hoping for a word of encouragement and wisdom from him. He invited her to his home for a farewell dinner, a rare opportunity for Sonnet. His wife and daughters showed her the same cordial welcome they'd always extended to her, none of them bringing up the ugliness of the scandal. Now Sonnet realized she would always be the outsider, no matter how big she dreamed and what she achieved. Her own family wasn't here in the opulent, comfortable home. She belonged to Nina, the mother who had sacrificed everything in order to give Sonnet a good life. Her father had sacrificed nothing for her sake, and his regard for her was tied to her performance.

After dinner, Sonnet opened up the box of Godiva chocolates she'd brought to share.

"So are you excited about Bhutan?" asked Layla.

"Totally. I feel really lucky that the opportunity is still there for me."

"Luck had nothing to do with it."

"Ah, thanks. I appreciate the vote of confidence."

"That's not what I was talking about. I mean, you're totally smart and all, but the luck? That came from Daddy."

A small chill touched the back of her neck. "Did he tell you that?"

"Nope. Just overheard him talking about it to Orlando."

Orlando?

Her expression must have given her away. Layla touched her arm. "Listen, I know you probably think I've always had the perfect life with our dad. Don't get me wrong—he's amazing, but he's the same guy with me as he is with you—demanding and difficult. My mom's a perfectionist. I feel the pressure, too. It's not easy."

"Wow, I... Thanks for saying that." She felt a tiny bit closer to her half-sister. "Have some more chocolate," Sonnet said, handing over the whole box. She herself had lost her appetite entirely. "I'd love to hear more."

A short time later, she stood in the doorway of her father's study. The room was like the Oval Office in miniature, with a massive desk set in front of the bay windows, a braided navy area rug, a sitting area with a sofa and two wing chairs. On a credenza were several laptops, each with a different window open on the monitor. The space seemed to radiate power and control; in that way it was perfectly suited to her father.

He was at his desk, writing something by hand on a yellow legal pad. He was left-handed, like Sonnet. She used to always like the fact that they were both left-handed.

"I came to say goodbye," she said.

He smiled and stood up. "You must have a lot of packing to do."

"You would know."

Her tone caused his smile to fade. "Know what?"

"Everything that's involved in getting me to leave the country."

A brief, dry laugh escaped him. "Why do I get the feeling you're taking issue with me about something?"

"Because I am. You engineered the fellowship for me—both times. Just to get rid of me during your campaign."

"You are eminently qualified for that fellowship. Past winners went on to worldwide recognition."

He was a politician, she reminded herself. A good one. He

would admit to nothing. He was trying to flatter her instead of taking responsibility. He had concocted a plan to send her overseas to avoid having to answer questions about his past. Then when she turned down the fellowship, he'd tried getting her engaged to Orlando to up her respectability quotient. When that backfired, he went back to the fellowship solution. She'd never have been offered it on the strength of her qualifications alone. She should have known better.

"I really don't want to argue," she said. "I only want you to know, I've made other plans for myself. You're a really wonderful candidate, and I don't doubt for a moment you'll get elected, despite what your opponents say about the past. I'm not at all worried about your chances."

"Sonnet—"

"It's all right. I'll let you go now. I can see you're busy." She felt strangely liberated. She was no longer his to manipulate. She couldn't be swayed by his influence. In his way, he cared for her, but it was so very, very limited. His love for her was conditional. It depended on her ability to strive for lofty goals, to wear achievements like the leaves of a laurel wreath.

Out of habit, she checked her phone for messages. There was a text from Zach: Your buddy Orlando leaked the video. Ask him about it.

Very slowly, she put the phone in her bag. "About that video…"

His brows came together in a frown. "Like I said, Orlando's handling it."

"You mean, Orlando *handled* it. How about you ask him how it was leaked in the first place?"

"What are you saying?"

"He leaked it. I don't know how, but I think I know why."

"He'd never leak anything so damaging to my campaign."

"Unless," she said, thinking about Orlando's true colors, "he's doing a favor for Delvecchio." Yes, she thought. Orlando was all about attaching himself to the winner. Now that Delvecchio was the frontrunner, he might easily shift his loyalty. Because to a guy like Orlando, loyalty was a moving target.

"That's preposterous."

"Then you won't mind asking him," she said simply.

"Fine, I'll do that. But you're reaching, Sonnet."

"Ask him."

"I said I would. The quicker we put this behind us, the quicker we can move on. You're still planning to accept the fellowship," he stated.

She nearly laughed. He simply didn't get it. "No. Like I said, I have other plans."

"Listen, I understand you've let something upset you, but don't let the children of Bhutan suffer because of it. They need you, Sonnet. You were chosen for a reason. This could open so many doors for you."

It was the same spiel she'd heard ever since she'd gone to American University and he'd taken her under his wing. She had to admit, he was persuasive. Like any good politician, he knew how to draw someone into his way of thinking.

The fellowship would be a feather in her cap for sure, and a way to make her father proud, but she was done living her life for her father. "I've always been a planner and in a way, that's been my downfall," she confessed to him. "I've been so busy making plans and sticking to them like glue that I forgot who I was. I lost my way. I only hope I can find my way home."

"You are home," he said. "Your mother is all right. That was your goal when you went back to Willow Lake to take care of her. Now it's time to get on track once again."

"That's exactly what I intend to do." She went to the door. "Good luck in the election. You've always had my vote."

CHAPTER
24

Back at her apartment, Sonnet did a final walk-through, moving like a wraith through the place she'd lived for the past five years. She'd cut herself loose from everything—her father, her career path, the life she thought she was supposed to have. The old Sonnet would have panicked at the prospect of having a life with no plan. Now she felt liberated—albeit excited and nervous—at the prospect of all this open white space.

There was sadness, too. She had walked away from Zach. And he had let her. She came across a stack of mail, mostly catalogs filled with items she would never, ever buy. Among the letters was a card from her mother, including a shiny silver disk without a label. Nina's handwriting was strong and sure. Her brief message read:

Zach didn't tell you *everything*. Here's a video I asked him to make for me—and for my family. There were things

I wanted to record in case things went badly for me. I couldn't have gotten through this without you, baby. You've been there for me even when I didn't know I needed you. I love you more than words can say.

Sonnet's hand shook as she put the disk into her computer. The screen resolved into a shot of her mother sitting on the porch of her house, with trees blowing in the background. It was the start of a beautifully produced video chronicling her mother's pregnancy and illness. There were short and long sequences showing Nina's journey, punctuated with some of her favorite things—music and nature, views of her world, even a cooking lesson and a few housekeeping tips she'd gleaned from running the Inn at Willow Lake. There were family stories Sonnet had heard before, and a good number that were brand-new to her. Nina was very much herself—frank and funny, emotional. There were a couple of parts showing her completely in despair and filled with terror—bruised and exhausted from chemo, speaking through painfully cracked lips, and a post-op sequence that was brutal to watch. She put everything in front of the camera, holding nothing back. Sonnet could only imagine how Zach felt, filming it.

Like all of Zach's work, the video was sensitive and honest. He'd been working with Nina all along, and he'd never said a word about it.

Sonnet clicked on an icon toward the end of the video series. There was her mother, looking completely exhausted, her cheeks hollowed out by fatigue. She wore a scarf and no makeup. Her smile was tremulous but still glimmering with hope. "I've been counting the blessings in my life," she said, "and I've lost count. It's a good problem to have, right? But it helps me realize that it doesn't matter what happens. If everything ended in the next moment, I would still be blessed. I'm completely bald, I'm eight months pregnant and I have only one breast. And this morning, Greg told me I'm beautiful. It's kind of a miracle, right? Actually, the miracle is not that he said that. It's that he made me believe it."

The screen blurred before Sonnet's eyes. What her mother was saying was something so obvious, yet so difficult to grasp. It was terrible, what her mother had gone through, but now, Sonnet truly understood the gift of being pushed to the brink of despair. There were only a few things that truly mattered. Family and friends and connection. Understanding and selfless love.

Zach went to the Sky River Bakery to celebrate making his final payment of restitution to the town of Avalon, and to wait for the last person he expected to see here—his father.

Matthew Alger had made parole.

Everything felt completely surreal to Zach. It was ironic that working on a project about the town his father had defrauded had ultimately given Zach the power to make amends. *Big Girl, Small Town* had turned out to be a surprise hit for the network. He sat listening to the familiar sounds of the bakery—acoustic music coming from the speakers, the murmur of conversation, the hiss and gurgle of the espresso machine. A pair of workers in white aprons emerged from the swinging doors, wheeling a stainless steel cart with a tall wedding cake surrounded by flowers. Around the edge of the cake was a message written in icing: *The beginning of forever.*

Good luck with that, thought Zach, looking at his phone. He wasn't sure he'd done the right thing, sending the message to Sonnet about Orlando Rivera. Zach knew he hadn't been mistaken. Perla Galetti, his assistant on the *Big Girl* show and resident digital geek, had pinpointed the ISP of the "anonymous" video uploader. For a smart guy, Rivera didn't seem to understand that nothing done on the internet was truly anonymous.

Sonnet hadn't called him back or responded to the message. Was she pissed at him? Or had she already left to go save the children of the world? Damn. He wished she could see there were children who needed saving right in her own backyard. But that wasn't exotic or prestigious enough, he supposed.

"You look like you could use some cheering up," said Glynnis, bringing him a freshly baked kolache and a big mug of coffee.

"I'm cheerful," he said. "I'm cheerful as hell."

"Sure." She set his tab on the table and moved on.

He reminded himself of something Nina had said in one of her video monologues—there are some things you don't have a choice about, but there's plenty you can choose. Like happiness. Like focusing on the positive.

And there were a lot of positive things happening for Zach. Executives, test audiences and critics couldn't stop talking about *Big Girl, Small Town,* already known by its initials, *BG/ST.* The impact of Jezebel, her connection with the kids and the strange juxtaposition of an urban icon with the beauty of Willow Lake were irresistible. There was even talk of award nominations, because despite the commercial intent of the series, a deep message of hope and healing through good works shone through.

These days, offers poured in for Zach and he had to engage an agent to juggle everything. For the first time in his career, he could name his price and his program. The industry considered him a seasoned and sought-after professional. He had offers to work all over the place—L.A., Vancouver, Austin, New York...*New York.*

He pictured himself going to Sonnet and telling her he wanted to be at her side no matter where her travels took her...but it just didn't work like that. If they couldn't figure out how to put their lives together, even love wouldn't save them. Still, he kept thinking about what Jezebel had said, that there was a reason he stuck around Avalon, and it wasn't just due to a lack of options. This was the home of his heart.

The bell over the door chimed. Somehow, without even looking up, Zach knew it was his father.

Sure enough, Matthew Alger walked into the bakery. He was pale and moved with a certain tentativeness, as if he was feeling his way through the dark. His trousers and shirt bore creases of newness, though he wore the same scuffed shoes and wristwatch he'd had at the start of his prison term. No one in the place seemed to recognize him. People moved on, Zach thought. Everyone was absorbed in his own drama.

"I did it, finally," said Matthew, spreading his arms. "I made parole."

"You did." Zach rose to his feet and extended his hand. "Have a seat. You still a coffee drinker?"

"You bet. It's really good to see you, son."

As they sat together drinking coffee, watching people come and go, a subtle rhythm took over. It was as if no time had passed. They were just a guy and his son, talking about the weather, the local baseball team, the merits of the strawberry rhubarb pie his dad had ordered.

"So you filmed a hit TV show," Matthew said after Zach filled him in on the production. "That's great, Zach. Sounds like everything is on track for you."

"Yep. Sounds that way."

"Actually, it doesn't. What's bugging you?"

"Sonnet Romano," Zach muttered.

"Hey, I remember her. She was always a go-getter. Pretty little thing, too."

And that was when the floodgates opened. Zach found himself spilling everything—the crazy reunion at Daisy's wedding, the summer they'd spent working together, the fact that no matter how hard he tried, he couldn't get her out of his mind.

Matthew grinned from ear to ear. "You're in love. That's nice to see."

"It won't work. She's on her own path, and I'm on mine. She's only ever wanted to get away from this place, travel the world, do humanitarian work. And I…hell, I can't see myself fitting into that picture."

"Then look harder," his father said simply. "There was one great love in my life—your mother. I ran her off, and didn't realize I'd lost something special until it was too late."

"You never told me that."

Matthew shrugged. "I'm telling you now. Maybe you'll learn from my mistake. If you love Sonnet Romano, then you'll do what you have to do to be with her. If you have to follow her halfway around the world just to be with her, you do it. Just don't let her walk away."

"You're oversimplifying it," Zach said.

"You're overcomplicating it," his father replied. "Hell, while she's off working on her international projects, you could be with her, filming and documenting."

"That's not exactly what I had in mind for myself."

"Love is compromise, and this sounds like one worth making."

Zach finished his coffee and paid the check. "Prison made you smarter."

"I had a lot of time to read. Promise you'll give it some thought, son."

"Yeah. Okay."

"Now I don't know what I'll do," Matthew said. "They're setting me up with an employment counselor to see what I'm qualified for."

"You're going to be all right," said Zach.

"I hope you'll come around and see me. Maybe we'll have a game of cribbage."

"Cribbage sounds good."

CHAPTER
25

Sonnet returned to Willow Lake to take care of one final piece of unfinished business—Zach. The idea of facing him and telling him what was in her heart was terrifying, but if she didn't speak her truth, she knew she would always regret it. She'd learned a lot from her mother about having emotional courage and the clarity that could bring.

The time she had spent in Avalon had brought her unanticipated gifts, but that hadn't become clear to her until she had tried going back to her old life. At Willow Lake, she'd found herself with blank space in her life, space that used to be filled with rushing around with work and trying to be the daughter she thought her father wanted. The time away gave her good breathing space she hadn't known she needed. She had not been feeling like herself for a long time, she just felt like someone who was trying to stay on a path she hadn't picked, trying to convince herself that she'd made the right choice. In reality, she'd been using all the busy-ness and chaos of work and the city to avoid thinking about the things that really mattered, like the importance of living a life that felt like the right fit for her, not for someone else. She'd spent such a long time chasing down her father's dream that she'd forgotten to chase her own.

Everything had changed, from the inside out. She felt completely different, excited and nervous about the future, but not at all scared. It was funny, she'd been scared without knowing it, scared to face a future that might not be big enough or impressive enough for people like Orlando or her father.

There was a peculiar sense of peace that came from knowing she'd finally made the right choice for the right reasons. Even if she discovered that Zach had left, or that he didn't want what she hoped he'd want, she would always have the peace of mind of knowing her future was going to be built on her own choices. There was a way to save the world starting right here, right now, with children like the ones they worked with at Camp Kioga. She didn't need to travel halfway around the world in order to find kids who needed her.

She belonged here, at least for now, close to her mom and tiny half-brother. Her plans had changed—but they were still big plans and this time, they felt like the right plans for Sonnet. As for Zach, she couldn't guess what he might think of her big change. She'd find out soon enough.

She couldn't regret anything that had happened. She would forever be grateful that he was the one who had always been there for her. He'd been there when she was confused and difficult, and she hoped he would be there now that she knew it was time to start opening up and trusting her heart and saying yes to things that used to seem so impossible to her. Being with Zach reminded her that life was beautiful, that love and adventure were possible even when times were hard or frightening. The two of them together could be magic, but there was just one thing she had to do—she had to tell him.

She'd sent him a text, checking to see if he would be in town.

After *Big Girl, Small Town* was a major hit, who knew where Zach would be? He was a key player in the success of the series; he'd be able to write his own ticket with any number of production companies now. He might be heading to the West Coast or anywhere in the world now.

Propitiously, he was in Avalon. He sent her a message saying he'd meet her at Blanchard Park. She tried to read meaning into his choice for the rendezvous. The town's lakeshore park was a part of their shared history. It had been their regular meeting spot from the time they were old enough to cross the street without adult supervision. They'd met at the old town park for swimming in the summer, skating in the winter, boating whenever they'd been able to scrape together the money to rent a skiff or catboat. Did he want to meet there because the place on the lake was special to them?

Or because it was an appropriate spot to say goodbye?

She felt exhilarated by the sense of risk, but she wasn't afraid. After watching her mother's ordeal, Sonnet understood what it was to be truly afraid. She would be devastated if Zach sent her away, but she refused to let fear keep her from telling him what was in her heart. It took no special bravery to be honest about her emotions.

He was waiting when she got there, his tall silhouette dark against the deepening light, his long pale hair catching the last of the sun's rays. He looked so good to her, just the sight of him made her pulse race.

"Hey," she said, unable to keep the smile off her face.

He turned to her, and the breeze lifted his hair. "Hey."

"I'm glad you said you'd meet me," she said, nervous in spite of her resolve. "Let's walk."

They wandered down to the lakeshore as twilight gathered and the first stars appeared. No one was around. It felt like just the two of them together, and it was a wonderful feeling. If she had to spend forever with just one person, she would want it to be him. The thought took root inside her and gave her courage.

"I came back because I have something to tell you. You don't have to respond or say anything back to me. It's just…something I need to get out there because to do anything less would be cowardly of me, and I'm done being scared."

He stared at her aghast, as if she was going to confess to having an STD or something. "Uh, okay. I'm listening."

"What I need to say is that what happened at Daisy's wedding was not some sweet, drunken mistake. Maybe I didn't know it at the time, but it was life-changing. I started falling in love with you that night, Zach, not the way I've always felt about you, but…deeper. More intense, and it scared me, so I backed off. Pulling away from you didn't work, though. I just…kept falling. So I came to tell you I love you, Zach. And not the way I felt when we were just friends, or kids growing up together. But as the person I'll love for the rest of my life, with every inch of my heart."

He stood statue-still, his face unreadable.

"Sorry to blurt it out like that." She tried to keep her heart from sinking. "If you don't feel the same way, I understand. I wouldn't blame you for giving up on me."

"Tell you what," he interrupted. "How about you let *me* explain how I feel?"

"Oh. Yes, sorry." She flushed, aware that she had a habit of getting ahead of the conversation.

"Listen, I'm not good with words," he said, "but ever since I got your message, I've been thinking about what I need to tell you."

She braced herself. Made herself be still and listen for once.

"So I was watching this video clip online," he said, "about these Chinese watermelon farmers who gave their melons too much chemical growth accelerator."

She frowned. He was always watching clips of strange phenomena, filing them away in his mind like bits of fluff in a lint trap. "Interesting, but what does that have to do with us?"

"I'm trying to make a point here, okay? Anyway, the watermelons are all starting to explode. That's right, they're exploding from growing too fast. Sometimes I feel like my heart is like one of those giant watermelons that is about to explode from being too full."

"Oh, Zach." Her arms felt chilled. She started to tremble all over. "Don't ever say you're not good with words."

"It's the best way I can think of to describe how my heart feels. What I'm trying to tell you is that I'm in love with you, too. You're right about Daisy's wedding. Something happened that night we were together. We both felt it. That night changed everything. I kept waiting for it to go away, or to fade, but that's not what's happening. This is the kind of love that's going to grow and withstand time and keep growing until it becomes this immovable, unconditional love that people always dream of finding and only a few ever do."

"Oh, Zach. Really? Oh, my God…I was afraid you didn't feel the same way I do."

"You should have checked with me before assuming I didn't."

"I know. I'm sorry." With every cell in her body, she wanted to touch him. No, she wanted to wrap her arms around him and never let go. "So…now what?"

"Hey, check it out." Something glimmered in the light. He pointed out a clear glass bottle bobbing against the lakeshore.

"Looks like somebody littered." She walked over and picked up the bottle. "At least they have good taste in champagne— whoa, there's a message inside." She held the bottle up to the light, immediately thinking about the last time she'd found a bottle floating in the lake. "Maybe it's the same one I threw out into the water at Daisy's wedding."

"You should check it out."

"No, I should throw it back into the lake and continue this

amazing conversation with you," she said. *I'm in love with you.* Had she heard him right? She was starting to think she'd imagined it. Exploding watermelons and unconditional love…

"Just open the damn bottle," Zach said.

She thrust it at him. "You do it, then. I don't want to be responsible for prying into someone's private business."

"Jesus, Sonnet. Could you just open it?"

She sighed in exasperation. "I don't want this conversation with you to end."

"Trust me, it's not going to end."

The expression on his face startled her. She saw tenderness and honesty in his eyes, and she recognized that this was the way he'd always looked at her. And she realized he was the only one who ever had. He saw her. He saw who she was, and he loved her. She didn't take her eyes off him as she worked the cork out of the bottle with hands that couldn't stop trembling. Then she glanced down at the scrolled note in her hand. The slender tube was bound by an elegant diamond ring.

"I have goose bumps," she whispered.

"Don't be afraid. It's okay. Read it."

She unrolled the slip of paper, instantly recognizing his handwriting. There were only two words: Marry me. On the back of the note was one more word: *Please.*

Her eyes filled with tears. "Zach…"

"Don't cry. Here, try the ring on."

It was a simple band of white gold with a glimmering diamond solitaire. She handed it to him. "Put it on me, Zach," she whispered. "My hands are shaking too much."

He lifted her hand to his mouth and gently kissed it. Then he slipped the ring on her finger.

"It fits perfectly," she said.

"Your mother told me your ring size."

"My mother? She knows about this?"

He nodded. "And yes to the next question—she's totally cool with this plan."

He had a plan. She shivered even more.

"That last bottle, the one I found the night of the wedding... was that planted by you, too?"

"It was, actually. And yeah, you were meant to find it."

"Oh, God. Please tell me there wasn't a diamond ring in it."

He laughed softly. "Nah, just a note."

"What did it say?"

He laughed again and took her in his arms, then leaned down to whisper in her ear.

"Okay, my goose bumps just got goose bumps."

"That's a good sign," he said. "There's one problem, though. You haven't given me an answer...to either question."

Happiness radiated from a deep inner core, shining through her. It seemed so long ago that she'd fought with herself, determined to tell him no but desperate to say yes. Everything was clear now. The answer had been written on her heart forever, and she could finally see that, finally give voice to what she'd wanted all along. She threw her arms around him and kissed him, at the same time whispering a single word against his lips. *"Yes."*

PART
5

Must-Do List (last one, promise)

✔ really fall in love

Being deeply loved by someone gives you strength,
while loving someone deeply gives you courage.
—Lao Tzu

EPILOGUE

Moments before the wedding was to begin, Sonnet Romano shuddered with a wave of nervousness. "Mom," she said, hurrying over to the window, which framed a view of Willow Lake, "what if I screw up?"

Her mother turned from the window. The misty light of a rainy afternoon shrouded Nina's slender form, softening her features like an airbrush. She looked fantastic in her form-fitting dress of champagne-hued damask silk, her dark hair still short, beautifully styled and highlighted with a sweet spray of flowers. Reconstructive surgery had given her back her figure, and despite the fatigue of having a nine-month-old, she was glowing.

"You're not going to screw up," Nina said. "You're going to be fabulous. You look amazing in your gown, you've memorized everything you're going to do and say, and it's going to be the best day of your life. Everything's ready. We just have to wait until all the guests arrive."

A chorus of squeals came from the adjacent room, where the

rest of the bridal party was getting ready. Daisy was matron of honor, of course, and Sonnet had asked her half sisters, Kara and Layla, to take part. Daisy's son, Charlie, served as ring bearer, taking his duties seriously. He'd insisted on wearing not just a tux, but a top hat as well.

Sonnet felt a thrum of emotion in her chest. She was about to marry the love of her life. It was like a dream come true, only better. Zach had come back into her life when she didn't even know she needed him. It had taken her a while to listen to her own heart; in all the bustle and haste of her career, she'd grown so distant from who she was and what she wanted. Now she understood exactly what she needed, and it wasn't an impressive resume or important friends or a list of accolades. It was making a life with Zach—her best friend, the love of her life, the keeper of the deepest secrets of her heart, the one person she would share everything with, from here on out.

If only she could get through this day. She paced back and forth, the yards of tulle swishing around her legs. "I might need to pee again."

"You don't need to pee. You just went, and it's a huge pain in that dress."

She was right about the dress. Only a short time ago, Daisy and Olivia had helped her in the ladies' room, forming a forklift with their arms to hoist her up and hold the gorgeous dress out of the way. It was a full ball gown with a train, as ornate and multilayered as the towering wedding cake from Sky River Bakery.

Before that magical night by Willow Lake, she had never dreamed of being this kind of bride—the fairy-tale kind, with all the trappings, from the tiara crowning her still-short hair, right down to satin dancing shoes encrusted with crystals. Previously, she'd pictured herself doing something tame and well thought out—a tasteful dress that could be worn again, a quiet transaction at city hall.

But being in love with this much passion and joy had given

wings to her heart—and to her imagination. She'd wanted it all, the gown that could barely fit through the doorway, the candlelight ceremony, the party complete with a live band called Inner Child, friends and family from near and far. There would be a surprise appearance by Jezebel herself. And most of all, the bridegroom who had changed her life.

She joined her mother at the window. "The rain's not letting up."

"Rain on a wedding day is good luck, or so I hear."

"That's a nice thought." Her heart sped up as she saw guests arriving up the walkway to the rustic pavilion below. Umbrellas popped open like flowers in the rain. With a thrill, she saw all the people who had come to see her and Zach—Kim and Bo Crutcher, who had given them such good advice. Olivia and Connor Davis, now eager to move forward with plans to create a summer program at Camp Kioga for city kids. And Jezebel herself, dressed in a simple but fabulous dress of royal blue, more diva than hip-hop star.

"There's my father," she said, pressing so close that her breath fogged the window, and her pulse kicked up another notch. With his trademark military bearing, Laurence Jeffries strode toward the pavilion. Instead of carrying an umbrella, he wore a dress blue overcoat and an officer's bullion visor hat. An aide accompanied him a few steps behind. People nearby noticed, and Sonnet could see the buzz of excitement ripple through the crowd. "Okay, I have to admit it's pretty cool, having a United States senator come to my wedding."

Despite Delvecchio's attempt—aided by Orlando—to taint Laurence's reputation, her father had won the election by a healthy margin. The voters had cast their ballots in support of her father's leadership skills, his vision and ideas rather than focusing on his past. Orlando, who had expected to ride Laurence's coattails to the nation's capital, had been fired. Sonnet and her father had settled into a cordial but somewhat distant relationship.

"He is one good-looking senator," her mom said. "Reminds me of Denzel Washington. How did he take it when you said I'd be walking you down the aisle, not him?"

"He was okay. I think he gets it." There had been a time when Sonnet would have felt obligated to include him in the traditional role of giving away the bride; she used to be afraid to flout her powerful father. Now it was easy to be in her own skin. Her father was a brilliant man, but he wasn't wise. Her mother had been present for every moment of Sonnet's life, and it was only appropriate that she be the one to do the honors.

"I'm happy for you that he came," her mother said.

"Zach's dad is coming, too," Sonnet reminded her. "I hope it won't be too weird for him." Since his release from prison, Matthew Alger had been living in the nearby town of Phoenicia. He had a job teaching bookkeeping (of all things) at a small community college and was putting his life back together. Zach went to see him once a week for a game of cribbage.

Lightning seared the sky, and the arriving guests hurried faster up the main walk. "I wonder if that's considered good luck, too," Sonnet mused.

"It's lucky you didn't insist on being outdoors," Nina said. "I have no problem with an indoor wedding on a day like today."

"Me neither."

"The pavilion downstairs looks incredible. Have you seen it?"

"Olivia didn't let me look. She wants me to be surprised." Knowing Olivia, who had exquisite taste, Sonnet felt confident it would be fantastic. Her only input had been to choose her two favorite colors—the bright orange of Cheetos and the cool blue of window cleaner. Having filmed more weddings than he could count, Zach had only two requests—great food and a great party. Sonnet was pretty sure they could deliver on that.

"Good idea," Nina said. "I can't wait to see the look on your face when you see it. Your smile is my sunshine, remember? Come here, you." Nina opened her arms and Sonnet gratefully slipped into her mother's embrace.

"This feels nice. I'm glad I came back." Sonnet turned her face to the warm breeze blowing in through the window. "I hated the reason I came back—you getting sick—but I'm happy about what happened while I was here."

"I got better and had your little brother, and you fell in love. Seems pretty perfect to me."

"It feels pretty perfect. I thought I was supposed to be off saving the world."

"There are lots of ways to do that," Nina said. "Your children's program at Camp Kioga is going to change lives, just the way it did last summer."

"Only not on camera, *please,*" she said.

"Zach's got other plans for his camera," Nina said.

"We're going to make it work, Mom," Sonnet vowed.

"There was never any doubt."

The window had fogged up, so Sonnet used the side of her hand to wipe a spot. "Zach just got here," she said. "Mom, come look."

Even now that Sonnet was used to being in love with Zach, she still found the sight of him thrilling, especially today. He was the tallest guy in the wedding party, hurrying toward the door amidst his buddies.

In a tailored tux of black superfine, he moved with lanky grace, his long pale hair flowing out behind him like the cape of a superhero. She couldn't take her eyes off him.

"Why didn't I see it?" she asked her mother. "When we were growing up and going through school together, why didn't I realize he was my future?"

"Because we humans are complicated, aren't we? Sometimes it takes a long time to see what's been in front of us all along."

"And then I almost lost him," Sonnet said, her breath misting against the glass. "I got scared and I almost blew it. Don't let me do that again, Mom."

"I'm not worried. The two of you are going to be great together."

"I just remember standing here before Daisy's wedding, thinking he had no possible place in my future. I've been trying to figure out how he changed from an old high school friend into Prince Charming. Then I realize I'm the one who changed, not him."

"I feel another embroidered pillow coming on." Nina laughed at Sonnet's expression. "Kidding. *Maybe*."

Olivia and Daisy helped Sonnet down the stairs to the anteroom located just outside the main hall. One by one, the members of the bridal party stepped through the double doors, made a pivot turn, and headed down the aisle. Sonnet couldn't see what was happening but she knew the hired videographer, a kid just out of film school who had been handpicked by Zach, would capture every moment.

A few minutes later, Sonnet found herself alone with her mother again. Just beyond the doorway, the ceremony was about to get underway. Murmurs of excitement and a drift of sweet music reminded her—she was about to get married. She would leave this place a different person than the one who had entered.

A flurry of butterflies took flight inside her. "What do you say?" she asked her mother. "Shall I go get married?"

Nina grinned. "There's no time like the present."

"Then let's do this thing." Sonnet's voice was on the verge of breaking. She took a deep breath.

Nina's grin turned to a soft smile, and her dark eyes took on an expression that pulled Sonnet into days gone by, when it had just been the two of them, making their way in the world together. There had been hard times and frustration, but plenty of love and laughter, too. A wave of gratitude swept over Sonnet. "Mom, I'm glad you're here."

They both knew what she meant by *here*.

"So am I," Nina told her, and tears sparkled in her eyes.

"You're going all mushy on me, aren't you?" Sonnet said, fighting the prickle of emotion in her throat.

"Yeah, baby. I am. My fabulous, amazing daughter is a *bride*. My mind is blown. I hope I can remember what I'm supposed to do and say."

"You will, Mom," Sonnet assured her. "You'll rise to the occasion. You always do."

"I've heard that before."

The music gently shifted to the song Sonnet had chosen for their processional. Eddie Haven, the lead singer of the band, launched into an acoustic version of a sweet song to accompany Sonnet and Nina down the aisle.

"Wow," said Sonnet, "it's really happening, Mom. Finally."

"Yes," Nina agreed. "Finally."

They paused to collect themselves one last time. A small, mullioned window in the anteroom offered a view of Willow Lake. The rain's silvery mist softened the colors of the trees and gardens outside, and a muted hush made it seem like the world was holding its breath. The sheer beauty of the lake, nestled between the gentle swells of the Catskills, made her heart ache. She was home now. *Home.*

Nina took her hand and together, they stepped through the door.

★ ★ ★ ★ ★

ACKNOWLEDGMENTS

A very special thank-you from me and PAWS of Bainbridge Island to the ever-generous Judy Hartstone and the adorable Jolie.

Winston Churchill once said, "When you are going through hell, keep going." Life threw me a lot of curveballs during the writing of this book, and I am deeply grateful for the steady support of my beloved family and friends. You know who you are, so I won't embarrass you by telling your names to a bunch of strangers.

Writing a book can be a lonely business. Picture yourself shouting down a well, wondering if anyone can hear you. A lot of the time, the process feels something like that. Thank heaven for my first readers, fellow writers Elsa Watson, Sheila Roberts, Lois Faye Dyer, Kate Breslin and Anjali Banerjee. I'm also privileged to work with the best in the business—Lindsey Bonfiglio of Beyond Novel, my editor Margaret O'Neill Marbury and the team at MIRA books, and Meg Ruley and Annelise Robey of the Jane Rotrosen Agency. For someone who makes a living with words, this is a hard thing to admit—there are no words.

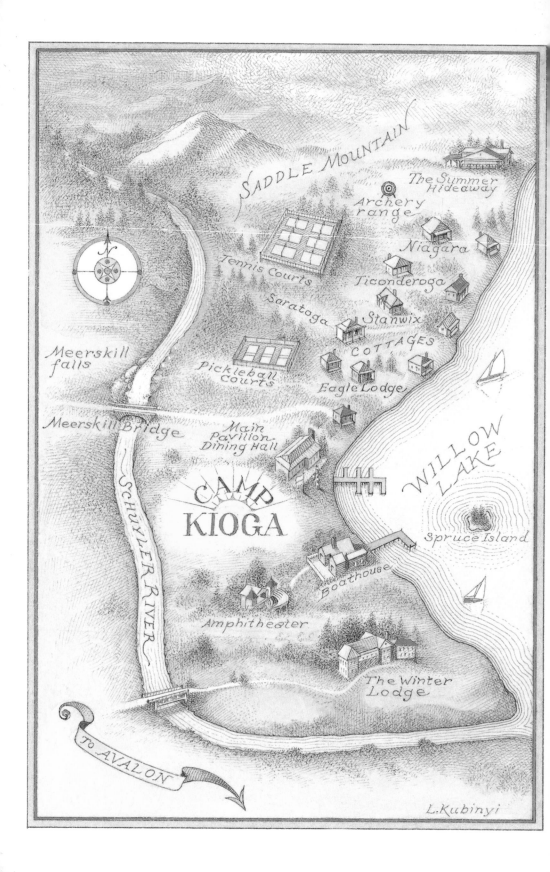